TEN DATES

RACHEL DOVE

Boldwood

First published in Great Britain in 2023 by Boldwood Books Ltd. This paperback edition published in 2024.

1

A CIP catalogue record for this book is available from the British Library.

Paperback ISBN 978-1-83533-952-7

Large Print ISBN 978-1-80483-607-1

Hardback ISBN 978-1-80483-606-4

Ebook ISBN 978-1-80483-604-0

Kindle ISBN 978-1-80483-605-7

Audio CD ISBN 978-1-80483-612-5

MP3 CD ISBN 978-1-80483-609-5

Digital audio download ISBN 978-1-80483-603-3

Boldwood Books Ltd
23 Bowerdean Street
London SW6 3TN
www.boldwoodbooks.com

To Nicola and Annalease. Love you lots.

1

ALICE

My eyelids are stuck shut. Did I sleep with my lashes on again? Damn it. Well, this is going to hurt.

Not the most original thought she'd ever had, but it was the first conscious thought Alice remembered having after. When she played the moments over and over in her addled mind, searching for some clue that would make the whole chaotic mess fit together. That thought, and the smell. Cleaning products. Something sharper. Bleachy. The smell of it was thick in her nostrils, as though she were sitting shut-eyed in some kind of sterile space. It made her want to wrinkle her nose. The chemicals weren't the only thing she caught the whiff of. There was... was... what was it she could smell? It was... familiar, in a way. She lay there, trying and failing to place it.

Something else was there, in the air. It rose above the bleach stink but didn't overpower it. It carried a different energy to it. Something spicier. Muskier. That smell danced in her nostrils, but the origin eluded her entirely.

When she'd first woken up, that was what her brain offered up.

The first profound offerings her mind spat out at her. Hardly a reboot, was it?

She'd tried to open her eyes, the action not even planned. It was just something her body did day after day, wasn't it? She couldn't think right now. Her brain felt... woolly. She tried again, but everything was just too heavy. Her eyelids being one of those things. She couldn't get them to do her bidding. They were trying though; she could feel her lashes being ripped out now and again. The odd tiny flash of pain when she tried to strain to see her surroundings.

There was an annoying beep in the corner. It was methodical, robotic. As she tried to move her limbs, the beep got a little quicker. The space between beats shortening, more rapid fire. It was bloody annoying. Beep-beep-beep-beep. She wanted to reach out and stop the sound, kill it. That would need arms though, and if she couldn't lift a pair of eyelids, arms were just not going to happen, were they?

'Mmmff.' She tried to speak but her lips were like rubber. Her mouth felt so dry, like she had licked the Sahara sand itself. Panic started to set in. There was something wrong. She felt trapped in her own body. Was that why her eyes wouldn't move too? Oh my God. What the hell was going on? Had she been kidnapped? Behind her closed eyelids she could make out a bright room. She could make out the light. It wasn't a dark dungeon and she wasn't lying in some sack on a cold stone floor. She couldn't feel the lick of hell fire flames around her either, so that was something. She was in a bed, she knew. How had she gotten here, though? She tried to remember the last thing she'd done. The last place she'd been. She wracked her brain, but all she got back were flashes of memory. Images she couldn't recall seeing before. Snippets of things she couldn't marry together. What the hell was going on? She tried to take a deep, steadying breath and felt a hand on her arm.

'Whoa, whoa. Don't panic,' the voice was deep, unmistakably male. Gravelly, and full of concern. 'Nurse!' He shouted that last word, and the sound rattled around in her brain like a bullet. She raised her hands to shush them. Or thought she did, at least. She felt pain instead. Her arms ached and felt as though they'd just been stuck onto her body.

'Sorry, sorry, baby. Don't panic, okay? I've got you. I'm here, babe. I'm here. Can I get some help in here, now!'

She heard the slam of a palm against the wall. A click. Another beeping noise started up behind her. This one was like a bloody siren, and the noise pierced her brain. Blurp! Blurp! Over and over.

She tried to shush it, to move, but everything was too hard. She wasn't in control of her own body. She heard noises from further away. The bang of the door as hands pushed it, the squeak of rubber-soled shoes as feet surrounded her. The hand on her arm didn't move or make any attempt to pull away, even as she felt other hands on her.

'Sir, please! Let us work!'

'Just tell me what's happening. Alice?'

'Mr McClaren, calm down!' Another stern female voice that time. She heard the male voice chunter something back, but she couldn't make it out. 'Let the nurses work!'

Nurses. It clicked. She was in a bed. In a hospital. The heartbeat monitor beeped faster still.

'Alice, calm down.' The male voice again. Mr McClaren, they'd called him that. *For God's sake, why can't I open my eyes? Too bright. Too scary. I need to look. Look...*

'Mr McClaren, we will force you to leave if you continue.'

The hand never moved from hers; it squeezed a little tighter. *Don't let go,* her brain screamed silently.

'Listen, I've been here the whole time. You'd know that if you'd been here, and my damn name! I'm going nowhere.'

'I'll call security!' The annoyed female voice half shouted back over the beeps and the movement of bodies. Alice was being prodded and poked, and people were talking to each other using medical terms she couldn't decipher.

The gravelly voice fell off a cliff, his tone solid, dark. 'Try it. I fucking dare you.'

The hand holding hers was ripped away. *No. Stay with me. I'm scared.*

'Get off me man! Alice!' The growl was desperate now. She had never heard her name sound so full of panic and pain before. 'Alice! I'm here. I'm not leaving!'

Dad? It didn't sound like Dad. Or her brother, Lewis. He was softer spoken than most men. Her dad was deep, but it didn't register. He didn't growl like that, but that was the Mr McClaren she'd first thought of. Two women were talking to the voice, and another one was trying to get him to leave the room, but he was having none of it. She tried to reach her hand towards him, feeling like she needed him to stay with her. She tried, and barely managed to lift it off the sheet. There was a commotion in the room, the man growling his refusal to leave.

'Fine!' She heard one of the nurses say. She felt a calloused palm clamp onto her hand. It engulfed it entirely, but it was soft too. She tried to look at the hand, to really see it there, in hers. Dad's felt different to this, and she burned to finally see what the hell was going on. The lid on her right eye had started to lift, choosing now to finally cooperate, but all she saw were retreating fingers as they were being pulled away. Her own flexed towards their retreating form.

She couldn't move, the nurses were still talking to her, and then she was coughing and gasping and the beeps were like a cacophony of sound assaulting her eardrums. She wanted it to stop. She wanted it gone. The noise was too much. She couldn't see, couldn't get her body to do what she needed it to. The growling voice never stopped talking. Telling her he was right here. Would always be there. She could hear the deep voice shouting, but she couldn't feel him any more. He sounded so different. She could *feel* the terror in his voice. Could feel her brain getting darker again as events overwhelmed her.

Before the lights went out again, she heard a distinct shout. 'Baby! Don't leave me! Fight, sparrow, fight!'

Sparrow? What the hell does a sparrow have to do with me leaving? That was the last thought she had before she lost consciousness.

2

ALICE

The beeping was there again. Incessant. Monotonous. She squinted one eye, to see if her eyelid worked. It opened, but the bright light dazzled her. She tried to focus on something, anything, to ground her. Her eyes stung, making them water. It was quiet now. The panic and the people were all gone. She listened for the voice again, but heard only muffled conversation, far away. The other side of the door, she guessed. When her eyes finally adjusted, she realised it was night-time now. She could see the moon right outside her window, big and full. As if someone had brought it there to show her that she was still on the planet. She looked at it for the longest time before she could bring herself to look away. The pain she felt whenever she tried to move wasn't making her want to rush. Every-thing felt sore, stiff. Something bad had happened. It didn't take a genius to work that out. But it was like her brain didn't want to think about it. Or couldn't, which scared her more to contemplate. She felt movement, a squeak of something on the floor. She realised that there was someone else in the room.

Through her peeking eye, she just about made out a blue shape next to the bed. Opening both eyes gingerly, and after a whole lot of blinking, she finally focused on the room around her. Her tired, stinging retinas revealed a man who was using a faded blue denim jacket as a blanket. Not the shape of her dad. Bigger. A lot bigger. His body filled the chair entirely and then some. His face was crinkled up, even in sleep. His head was turned away from her, a grizzly beard obscuring the rest of her side view. She tried to see who it was, but her eyelids were already dropping again with the effort of thinking about it. She lifted her left hand, a double cannula taped to the back of her wrist. She tried to lift her other arm and stopped when she felt a stab of pain run up her limb.

'Fssshhh...' she grunted, and the man in the chair jumped up from his seat.

'Sparrow? Oh my God! Baby!'

'Oww.' She dropped her arm onto the bed without thinking. Hissing when a fresh bolt of pain ran up it. Her whole body felt sore. Alien to her.

'Sshh...' she tried to tell him, but the jacket was flung onto the floor, and he was running out of the door shouting at the top of his bloody lungs. What the hell was he doing here anyway? He was a bit scruffy to be working there, surely? Dad. Dad was here, she remembered. Was it Dad? She felt fuzzy on the details. Did Dad send him here? Not Dad, she remembered. Different voice. Familiar though. One way to find out.

'Dad?' Ai-chihuahua. That hurt. It felt like she'd banged her head against something hard. Just from saying one word. It didn't even come out of her mouth properly. It was like coughing up dust, not a name she'd said all her life.

Her throat. She remembered she was busted up, in a bed. She wracked her brain. Facts. She needed facts. Why was she here? What the hell happened? What did she remember last?

When you lost something, you always looked in the last place. That was the rule.

She remembered something about the weather. Wet. She'd felt wet. And cold. She shivered at the memory, pain letting her know it was there in about fifty different places. Jesus Christ. Her vision swam, and the beeping got faster. The bloody beeping. Over and over. Faster. Quicker. Her head banged with pain. Like a drum that never stopped, with the bloody beeping like the insistent water out of a leaky tap. Like rain. It was raining. She remembered. Did she fall over, hit her head? Hurt her arm trying to catch her fall? It didn't feel like it. She felt like she'd been hit by a damn truck. A big truck, filled with something heavy. Like lead, or bricks. None of your rice cake transporting tiny wagons. A real-life Arctic frigging truck. Filled with frozen Arctic rolls. Those things were like breeze blocks before you defrosted them.

The door opened, and the room started to fill with people again. *Jesus, the noise.*

'Will you please be quiet?' She tried to half shout, but her throat was sore, cracked. Craggy, with a couple of puffins' nests clinging to the sides, full of tourist fluff by the sounds of it. She was so parched. 'Drink?' Looking back at her were two doctors, one of them a grey-haired, official-looking man who was obviously some kind of consultant, and the other who was a rather nerdy-looking young man with large, horn-rimmed glasses on. They were far too big for his face, and she had to resist the urge to laugh. Not that she had the saliva to spare to do that. She realised as her vision swam again that she might be on some kind of drug. Given that she had wires coming out of her like the creature from *Stranger Things*, it was a good guess. 'Am I... drugs?'

The senior fellow opened his mouth to speak but was pushed from behind. *Dear God.* Her mother came running across the room, tearing up the second she saw her daughter lying in the bed. *Well, I must be a mess.* Her mother wasn't prone to drama. She was normally bloody stoic. Annoyingly at times. She was definitely a glass half full type of person, but she was looking at her like a broken tumbler she couldn't stick back together. Alice felt a wave of relief when she first set eyes on her. Her mum was here, things would be fine. Except the look on her mother's face. The beeping got a little faster.

'Mum.' She tried to lick at her lips. Her mother tutted and, eyeing the doctor, she filled a tumbler with water from a jug that Alice hadn't seen before. It was sitting on a dresser that she hadn't clocked. The room was very different to what she'd expected. Not that she'd seen more than a chunk of bright light before. It didn't look like a typical hospital room. She was in a private side room, not a ward. She'd guessed as much already. It was full of crap, for one thing. Gaudy explosions of colour along the windowsill and surfaces that hurt her eyes almost as much as the bright lights.

Once her mother had lifted the glass to her lips, she took a big drink through the straw sticking out of it. Her mother held it still, making her feel like a toddler. She was parched. It eased her poor throat and felt like she could finally speak. She turned to her mum, a million questions on her lips. Only one pushed itself from her mouth. It was the one that burned on her tongue the most.

'What the hell... is all... this shit doing here? Am I... someone's else room?' The two sentences had taken her an age to croak out, every other word a shadow of itself. She turned her gaze back to the doctors. 'Did someone... just die in... here or something?' The doctors just looked at each other. There was stuff everywhere. Cards, a little cushion with a small brown bird on the front, chocolates in puke-inducingly cute packages. A fruit basket. More cards hung from a string on the far wall. The worst thing she'd seen though, by far, was a soft toy gorilla. She hated gorillas with a bloody passion. Who the hell would send her that? That was when something clicked. The taxi.

'I was in an accident. A taxi.' Now they were all just nodding at her. She didn't feel right. 'Did I die?' She looked at her mum, but she was now crying like a loon. She couldn't get any sense out of her. 'Did I die? Am I dead?' The doctors went to speak, but someone pushed forward into the room.

The guy in the denim blanket. She recognised him from somewhere. *The beard.* It sat oddly on his face to her, looked strange. He didn't normally have a beard like that. She wasn't sure how she knew, but it was glaring. She knew him. His name was on the tip of her dry tongue.

'No, you didn't die, Alice.' When he spoke again, said her name, it clicked. She knew exactly who it was. Gravelly voice too. *What did that remind me of? Last night? God, I wish my brain would work.* 'You were hit by a drunk driver. Going home after a night out in town. It was raining heavily and the other driver, he... lost control. You didn't have your belt on.' He looked angry. She could see movement by his side. When she looked, his fists were clenching and unclenching. She looked at her mother, but she was still crying. The nerd doc was talking to her in soft, hushed tones. She looked back at the man before her, and it clicked. Bringing with it more confusion, and a little lick of anger of her own.

Why was *he* telling her this? She knew exactly who this guy was, and she didn't need to hear anything from him. She was still hopping mad at him. He'd been there, that night. She levelled her gaze at him. He kept jabbering on, and she tuned back in.

'I'm so sorry, I wish I'd been there, with you.'

'Why on earth would you want that?' She looked aghast at him, pointing with a stiff arm to her injuries. 'Then you'd have been in here with me, wouldn't you? And I'm still mad at you.' Her hoarse voice was getting better, her anger helping her to push the words forth. She pointed a finger towards his face fuzz. 'Do you always skulk around hospital beds, looking like a reject from *Swiss Family*

Robinson?' He didn't have a beard before. Was she losing her mind here? She felt like she was hallucinating on the drugs she was on.

'Ali—'

She kept going, cutting him off. 'What's with the face fuzz? You in witness protection or something?' *What is he doing here, being the spokesperson? Am I being pranked? My brain is not working at all.*

His head snapped back at her question, but she turned back to the doctors and dismissed him. Before she could even open her mouth, he was piping up again.

'It's me. It's Callum, Ali.'

She looked at him again, wondering why he was stating the obvious.

'It's me, babe. It's Callum.' He rubbed at the monstrosity on his face. 'I haven't had time to shave for a while.'

She took him in again. He looked awful. His eyes were bloodshot. The bags underneath could cater for the Kardashians next trip with ease. Faking a beard though? It was a bit much. Was he incognito or something? She'd slapped his clean-shaven face only hours before. Right before she'd got into the taxi that would later crash.

'You really are an idiot. Take it off. I don't get why you're trying to make a joke right now. And where's Lewis? Did my stupid brother put you up to this?' She started to look towards the door, half expecting Lewis to pop out wearing a wig and a fake goatee. They were always pissing about when they were together, but she wasn't in the mood for this.

'Lewis is at work, Alice. He couldn't get cover, or he'd be here. Michelle too. He didn't put me up to anything. Take what off?'

'The fake beard! I'm in no mood for your jokes.'

He looked at the doctor, and then down at himself. She turned back to the doc, ignoring him completely.

'What happened? What's wrong with my body, and my head?'

For men who looked struck dumb, the two medical professionals were pretty animated by her question.

'Miss McClaren, you were involved in a road traffic accident. You were correct, you were in a taxi vehicle at the time. Now, we need to do some checks of course, but I just want to ask you a couple of questions first. We'll explain everything, I promise.'

The room was quiet now, her mother was looking straight at her as if she were a newborn baby. She must have given them a scare; she knew she was in bad shape. She could feel every little and large injury, and she didn't even know what they were yet. Callum's face was what shocked her the most, though. Other than the beard. He looked so upset. Maybe he'd realised he'd been an idiot that night. Maybe it was guilt, she thought rather petulantly. She giggled without meaning to and noticed that only made Callum's expression worse.

'Doc, is she okay?' His eyes slid from hers to the doctor in front of her and she wanted to tell him to leave now. She wanted to be alone with the doctors; looking at the faces of the people she knew and loved was freaking her out. What was Callum's deal anyway? They didn't tend to hang out alone together. He was with his friends, namely her brother. She was with hers. They often just crossed paths that way. She was close with her brother and best friends with his fiancée Michelle, or Migs as she was known to them. They'd grown up in the same neighbourhood. Migs and Lew had gotten together in high school, stayed together ever since. They were a little gang, but hanging just with Callum?

They were what she'd describe as frenemies, mixed with a rivalry that often sparked fierce debates. Callum wasn't the one she'd call first for help. Him being here, without Lewis or Michelle, it was weird. Everyone was acting strangely, she decided. Her mother had just hugged the nerdy doctor, she was sure of it. Callum was still looking at her. His facial hair blocked any attempt of working out what he was thinking, not that she considered herself an expert. She was still mad at him for trying to chat her up. And what had he said again? Right before she'd slapped him?

I've always wanted you. I've been a coward for years, but I can't take it any more. Go out with me, Ali. Please?

That was it! She remembered how earnest he'd looked. How sincere he'd been, even with half a bottle of Jack singing through his veins. He'd been weird all night, drinking more than he usually did, being all extra moody. *Take what any more?* He wound her up, she wound him up. Coward for years? What did that even mean? He made himself sound like a star-crossed lover. Even if she occasionally did find him attractive, the girl crush she'd had on him had been secret and short lived. Well, mostly. She'd learned to stuff it down quite well over the years. It was a bit like fancying a movie star. You could look, but the reality was, it was never going to happen. She'd forget about it. A product of misplaced horny teen hormones, she'd reasoned.

She used to think he might like her, years ago, when Lewis and he had been friends at school, played football on the same team, but nothing ever came of it. He was one of her brother's friends, the annoying one. He seemed to enjoy winding her up most of the time. He always called her Ali, even though no one else did, and she liked it that way. Hearing it from his lips always made her feel odd, but she'd stopped trying to correct him after the first hundred times he said it. It just seemed to stick.

That night though, he hadn't been joking. He'd seemed to be almost in pain, trying to get his words out. It hadn't gone well, of course. She'd been too shocked and annoyed to give it any real consideration. Plus, she'd had one or two drinks herself by that point. She didn't trust her alcohol-lubricated tongue to do anything but tell him she wasn't interested. For one thing, Callum had never had a serious relationship, and even regular dating wasn't something he ever did. So where was he going with this, she'd asked herself, before chewing him out and getting into that stupid bloody taxi. He'd tried to ask her again. She remembered now, his white knuckles gripping the top of her car door. Trying to stay her exit. Eugh, and then he'd tried to bloody kiss her! As if! She wasn't one of his groupies.

God, she'd been so mad at him in that taxi. She remembered talking to the driver about him. How shocked she was. *I remember feeling flattered too*, she reminded herself. She knew her brain wasn't lying to her on that one. The point was, at the moment of impact, Alice had been doing nothing but thinking about Callum.

Suddenly, she needed him to go. She felt like she was suffocating with confusion. Him calling her baby and being all caring wasn't exactly helping. The beard was just the icing on the cake.

'Callum, I think you should—'

She was thwarted in her attempts to push him out of the room by the senior doctor taking a cautious step forward and breaking her line of sight to Callum the bearded wonder. She saw him lean close to the other doctor, whispering something, and the other doctor nodded and left the room. She'd turned back to Callum, to look at his face again. Just before she lost sight of him, she could see he'd been waiting for her to finish. Focused on her so intently she couldn't help but look back. The penetrating, sullen stare he usually sported wasn't there. He looked so... different. She couldn't tear her eyes away from him.

The doctor's face swam back into view, and she realised she'd leaned forward a little to see the last bit of Callum's face. *Yep, you definitely hit your head. He's irritating, remember? What are you gazing at him for?* Concussions were weird things. The banging pain in her head was testament to the possibility. That was it. Having him declare his... whatever, it had shaken loose a knot of the old crush, that was all. The drugs were mingling everything together. Why she was still just looking at him didn't make sense, but she found she couldn't stop. Everyone else in the room blurred in her vision. She felt this weird... something. Aside from the faux facial hair, he didn't look the same. Maybe he just looked so different because he'd been worried he'd killed her off. Hence the fake beard, so that he could hide his stupid shame. After all, she had spoken to him last night. Before this, he looked like a different bloke. He looked older somehow. Grizzled. Less pretty boy. Not that he really was, not in a really bad way anyway, before today but—

'I want to ask you what year it is. Can you hear me, Alice?'

Shit. The doctor was talking to her, leaning in ever closer. She caught a whiff of coffee on his breath and tried hard not to gag. Her stomach felt weird. She couldn't remember the last time she'd eaten anything.

'Alice?'

'Yeah?' Shit. She'd done it again. Her mind was wandering off. 'I know the year.'

The doctor nodded once. 'What is it?'

'2020.'

'Are you sure?'

'Yes, it's 2020.'

Her mother gasped, and Alice eyed her.

'Mum? What's up?'

'Er, nothing dear.' Her mother looked flustered and didn't speak again. Probably because her dad had just arrived, smiling at Alice. He was gripping her mother's arm so tight his fingers were turning purple. Callum came forward again. *I've got a bad feeling. It's started to feel like I'm in some kind of weird nightmare.* She tried to pinch her own thumb but couldn't do it. Her fingers were still weak, like thin little sausages strapped to her equally wobbly hands.

'Babe, what year is it?'

'Why are you calling me babe? It's 2020. Same as last time I answered. Next question, doc.'

Callum came to sit at the side of her bed, and she tried to push him off when he reached for her arm. He frowned but kept his hand close. 'Next question, doctor.'

Watching her, Callum placed one hand over the rail of her bed. She tried to flick his finger with hers, but she wasn't very strong. Her finger just pinged off his. He didn't move, but she saw his lip twitch. Her parents were silent, still gripping each other. This was some kind of nightmare. She wiggled her toes and was relieved that she could feel them moving. She saw the covers move, just a little. She wasn't too bad then; she could walk. The rest she could cope with, she was sure. If everyone could just stop being so damn odd. 'Ask me.'

'What's the last thing you remember?'

'Being in a taxi. Being mad at Callum.' She side-eyed him. He had his head in his hands, but his head snapped up as if he knew she was watching.

'Ba... Alice, you weren't mad at me.' He muttered half to himself, 'You were the opposite.'

'Oh... like I wasn't!' She winced with the violence her words wracked on her own body, but it was worth it. She *was* mad at him. Just because she was in this bed, it didn't change a thing. She felt like a cornered animal and she knew just who to strike her claws at. 'You crossed the line.' Callum's brows knitted together, and he stared at her. He didn't take his eyes from hers. She scowled right back.

'Ask her something else.' Callum's voice.

The doctor did his little nod, and Alice noticed how tight his lips were before he asked her these questions. His shoulders were tense. Something was wrong. Badly wrong. Shit hitting the fan wrong. 'Please.'

'Where do you live?'

Easy. '322 Merkin Avenue, Hebblestone.'

The doctor looked at Callum for confirmation and he nodded.

'And who do you live there with?'

'I live alone.'

Callum did a strange kind of whimper. She glared at him. He was shaking his head at her.

'Callum, what is your problem? Why are you even here? This wasn't your fault. You didn't drive drunk into me. You can tell my brother he's a dick for even making you come here and miss work.' She winced again as she tried to sit up. 'Oh God, this fucking hurts. Can we just get on with this please?' She looked back at Callum and her statue-like parents. 'I just want to get on with this and get home.'

The doctor's lips all but disappeared.

'Alice, I need you to listen to what I am about to say to you and try not to panic.' He looked around at her monitors, and back to her. 'You are stable now. Your recovery has been remarkable, but you are still coming off the effects of some heavy medication, and your body has suffered severe trauma. You have healed a lot, remarkably well in fact, while you were... asleep, but your injuries were, I'm afraid, extensive.'

He paused, as if giving her time to take it in, but she already knew some of that. Her first inkling had been the fact her body felt so destroyed, weak. She wasn't daft. She'd seen the faces of concern. She was the ruddy one with the injuries. 'And?' she pressed.

He eyed her parents, and then Callum. They were all nodding at him like he was walking a plank and they were cheering him on, hoping for the best. 'Are you following me so far?'

Alice blinked rapidly. 'Yes. Tell me.'

Dr Berkovich pressed his lips together. 'You suffered fractures to both of your legs, and during the collision you also suffered four broken ribs, a broken arm, a dislocated shoulder, and a head injury.'

He paused again, and this time she needed that pause. She catalogued her injuries. She already knew both her legs had been damaged. She'd felt it when she'd wiggled her toes. She'd just not registered why. Only that she was in bad shape.

'The head injury caused your brain to swell, and you arrived at the hospital unconscious. A few hours later, you fell into a coma. The neurological team monitored you, with a sedation and intubation plan if you needed it. The coma helped to slow, and eventually stop the swelling forming under the skull. You could breathe on your own, so we managed your pain. Assessed and treated your other injuries. When you showed signs of consciousness, we lowered the sedation over the last couple of days, but it took you a while to wake up.'

A coma. Not just drowsy from the pain pills then. She'd had an extra scary nap on the way here. A coma. *How long have I been here?* She looked at Callum's beard, and her fear escalated.

'How long?' She suddenly thought to ask out loud. How long was that death-skirting slumber?

'You woke up last night, but we'd been waiting a while,' Callum cut in, a bleak edge to his voice. The doctor closed his eyes but didn't add anything else. 'Tell her, doc.'

'Tell me what?'

'Alice, your coma was for over two months. You had your accident in December 2022.' Another pause. 'Tell me what year it is again.'

Never before had two sentences ripped her world apart, but there they were. Two months. She'd been in the hospital that long? 2022? December 2022? She looked up at the medication bag hung above her. It was half full, and she tried to read the label.

'What is this?' She pointed, her panic rising. She went to tug on the cannula, but Callum's hand was faster.

'Don't! Alice, it's okay.'

'Okay?' She tried again to pull the needles from her arm but gave in when her fingers refused to help her escape. 'How the hell is any of this okay? Two months?' She felt a tear spill down her cheek. 'Really?' She tried to stare the doctor down, as if sheer will could *make* him to take the words back. He didn't.

'This can't be right,' she said, looking around her for some kind of answer. 'You said my coma was for over two months, right? So it should be what, February 2021?' She eyed the doctor, half wild and also proud of her maths skills.

'March.' he nodded. 'You have been here for almost eleven weeks.'

She tried to make the dates fit. Make sense of what she knew.

'March? But it was December 2020. I'd been out to a party. I was with all of you lot, celebrating Lewis and Migs's engagement.' She saw her dad shake his head and carried on. 'I spoke to Callum. Got a taxi home. Ended up in here. That was 2020.'

The doctor nodded grimly. 'We will have to do more tests, but we did fear this. Brain injuries are difficult conditions to predict, Miss McClaren. It appears some memory loss has occurred. We will know more after the tests.'

'So I lost what, two years?'

He nodded slowly, his eyes wrinkling with warmth in the corners. 'It would appear so, but it's early days. I know this is difficult, distressing, but try to focus on what we do know. You are healthy and recovering. You suffered quite a traumatic event.' All she could do was nod, but inside she was frantically running around inside her brain, pulling out drawers and looking under rugs for some kind of memory that would spark something in her.

All she could remember was Callum asking her out, her leaving into the night in the back of that car.

'What happened to the drunk driver?' She suddenly thought of the others involved.

'The police are dealing with him,' Callum half grunted. 'Your driver was okay, he's back at home.'

'Good.' She nodded, dazed by everything they were telling her. 'Just me that's screwed then.' She laughed, but it was hollow. 'Where's Lewis again?'

'Stuck at work, he's going to come as soon as he can. Migs sends her love.'

'Oh, okay. Well, I'm...'

She didn't know what she was. She couldn't take it in. She needed to digest it all. Scream into a pillow maybe. Callum ran his fingers along the back of her hand, and she pulled it away. 'You must need to get back to work too.' She threw him a deflated-feeling half smile. 'Thanks for coming. Sorry I snapped.'

Callum's face dropped.

'You want me to go?' He sounded gutted. She needed him to go, though. His hand had felt nice, in that moment. He was being so kind. It was adding to her confusion tenfold. 'Alice, I can't. You need to listen to what we're saying. I can't leave.' His jaw flexed beneath the bush. 'I won't.'

'That's right,' her mother said, suddenly rushing forward. 'He can't leave. Oh, what's wrong with her, doctor? She's not right!'

'Mother!' Alice made sure to call her 'Mother'. To tell her in no uncertain terms that she was pissing her right off. A remnant of a code from her teens that had stuck. Her mum narrowed her eyes instead of backing off.

'Don't you "Mother" me. My dear, it's March 2023. The twenty-seventh of March 2023. You were in an accident in December 2022. You were in a taxi coming back from a night out with the others, but you were going back home to meet Callum. He'd been working late and had to miss it.' She looked away then, her determined features flashing a touch of vulnerability before she went on. 'You were badly hurt. Your head, oh your head. Your heart stopped.' She saw Callum's fist clench again.

'My heart what?!'

'Mrs—' Dr Berkovich tried to cut in. She shut him down with a mother's stern look.

'She needs to know. She's my daughter, I know what's she's like. She's always been so independent.' She sniffed. 'She's a tough cookie, my Alice, but she's a problem solver. She'll worry at this till she knows every little detail.' She was snarling at the doctor, but when she looked back to face her youngest child, she was the picture of maternal kindness. She licked at her lips. 'I'm sorry, darling, but here it is. And remember, you are here now. With us.'

Alice nodded slowly. 'Tell me. You're right.' She flicked her gaze to Callum. 'I need to know everything.'

Her mother smiled, taking a slow, even breath. 'It was a bad crash. The other driver was going too fast, even before he hit the black ice. You were hurt the most. He slammed right into your door.' Her voice broke, just for a second, but Alice watched her mother take a deep breath. Her voice was stronger when she spoke again. 'Your heart stopped in the ambulance. They blue-lighted you all the way. People all came to help you. Called for help.' She smiled, but it was watery. 'Everyone's been so kind.' She dabbed a tear away from her cheek, cleared her throat.

'There was a lot of trauma to your body from the crash. You were in a coma for just shy of three months, like the doctor said. They warned us that there might be some damage, that you might not ever wake up, but I knew you'd fight. I knew it.' Her mother's voice broke down completely, and she sobbed into her father's shoulder.

Damage. That was the one word that sent a chill through her. She knew that she was high on drugs and had a head injury. She had been semi amused up to a point, but now reality was sinking in. Seeing her mother so broken. It sounded so bad. She wished she could remember. Anything. Even the crash. Anything to help her make some sense of this. No matter what she probed at, it was like dead space. A void. Worse than a void. Non-existent.

'My memory? That's it, right? You weren't joking? It's real, isn't it?'

Their faces said it all. She heard Callum grunt a 'yes' under his breath.

Her mother smiled, as if she'd won a prize. 'Yes! She's getting it!' She turned and stabbed a finger in the direction of the doctor. 'See, I told you she was smart.'

'She's the smartest. This is going to drive her crazy.' A gravelly voice from the side of her sighed heavily. And just like that, her anger rose above everything else swirling around.

'Callum, why are you still here?'

'I'm here for you. Listen to your mum, Alice. This is real. God, I wish I'd not worked late that night. We never went out without each other normally. We didn't want to.' He grinned, but it faded fast. 'You were coming to see me in that taxi. We were on the phone at the time.'

'No,' she was already shaking her head. 'That's not what I remember.'

He looked nonplussed for a second, and then his legendary steel jaw clenched tight. She used to wonder why he always seemed to clench it so much. She wondered if he had an uncontrollable twitch. She'd watched him when he was with her brother though. No twitch. It just seemed to be around her. Weird.

'That's what I'm trying to say, baby.' *Baby.* There it was again. Her addled brain chose to focus on that. He was saying things she didn't understand, didn't want to comprehend. She could only process one emotion at a time. She chose anger. And she levelled it right at Callum.

'That's not what I remember. I don't know why I'd have been coming to see you. I remember *leaving* you, getting into the taxi.' He looked at the people standing near the bed and she felt stupid. Like she was failing some test she didn't get a chance to revise for. 'And as for that night, I don't get why you even tried it on with me anyway? You look like you want to tell me to go away half the time. Which is why I feel fine about asking you to leave now. Go back to work, I know you have that big contract on the industrial estate, right?'

'You're focusing on that, now? I don't give a stuff about my business. That contract was in 2020. I didn't try it on with you that night, I don't get what you mean. Do you remember anything about us?'

'I remember your "I don't want to be a coward" speech. You said that. It's annoying that you're denying it.'

'When? Just now? Baby, I wasn't—'

'I asked you to leave.' She turned to her father, who was right in the back of the room. 'Dad, tell Callum to bugger off.' She looked back at him triumphantly. 'You did try it on. I told you to jog on and got into the taxi. Here I am. Not your fault.'

'The night I first asked you out?' He said it slowly, as if he didn't want to ask her in the first place.

She nodded, very slowly, back. 'Yes, Callum. The same night. The night of the accident.' Her voice petered out. 'But... but...' She tried to collect her thoughts. 'That was in 2020, so...' Jesus, her brain really was like a wet noodle.

Callum's face fell. 'Oh my God, that was the damn night you remember? The last thing? The night we fell out after the engagement party?'

'Yes! The night you whispered slobbering nothings in my ear, tried to kiss me, and then declared your undying love. Yeah. Last night.' She frowned. 'Or maybe three months ago last night. Or two years and three months ago. I dunno.'

Her mother laughed hysterically. It sounded like a hyena had walked into the room.

'I think she's in shock,' her dad announced to the room. 'She did that when I told her my mother had died.'

'Oh God, what are we going to do?' Her mother mouthed her words to Alice like she was a toddler, over-enunciating every syllable. 'You're a bit confused, darling. It's March 2023. Twenty. Twenty-Three. We came second in the Eurovision! The women won the Euros! That's good, isn't it!'

'It's not good, Mum. None of this is good. Oww! For God's sake!'

She'd punched the bed rail. Or tried to. Anything to stop her emotions from taking her over completely. She was in a cold sweat, trying to make sense of things that in her head were just not there.

'Language, my girl,' her otherwise seemingly mute dad chimed in. 'The man upstairs brought you back. Be nice.'

Callum's hands were around her injured one in seconds. She didn't brush him off this time. He was gentle, soft. He didn't crush her in his big meat hooks at least. She let her hand just lie there, sitting in his. She felt his warmth. Something within her calmed down, just a little. She noticed a ring on his wedding finger. It was chunky, like his hand. Silver, with a little bird etched in black on the surface. Not something she'd ever seen him wear before. It wasn't a man's usual trinket.

'Cute ring,' she pushed out before thinking. The drugs combined with the day were making her feel odd. Unfiltered. His eyes crinkled at the corners as he looked from her to it.

'Thanks. It was a gift.'

'From one of your chicks?' She pouted, a little scowl crossing her features that she'd spoken it out loud. *Good comeback though. Yes, brain. Still got it. You saw the bird, delivered the zinger. It's not all lost then. I've kept my sarcasm too. Small mercies.*

'No,' he cut through her thoughts. He was twirling the ring around on his finger. 'I don't have chicks.' Something about his expression made her bite back another retort. Bet it was from one of his hangers-on. He always had the attention of women, wherever they went. Like flies round the proverbial pile. He never seemed to notice like she did. Stupid ring. She hated it. *I hope it turns his finger green.*

She noticed both her parents were now huddled in the corner, talking with the doctor. Her father caught her looking, gave her the most awkward double thumbs-up she had ever seen, and returned right back to the huddle. She looked away. Unfortunately, her only comfortable position meant she was left looking straight at Callum. She realised he was still holding her hand, and she tried to pull away.

'Callum, I really think you should be going now. My parents will be going soon.' She had no idea what time it was, but she felt like she had woken from a long daytime nap. Woozy. A bit wonky. 2023. March 2023. She'd lost all that time. For three months of scary nap time. *What the hell.*

Callum made no efforts to move, bar his usual jaw clench.

'If that's what you really want,' he half muttered as he slowly released her hand. 'I was hoping we could talk some more. You must have questions. I know I do.'

He was on his feet before she almost caved in and asked him to stay. Maybe this was just amnesia, temporary. Maybe a key word would unlock everything. Her mother was right; she needed to know things. He was there and all she had for now. Her mum and dad were wrecks. Her mother was beside herself, and her dad just kept looking at her like he couldn't believe she was real. They were no good, and her mother was speaking to her like she was stupid. She needed to figure this out, and fast.

She'd almost asked Callum to stay back, talk to her. Fill in the blanks, but what would he know anyway? He was always on the periphery of her life, never at the centre of it. They knew each other well, really well, but he wasn't there day to day. They didn't hang out just the two of them, not like the others did, it was always with other people around. They weren't besties. Their unusual dynamic had been part of the angst to her teenage soundtrack. That and his groupies, she thought glumly.

She'd seen the ring. Obviously, a gift from a woman, and she didn't like it. He'd asked her out, told her things. Whether she was interested or not, the thought of her just being the subject of a pick-up line suddenly smarted. She felt like she'd regressed into teen-hood again.

Nope. Having him there would just be confusing. Having him in this room, looking so concerned, so different to the man she remembered.

Older. Worried. Callum was always carefree. Maybe he'd been through some stuff since she'd been asleep. No, she'd make him go. She had family, other friends.

She wondered how long her brother would take to get there. Whether her work contacts knew she was awake. Whether any of her clients were even aware of what had been going on. Being a self-employed interior decorator and designer was all well and good, but it didn't provide sick pay for comas. She had work to do still for some of her clients. Before this. Who knew what state her business was in now? What had become of the bigger commissions she'd started to land? One of them alone had paid for half of her kitchen refit costs. She'd been in good financial shape. *In 2020*, her brain screamed at her. *It's 2023. Do I even have a business to go back to?* The house. Her house was supposed to be part of her career. A professional showcase for what she could do. She had been planning to Instagram the whole renovation. She had gained followers already. But where was all that? Had it continued? Was there a feed out there somewhere, of the life she couldn't recall? Oh God. Her house had always been such a goal. A dream of hers. A forever place. She wanted to see it. *I want to go home.* Which presented another issue, given that her house was essentially a stripped back shell. Home. It was going to be so weird going home. *The house.* A terrifying thought took her over. Made her blood run cold.

'Callum, do I still have my house?' His movements stopped as soon as she spoke. His shoulders dropped half an inch.

'What?' He turned back to her, as if his body had already been desperate to do just that. 'Er... yes. It's yours.'

'What about the mortgage though? I mean, I'm in here. I... did Mum call them? What about the money? Dad didn't pay it, did he? He's saving for that camper van. Oh God, I need to get out of here.' She went to get up, but he stopped her.

'No, no,' he shushed when the panic of her new house going under the repossession hammer while she was pulling a Sleeping Beauty had sent the monitor into overdrive again. The doctor looked over at them anxiously, her parents still chewing his ear off. Callum shook his head at the doctor, who frowned, before checking the monitor and turning back to her folks. 'Everything's paid. Mortgage, utilities. The house is fine.' He bit at his lip again. 'That's the least of our worries.'

'Our worries?' she questioned. Callum's face did that thing again. Like she'd poked him in the chest. A stab of pain flashing across his normally closed off, sometimes damn-right haughty, features. Seriously, the man could make Mr Darcy look like Coco the Clown on his best scowling brooding days.

'Yes, our worries. The house is fine. Work's taken care of. You don't need to worry about any of that right now. I've got it covered.'

'What do you mean, you've got it covered?' She narrowed her eyes at him. 'Dad, what's he on about?' Her dad said nothing, just looked to Callum helplessly. It wasn't the first time, either. The people in the room had been deferring to him all day. Checking with him before they spoke to her. It was making her feel like she was mentally impaired. She knew she was, but why were they looking to him all the time? 'Callum, why *are* you here, exactly? What do you mean by *having it covered*?'

'He can't leave, love. It's not that simple.' Her mother again. Her dad was holding her up but wouldn't look Alice in the eye. He was looking at Callum like his own heart was going to break.

Her mother half shoved the doctor back over to the bed. 'Ask her something else.'

Her dad stood still at the back of the room, looking as though he was wishing he was anywhere else. She could relate. She wanted to go back to sleep again. Hit the reset button. She was wishing for the coma to claim her back. Maybe next time she woke up, things would make sense.

'Alice,' the doctor finally asked, 'who is Callum to you?'

3

ALICE

Callum groaned and sat back down heavily in the chair. The wood protested under his weight.

'I can't take this.' He sounded far off, his voice a cracked shell of a statement. Anguished. *What is his deal?* Something was missing from her brain, and somehow it was connected to the annoying hairy ding-dong in the chair. That smell was back too. Spicy. Had it been coming from Callum? An image sparked, disappearing too quick. She tried to catch it, but it flew away. Too fast to pin down.

She took him in, assessing what her eyes noticed. A 4D Spot the Difference challenge against her memory. She saw how much he'd changed, but somehow he still looked the same. Surreal. She'd always had a lot of cruel and clever ways of describing Callum in the past, but right now she couldn't think of a single one.

'He's Callum Roberts. We grew up in the same neighbourhood. Went to the same schools. He's my big brother's best friend. Mr brother is called Lewis. McClaren. Like me. Cos we're related.' She was rambling now. She'd almost told him the square root of pi, just to prove that she wasn't a total magoo.

The doctor nodded, in his annoying doctorly way. 'Good. That's good. What else? Look at him again.'

She sighed. 'I don't know. He's a centre back at football.' An image of him celebrating a win popped into her head. The school colours on his shirt. 'He has a building firm.' She'd passed him once, coming home from working away on a design project for a new salon in Leeds. High on a scaffold, hard hat on. He looked like a giant, even from up there.

She stopped, looking at Dr Berkovich expectantly. His demeanour had changed. He looked a bit more cheerful.

'That what you mean?'

'Yes, just keep talking. Say what you remember.'

She laughed. 'We'd be here all day.' She didn't miss the smile breaking through the beard. 'I've known him, well... forever.' She tried to think of a time when she didn't know Callum but couldn't recall. Her fuzzy brain threw up plenty of memories though. They came thick and fast.

Him punching a kid in the year above for twanging her bra strap in the Science corridor that time. Him glaring at her whenever he saw her at school. His eyes always seemed to find her. Sometimes, the little hairs on the back of her neck would tingle, and he'd be there, walking away. Turning his head. But she knew, and when she found herself looking for him, he would already be watching. His eyes were quicksand, which was one of the most infuriating things about their little indifference dance. He'd lock on to hers, the deep-brown tones of his eyes easy to spot, even under his ever-furrowed brow. Another memory. Him standing awkwardly in her parents' kitchen while she made herself a snack, her brother waffling on about some girl or other. Callum was always with them. He was an only child; his parents worked a lot. Most of the time, he came right from school. He had his own bunk in Lew's room. Her mother even set out a handmade stocking for him at Christmas, matching the others on the fireplace. 'I know who he is. I remember people.' Her head throbbed, and she rubbed at it ineffectually. The bandage on her cheek was irritating her when she spoke. She hadn't even seen her face yet. She shuddered at the thought, squashing it down. 'Is there a point to this?'

Another purse of the lips from the doc.

'I understand this is frustrating, but it is important. Your recovery has been extraordinary, but this is only the first hurdle. We need to know that when you are ready to go home, you will be able to cope with the changes. Too much too soon, and we risk moving in the wrong direction. Do you understand?' His eyes were soft, a comforting smile crossing his usually tight mouth. 'Now, when I asked you who you lived with earlier, you said you lived alone.'

'Yes, I do.' *If you could count living in my bedroom, which was the only room not looking like it had been destroyed in a tornado.* Renovations on her first house had been harder than she thought. 'I don't even know what it looks like,' she said feebly. 'Did I finish it, like I'd planned? Dad?'

Her dad made a strange noise, something spilling from his mouth along the lines of 'Well... er... don't worry, love...' till the doctor broke through the babbling.

'Don't focus on the house right now. Focus on who you were living with there.'

She huffed. 'I told you, no one. I moved from my parents' house. I saved my arse off for the deposit.'

'That was in 2020, right?'

She nodded back. 'Yes. When I... ended up here, I was living there. On my own.'

Her father bowed his head.

Dr Berkovich pressed on. 'That's right, you did move in alone.

But I've spoken to your parents and they tell me that eighteen months ago, someone moved into your house with you. Can you remember who that was?'

Alice wracked her brain for something, anything. Lewis lived the next street over from their parents in a place he'd bought with Migs. They'd bought their house early on, putting the wedding stuff on the backburner. They'd both been keen to start their lives, strike out into the world of work. Hebblestone was home, all of them settling close by. It didn't make sense. If she'd had a love life, she might have been able to come up with a name, something. The truth was, her love life had been on life support long before the crash. The slobbery kiss attempt from Callum had been the most action she'd seen in months. She just couldn't see it. Living with someone. Anyone. Her head throbbed, stopping her from digging any deeper in the dark for a nugget of light.

'No. Doc, this can't be right. I can't remember right now, but there is no way I would have taken in a lodger. My house is a shack. I bought it cheap to do it up myself, like a project. It had one room that was even habitable, and that was my bedroom. So unless some DIY show has been doing a special on coma victims, there is no way in hell that's true. Mum, what the holy fuck is going on?'

Her mother winced at her language, but let it drop for once. Normally, she was very prim on these matters, but she'd obviously read the room.

'Alice, the doctor's right. You moved in with your boyfriend. You're fixing the house up together, around work.'

Alice's mouth dropped to the floor.

'Shut the f-front door!' She gasped. 'A boyfriend? What boyfriend?' The monitor picked up, and she felt Callum place his hand on her leg over the blanket.

'Stay calm, Alice. It's okay.'

She took a deep breath. 'I'm trying. You try waking up and being told you live with a stranger!'

His hand flexed on the sheet. 'Try harder. Breathe.' His eye was on the monitor. 'That's it. Nice and slow.' The monitor slowed. 'Okay?' he murmured.

She moved her leg away from his hand. 'Yeah. I guess.' She shrugged. 'No. How is this real?'

He didn't reply. His hand didn't move from the bed. Dad, who had been acting like an innocent bystander in this Alice crash, stepped forward.

'It's real, love. All true.' His lips curled into a half-smile. 'It surprised all of us too, at the time. You never seemed too bothered about all that, with your career. When you bought that house, I thought that was it. You were always happy. Never a bother. You had your own mind.'

'Dad,' she half blubbed. Listening to her dad talking was setting her off. She felt like she could cry for a week. 'You never said.'

'Well, you were happy. Own house, big business all on your own. When you brought your fella home, well, it damn well knocked me off my feet.' He chuckled, wiping a tear away with a knuckle. 'I can't think why now. It's all I've thought about, day after day. You lay in that bed, all tubes and machines. How happy you were before. You actually quite like him.'

He smiled then, a huge toothy smile. Alice could see crow's feet that weren't there the last time she looked at her father. She'd lost two bloody years, and she was a stranger in her own life. Everyone had moved on, aged. She felt like Sleeping Beauty, but instead of getting a nice kiss, Prince Charming was nowhere to be seen, and she was told she'd been living with a bloke she'd never set eyes on. What were the odds that he wasn't a complete idiot? What if he looked like Gollum? She'd clearly lost her independent mind, maybe her marbles too. She couldn't think of a single person it could be.

She sank back into the pillows, taking everything in. Her dad patted her hand, and she grabbed at it.

'Dad, who is he?'

Her dad frowned. 'Who, love?'

'My boyfriend,' she pressed. Wondering who the hell it was that had made her consider living with a man. She wanted to rehome a shelter cat or a dog when the house was done, not adopt a man child. 'Who is the guy, and where the hell is he if he cares enough about me to move into my house?'

Her dad squeezed her hand and looked across at Callum. Alice was busy looking for answers in her own head.

'He's the bloke who's sat by your bed side every day.'

Alice wracked her brain but came up blank. She had literally nothing to reference about him. He just... wasn't in her memory. Not even here.

'I didn't see anyone, where did he go then?' She pointed to the stuff. 'This from him? Mum, pass me a card over.' Her mother did a little two-step on the spot, not really moving an inch. 'In a minute, love. Have a think.' She clicked her fingers. 'Something might spark, eh?' She shot a hopeful look at Doctor B, but he just tightened his lips a notch.

'It's early days, Mrs McClaren.' He looked back to Alice. 'It will come. Don't try to force it.' He turned to her folks. 'I think that's enough for today. She needs to rest. Process.'

Alice barely heard him. Her mind was stuck in buffer mode. Looping over and over.

Boyfriend. Boyfriend. Boyfriend. Boyfriend.

Been by your bedside every day.

You actually quite like him.

She still wasn't impressed. All she felt was trapped. Out of control of her own head. *Been by your bedside every day.* She took in the display of gifts and cards. Nothing sparked anything, apart from making her want to punch the stuffed gorilla in the face. *Where was he, this mystery man? How could her pops give him the seal of approval, knowing he wasn't there when she woke up?*

If he couldn't be bothered to show up now, that would be the perfect excuse to get rid of him. After all, she didn't know him. She'd lost two years of her life, not had a lobotomy. She wasn't going to bloody well live with him now, was she?

She was well within her rights to play the 'you weren't there when I needed you' card. Who could fault her, after all? Even her brother had sent someone to be there when he couldn't. Even if it was Mr Cute But Annoying. *Did Callum know him? Were they friends?* Picturing another face in the gang felt weird. The one half-decent relationship she'd been in hadn't gone too well. The lads never seemed to warm to him. Not that it lasted long enough to be an issue. Thinking of her limited dating history, another thought occurred to her.

Maybe she wasn't Sleeping Beauty in this scenario. Maybe she was Princess Fiona, and Shrek was on his way by donkey. She half giggled at the thought, making her doctor write something on his tablet again. He kept whipping it out, tapping away on it. She wanted to snatch it from him, read it to see what was going on. She never was one for feeling out of control.

Her dad moved to the end of the bed, gathering up his wife and their things.

'Dad?' she pressed. The whole room had fallen silent. All she could hear was the shuffling of her mother's feet as her father tried to make her leave. 'Why won't you tell me? Why is he not here?' A thought occurred to her. 'You don't like him, do you, Mum? Or Lew?

Lew hates him, right? Is that it?' She was started to babble. 'You said I liked him, but you were surprised.' She tried to think of possibilities. He could be a traffic warden. Dad hated them with a passion. 'Is he a Man U fan?' Dad had ensured that the only teams anyone was allowed to support was the one Lew played in with Callum, and Leeds United. He always moaned if she wore red on match days.

Callum laughed. Her dad shuddered. 'Heaven forbid.'

The doctor was staring at her as if she was in a test tube or on an operating slab. Like something he was trying to figure out. The fact that a medical professional was eyeing her like that just panicked her further.

'I like him,' her dad said eventually. 'We all like him, he's part of the family. Remember that, love, okay? You two have a long road ahead.'

'Okay.' Alice sighed, partly from relief, partly because she was feeling so anxious she could barely take a deep breath. 'Tell me who he is, please. Why don't I know him? Is he in the army or something? Why wouldn't he be here?'

Her mother went to speak, but all that came out was a scrambled squeak. Her father had jabbed her in the ribs. 'He's been here. Every day. You've been telling him to leave since the second you woke up.' Her dad levelled her with his words.

'What? I—'

Callum sighed in the chair. A heavy, bone-juddering sigh of defeat that she felt down to her marrow. She looked at him, and she saw it. The way he looked at her. His lips were pulled tight, tugged down at the corners as he ran his eyes over her. 'You?' she asked. He simply nodded his head. 'You? We're... together?' She laughed. 'No.'

'Hell yes.' His voice was stronger now. 'Coming up on two years. We're pretty happy.' His jaw clenched, and she looked to his fists. It was there, his tell. He was clenching them tight on his lap, and when he saw her looking, he straightened out his fingers. 'We were really happy, Ali.'

Alice could do nothing but stare open mouthed.

'Happy?' she echoed.

Callum's eyes flashed. 'Very.' He seemed to be reluctant to look away from her. She felt the same, so the pair of them just gazed at one another until her dad made a diplomatic coughing sound.

'I know it's been a lot, love, but we're so glad you're okay. We were so worried.' His face threatened to crumple, but she watched her father pull it back into himself tight. 'Me and your mother are going to get off. Let you two have a talk. We'll see you tomorrow.'

Her mother was crying, and her dad bundled her out of the door before she could lunge at her child for a final hug. Alice could hear her blowing into a hankie in the corridor. The doctor made his excuses and muttered that he would arrange for the tests, and then they'd talk again. Coming over to them, her dad touched Callum's arm in a comforting way as he left. A familiarity flowed between the two men. That wasn't surprising, given that he'd grown up with them, but it felt different to watch, given the revelation.

'Love you, son.'

Callum reached out his hand, and Alice watched as her dad wrapped his hand around it, pulling him in for a hug. Gerry McClaren wasn't a short man, but Callum still dwarfed him.

'Thanks, Gerry. I'll call you later.'

A pat on the back later, the swish of the doors heralded his departure, and then it was just the two of them, and the beeping of the monitor.

The waft of the hospital suppers being wheeled down the corridor sneaked into the gap through the door. Her stomach growled, but she figured she'd been having a liquid lunch for a while. Her body was no doubt craving solid food. She was battered enough to realise that she wasn't able to get out of this bed and run home. She was stuck here. In this room. With Callum.

Her boyfriend. Wow.

That knowledge was still fresh in her head. He was sitting forward in the chair, his head in his hands. She wanted to see his face, she realised with shock. She needed to see his face to see if anything jolted with this new information. He had changed from the image she'd had in her brain. It wasn't just the beard. He looked older, bigger than she remembered. Like his muscles had grown overnight. The knowledge of *her* night before though, the one she last remembered – with his sweet nothings, and her feeling of being thoroughly hit on out of nowhere – lingered. She closed her eyes, trying to remember... well, anything after that. Something more than the spicy scent of aftershave.

She came up with nothing but the guy in the blue denim blanket. The sleeping form by the side of her bed. That must have been Callum. She saw the jacket now on the back of the chair he was sitting in, and the pieces clicked into place. He'd been there every day, her dad had said. Waiting for her to wake up. She remembered the commotion when she'd first come to. The gravelly voice. Things started to match up, but without any knowledge of their relationship, it was hard to know what to feel. She'd heard the pain in that voice. A man suffering, panicked. She remembered his growled refusals when they'd tried to oust him. The voice that had shouted for her to fight. *Don't leave me.* He'd been there. Now she had to figure out how to feel about it.

Callum had moved to stand by the window, the muted light of the outside giving his skin a blue tinge against the tinted windows.

She was going to have to take this slow. She had so many questions, and this guy was here. Again. She felt bad for using him when she was probably going to dump him and kick him the hell out of her gaff, but her parents were gone, no one else was here. She would be careful not to give him mixed signals. That was only fair. She hoped her brain wasn't sending her down the wrong path. She couldn't exactly trust it at the minute.

'Are you going to ask me anything?' He broke the silence before she could shuffle her questions into any kind of order.

'Er... yes. I just don't quite know where to start.'

His shoulders slumped a little and he turned from the window. 'I bet. We can do this at your pace.'

She nodded, now wanting to ask whether he meant do *them* at her pace, or her recovery. She didn't want to know the answer to that. It didn't matter anyway. Whoever he'd been living with, it wasn't her. She'd had a secret crush on him for years, but she'd never let it slow her down before. She'd been living her life quite happy on her own. Setting up her business, sinking everything into her other dream of having a home of her own, all designed by her. She'd not bothered dating, happy to hang with her brother and Migs, their friends. Sure, Callum was always there, but she didn't automatically melt into a puddle whenever he was around. She'd had a lot of time to adjust to being near him growing up. Her teenage heart had put him in a box never to be opened. *Till now.*

It seemed in the two years she'd lost, something had caused her to break that box wide open. They were living together, in her house. Callum had his own place, she knew that. She'd been the last one to jump onto the first rung of home ownership. The baby of the bunch the last to fly the nest.

Callum had spent a lot of time at her parents' place anyway. His parents weren't the most attentive people on the planet, sure, but the fact that they were neglectful, workaholic parents meant that Callum had always been mature. She remembered how different he was from her brother, despite Lewis being a few months older. Callum had been born serious; she always used to tease him about it.

'Right, yeah. I... need a minute.'

The easy tilt of his head was all he replied with. He just sat there, watching her watch him. It was oddly calming. She tried to get herself back onto that street, in front of him. She remembered her shock, the slap when he'd reached for her. He'd not been handsy, but the way he'd pulled her to him, his eyes half closed, his head tilting... she'd reacted.

Hearing him speak about liking her for so long. He made it sound like he'd been pining for her the whole time. Which was nuts. He acted like he didn't even *like* her half the time. It was their thing. They were known for it, winding each other up. People rolled their eyes around them whenever they started bickering about things. They challenged each other on everything, competing. Correcting, teasing. Pranking.

Alice just couldn't see how in the last two years, so much had changed between them. She just couldn't believe it. Wouldn't, even, if he wasn't right here in front of her. It was the way he was looking at her. Like he did when they were kids, and first started hanging out in those early days. It was the look she sometimes saw on his face as an adult too, but it was always just a glimpse. Like his mask slipping, and then he'd cover his face back up in his trademark moody gaze. It didn't make sense. Why the hell would he be interested, when she'd given him a hard time for so long? He was here, talking about her leading things. Being there to support her, and she didn't remember a time when they weren't frenemies with a good dollop of sexual tension thrown in on her side.

Shit. Sex. Oh God, we've already done it. We definitely have. Eighteen months of living together? A certainty. Callum Roberts and I have been naked. We've done the horizontal mambo. He's probably seen me on the toilet. Heard me fart. Oh God. No. Coma, come back to me. Maybe if I go back under, my brain will fix itself.

'I know that this is really hard, baby.' He leaned forward in his chair a little, and Alice heard the wood creak beneath his six-foot-odd frame. 'Believe me, I fucking hate it, but I'm just so glad you woke up. We'll be okay, I promise. I took time off work. I'll be right here with you. At your pace.'

He threw her a look so hopeful she wanted to cry. He was hurting, and she felt like it was her fault. The way he looked at her, she just couldn't take it. Her head was banging. It was just too much. She couldn't remember Callum after that night. She had nothing to go on. Nothing to give her a clue to anything. Maybe she'd had a bump on the head back then, in 2020, and no one had noticed. Hence the twilight zone she'd woken up in. 'My pace.'

'Yeah.' He smiled, just a little one, from the corner of his mouth. 'We've got all the time in the world.' He sat back in his chair. Not that it was his chair, but with his size, he bloody well claimed it. He'd always been a big guy, not skinny, not thickset. Just muscular in an annoyingly effortless way. It had always irked her, when she had to run miles to keep the doughnuts she liked to eat at her desk off her thighs. *Oh God. Running.*

'Okay. First question: will I be able to run again?'

He nodded earnestly to that one. 'I already asked the doc. Your broken bones have already set; luckily there was no major damage. He says he has every confidence for a complete recovery, given time, rest and physio.' He looked away. 'Physically anyway. The other stuff, they're still going to be working on, I guess.'

Alice swallowed hard. She didn't ask anything about that. She didn't want to know. She couldn't take that yet. The thought of living her life with two years a blank forever terrified her.

'You'll be back on that track in no time.'

'You know about the track?' She always preferred to run outdoors, not on a treadmill in a fart-ridden, air-conditioned gym, and ran three nights a week at the local stadium track. She'd done it for years. Her little secret me time. 'So I still run?'

'Yep.' He smiled. 'Three times a week, like clockwork. We run it together.' He smiled again when her mouth dropped. 'Knew that one would get a reaction.'

'You do not run. You tease... teased me about my running!'

He laughed. 'I sure do. Lots has changed since your sleep, sparrow.'

4

ALICE

Sparrow. There it was again.

'Sparrow?'

His face fell a little. 'It's nothing,' he said, his fingers moving to play with the bird ring on his left hand. He looked disappointed. Hurt maybe? She didn't press him any further. She had to be careful here. He was part of her family. She couldn't blur the lines any further than they were. She'd get too confused. She'd heard that word before though. Childhood nickname? Nope. Hers were pretty unoriginal. Geeky Gail for one, before she'd got contacts, and later, laser surgery. She'd worn the biggest framed glasses known to man in her tweens. Her school photos were a hoot. She remembered her brother had always ripped the piss and she felt a sudden pang for him. And the urge to kill him. How the hell had this happened under his watch anyway? He'd always threatened to pound any of his friends who even spoke to his sister. Sure, Callum was the exception in that he always slept over at their house, and so she was always used to having him around. She remembered Lewis joking once that he could trust Callum around Alice, because his sister would rather die than date him. She could remember that as clear as day.

Callum and Lewis had been in their parents' kitchen, goofing around. Well, those two were. She'd come down in her pyjamas to get some cereal. It was the weekend and the boys had been dressed in their football home kits. Her parents had already gone out early, something about a garden centre and the front flower beds. Alice remembered her dad muttered something about wanting to have a nap in front of the cricket, but they'd trundled off anyway.

Alice's heart clenched at the memory. Her parents were so suited and still so in love. She wanted that, someday. Maybe. She scrunched her nose up, deep in thought. She also couldn't imagine being that co-dependant with another person. Being that linked with someone; she just couldn't see it happening to her. Which was fine, because she preferred to make her own plans anyhow. She focused again on the memory, pushing aside her feelings about her life plans. She side-eyed Callum. For someone who planned to just live her life, and not long for that happy-ever-after, she'd apparently changed her mind. Hitched her wagon to the one man who was linked to her in about every way he could be.

* * *

She'd padded barefoot in the kitchen that morning, still sleepy and looking forward to an easy day. 'Coming to the match?' Callum had asked, as he did every Sunday morning. And every Saturday morning when training came around, come to think of it.

'Nope.' He looked her up and down, and she blushed. She'd already started to regret wearing her Pocahontas PJs. She saw his eyes widen.

'Why, what you doing? Reading?'

'Studying,' she countered, filling her bowl with muesli. Trust him to suss out the fact that she was, in fact, planning to read the books on design she'd borrowed from the library. It was so annoying when he did that. Lewis was jabbering on, talking about the upcoming game. He always held a little strategy meeting before he played a match. Mostly with himself, Callum occasionally chipping in. If their dad was there, he turned into some kind of Yorkshire Bielsa and talked about strategy and game play. Lots of other stuff that Alice had no interest in listening to on a Sunday morning. Especially before she'd eaten. She got hangry pretty quickly.

Moving to the fridge, she'd realised that Callum was blocking it with his meaty frame. She could barely make out the corner of it behind him. She'd looked up at him expectantly, and he was already looking at her. And down her body. And back up her. He fixed his eyes onto hers and blushed.

'Morning,' he muttered.

'Morning.' She'd smiled back. 'Breakfast time.'

'Er, yeah,' he countered. 'I already ate. Protein pancakes. My mum made them.'

'Cute story, did she do little smiley faces with whipped cream?' She'd put her fingers to the corners of her mouth, pulling them out into a clown-like grin. His jaw had clenched, and she'd revelled secretly at the fact she'd gotten to him. It was so easy. The thrill of it was addictive. It gave her a reason to talk to him, she'd realised, but that didn't mean a thing. Not. A. Thing. She'd put her hands by her sides. Her fingers had brushed the front of his T-shirt by accident, and she'd felt him flinch. Lean back a little. She'd done the same, mortified at breaking the touch barrier. And feeling something when she had. She'd found herself wondering idly what was beneath the football jersey.

'Er, no. Blueberries.' It came out as a mutter. Lewis was shouting at the TV in the corner of the kitchen now, last night's highlights playing on the small screen.

'Cool, cool. Listen, can you er...' She'd moved in closer, and his eyes grew to saucers. The colour of them darkened, almost to black. She'd felt his breath on her face as he dipped down. Minty fresh as always. He always smelled nice, oddly different to the other boys at school. 'Move?'

He'd jumped a half-foot to the side when she spoke. 'Shit, sorry. I thought...'

'You thought what?' Alice and her brother had spoken in unison. Callum had made a weird sort of noise and blushed like a ripe tomato.

'Nothing.' He'd frowned. 'You ready to go Lew, or what?'

'Ah! Ha ha! You thought she wanted to kiss you! I saw it.' Lewis's face had lit up like it did when he was a kid. Gleeful at the development.

Her brother wasn't going to let this drop, Alice had realised with a groan. But had he been about to kiss her? Nah. As if he'd thought that, she'd just got in his face, that was all. As if he'd even looked at her that way. Eugh. She saw the girls that looked his way. She wasn't like them. Didn't really want to be, either. The thought of Callum liking her had bumped around in her skull, but she hadn't believed it. She'd got under his skin just as much as he did her. A bit like a blood-sucking tick that irritates the bejesus out of you till you twist the little bugger's head off.

'I fucking did not,' Callum had growled at Lewis. 'We off, or what?'

Wow. Alice had looked at Callum, but he wouldn't meet her eye. He had been so angry at the suggestion. Well, that had hurt. Stung a little. More than a little. That he didn't even see her that way shouldn't have bothered her, but she had still felt the sting of rejection regardless.

He had always had girls around him, asking him out, calling him up. He had always taken the calls out of earshot, but whenever he was round at their house, she had got the impression he had always had a girl on his mind. He had always shut down any ribbing from the lads on the team. If he kissed, he sure didn't tell. She had just sensed it sometimes, a quietness about him. Something beyond his easy nature.

Why he had tortured himself with so many hangers-on, she never knew. The fact that he had been offended at the thought of kissing her was a bit shit though. Still, she was the little sister of the douchebag currently winding Callum up. It had hardly been a shock he was annoyed.

'One more little joke, and I'll thump you.' Callum had looked like he was desperate to do it too. When Alice had looked at him, his fists had been clenched. When he had caught her looking, he hung them limply by his sides. 'Outside.'

Her brother Lewis, the annoying shitbag that he was, had laughed.

'I'm sorry, mate. Come on, I know that my sister is safe with you. Why do you think I let you hang here so much or stay over? The other guys know the score, but I definitely don't have to worry about you two getting together.'

She had noticed that Callum had clenched his fists together again.

'She told me herself.' Her brother had shot her one of his smug little looks. 'She told me she'd rather die than date you anyway. So we're cool. Let's go.' He had picked up his kitbag, nicked a piece of toast from Alice's freshly made plate, dodging her attempts to give him a dead arm, and headed out of the door. Oblivious about the bomb he'd left ticking in the room he'd vacated.

Callum had still been standing there, his fists clenching and unclenching like a cat kneading a blanket. Looking at her with eyes she could swear looked sad.

'Ignore him. I didn't say that.' Alice wasn't one for lying, but the truth hadn't been easy to explain without sounding too interested, or too mean. *The lady doth protest too much.* She had bitten at her lip. Shit. *Don't blush*, she'd urged her already hot cheeks. *Don't blush.*

'You didn't?' The scowl he had been sporting lifted a little.

'No,' she'd said, trying and failing at not feeling a thrill when his lips had thrown out his seldom seen half-smile. It had always felt like a win when she got one of them. Him trying not to laugh at her jokes produced the same result, so she'd done it more. To get that cheeky little reward for herself. The fact that she'd made Callum Roberts smile. Moody, sullen Hebblestone High heartthrob Callum. The same heartthrob that had still been looking down at her, waiting for her to finish.

'Not exactly that, it wasn't a big discussion or anything. One of my friends made a comment about you, wondering why you were always hanging around here. She said you might like me.' His fists had clenched up again, and her heart had sunk. For a second there, she had thought he might like hearing that. Stupid Alice. God, sometimes she had worn herself out with pretending she didn't give a toss. 'I said I would rather die to shut her up and Lew was there. Earwigging as usual. I didn't mean anything against you.'

'You don't have to explain.'

'I know I don't.' She'd rolled her eyes. 'But I meant I'd never date any of my brother's friends.' She didn't know why she had needed to make that distinction. To lessen the awkward air her brother had left there, like a bad fart. 'I didn't want you to think I was talking about you.'

'Don't worry.' He'd swung his bag onto his shoulder. 'I know the last thing you'd ever talk about is me.'

He had left before she could say anything else. Just as well. She never could think of the right thing to say to Callum. They just seemed to rub each other up the wrong way. He had always looked at her as if she was stupid. No, not stupid. Like she didn't know something she should all the time. That was it. It had really pissed her off.

5

ALICE

'How come my brother let you live?' Alice asked, the minute the nurse had left with the tea tray. Callum was sipping coffee in his chair. He chuckled at her question. She watched him laugh. He was different around her now. Less guarded. It was surreal. She half expected him to tell her a bad joke or tease her like he usually did.

'Lewis? He had a few things to say, at the time.' Callum's jaw flexed with his answer. He was getting angry again at something. She could see the same old stare creeping back onto his face. He was getting lost in his head like she was.

'Why are you mad?' She asked him in a tone that implied she was irritated and stopped. 'Sorry, it's just...' She went to run her hand through her hair and was thwarted by her tubes. 'I'm know I'm confused, but you just seem so angry. I mean, I'm the one who woke up to all this.'

'I know, and I'm the one you forgot.' He fired that back just as harshly, before cutting himself off with a heavy sigh. His lips were clamped so tight together they had lost all colour. 'Sorry. I'm not angry. Well, I am, but not at you. Never at you.'

She believed every word. She knew him well enough to know that. She trusted him with the truth.

'I'm so glad you woke up. It's been...' His voice cracked. 'Look, all I'm saying is it's not easy for me either.'

She hadn't considered that. She had been waiting for someone to start laughing at the beginning, as if they couldn't keep up the prank any more. It was the drugs, she knew. The wooziness from being awake after so long asleep. She got all that. She just hadn't really considered how everyone else might feel. Especially him. She hadn't even known there had been a 'him' to sit by her bedside.

'I'm sorry. I was single when I got into the accident. My head thinks I was, I mean.' *Happily single*, she almost added, but that wouldn't entirely be true. She did remember feeling lonely sometimes. Wishing that she had someone to share things with.

'I know. Of all the times we've had together, your brain gets stuck on that one. It's like some cruel joke.'

'Drunk drivers,' she quipped. 'So unreliable.'

He smiled, but she could see the strain in his eyes. Talking about this was hurting him. She could see it as plain as the nose on his face. And hated it. She'd hated that day, by the fridge. His last words to her before he left her clutching her Coco Pops. *The last thing she'd talk about.* As if he didn't even register on her radar. The same look of upset was on his face. A bleak look that took her breath away. A feeling they were already slightly out of step.

'Well, you're never getting into a taxi alone ever again, that's for sure. Not without me. Even then, I don't like the idea.'

God, she wished her heart wouldn't leap when he said things like that. It was so weird, hearing it from his lips. So strange to think that he considered her so precious.

'I can live with no more taxis,' she agreed. 'Did you really come here every day?'

For a split second, he shot her an incredulous look, before he beat it into submission with a tilt of his head. 'Every single day. I made a nuisance of myself, I think.'

'You were there by the bed when I woke up. You spoke to me. I didn't know who it was, but I heard it.'

He nodded, moving his chair closer to her with a flick of his body. 'I wanted to be there when you opened your eyes. Listen, I know that you're confused right now. It's a lot to take in, but I'm here. I will get us through this, I promise.'

He reached for her hand, but she pulled it away instinctively. 'I really think I should sleep now.'

He nodded slowly; his hand still outstretched. 'Okay.' The spring in his voice sounded dull now. He went as if to lean over her closer, but a nurse came in wheeling a trolley. She smiled awkwardly at them both.

'Right my lovelies, sandwich? Bit of sponge cake, if you like. Raspberry jam.'

'I'm just leaving actually, but this one is starving. Fill her plate.'

The nurse grinned, turning to make up a plate.

'My pleasure. Nice to have you back with us, dear.'

He turned to the door, and then back to Alice again. 'Sorry,' he said, his voice cutting out the closer he got. 'Don't hate me, but I'd like to kiss you goodbye...'

His lips were on hers as soon as she muttered a faint 'okay'. The woman, hell the room, seemed to disappear even before she closed her eyes in response. It was as though her body knew what to do, even if she didn't.

His mouth was warm, his lips soft. Chaste. Gentle. She'd imagined kissing these lips as a teenager, in her bedroom when he'd said something nice to her or teased her in his irritating way. For a creative person, it surprised the holy crap out of her that all that time imagining what it would be like was nothing compared to the reality. It wasn't a hard kiss, or even a sexy one. His lips had stayed sealed, closed to hers, the slant of his mouth turning to kiss the corner of her mouth before he pulled away. She felt his breath, faster than before. Saw the whites of his knuckles as he leaned over her bed rail.

He breathed her in, his lips a wisp away from touching hers once more. 'Sorry, sparrow, but I promised myself I would kiss you the second you woke up, and it's long overdue.' He touched his forehead to hers. The woman had already left, taking the noise of her task with her. The room was as silent as a pin, and full of questions she wanted to ask him. 'Goodnight, beautiful. I'll be here when you wake up in the morning.'

* * *

Callum had been gone hours, but she couldn't stop thinking about him. Trying to reconcile the man stood in the rain that night. The man sleeping in the chair. The boy in her childhood home. The way he kept trying to reach for her but stopped himself at the last minute. The way his kiss had seemed so controlled, as if he was trying to hold back, but struggling. It seemed unnatural for him not to touch her, and that's what kept her up. That kiss was not something from a casual dater, which she already knew he wasn't. She'd heard the timeline of their relationship. She knew that the fact he was living with her meant it was permanent. Pre-coma her was still her. Alice was still in the driving seat. She just wished she knew what she'd been up to. What her life now was.

It was all a mess. She was all talked out as well, after the doctor's sobering report. The police had been to see her too. It was hard to take in. The taxi driver really was okay, doing well. A man who she now knew to be called Thomas McKenzie. He'd been driving her home to Callum, they'd told her. Back to *their* home. She had an image in her mind of Thomas, his eyes in the rear-view mirror.

But she had to remind herself that the taxi driver she'd moaned to about Callum's clumsy pass wasn't the same man. Not Thomas. She didn't remember him. Or the night in question.

Thomas had been taking her home to her boyfriend, till they got shafted from the side by a minivan, driven by one Barry Evans. The police had laid it all out for her.

Barry had fallen out with his girlfriend while they'd been out drinking together and had failed to get a cab to take her home. Had decided in his beer-addled brain to nick one instead. Namely, a large, black, eight-seater minivan. It had been left running idle while the tired and busting for a wee driver had nipped to the loo between fares. The most stressful pee of his life, she thought to herself when the officers explained the accident. Barry wanted to meet his missus, thinking that his gallant behaviour would win her over. It didn't. He never got there. He skidded on some black ice and hit the side of their taxi at just under fifty miles an hour. The officers said they were lucky, given the size and condition of the vehicle. Poor Thomas had only got his new wheels the week before, at the urging of his missus to upgrade his clunker. It cushioned a lot of the impact, especially for him. Alice had come off far worse. Her head had hit the side window, breaking it, and fracturing her skull. Her brain had been thrown around, causing it to swell. Her body had shut itself down, the doctors eventually saving her, the coma doing the rest.

She'd been pulled out, blue-lighted to the hospital. Her heart had stopped in the ambulance. When they'd got her back, she didn't wake up. The doctors had told the police the odds. She got the feeling from the way they'd conveyed it to her that they'd been expecting the worst. As if they'd never expected to be taking her statement. Or lack of it.

Recovery would take a while, the doctor concluded. Her broken bones were already healing, her casts removed from her limbs. Her ribs were at a comfortable level of pain, almost healed. She wanted to punch him in the chest and ask him if he thought *that* was a comfortable level of pain. She didn't though; she just sat and listened to everything he said. Everything the nurses said. Everything the police said. About possible court dates, that Barry had pleaded guilty but was trying to claim he was mad on love. The officer rolled his eyes when he said that bit. The police sounded almost bored of speaking about them. Barry was locked up till he faced justice, but they felt sure, now she was awake, he would change his plea. Probably now he wasn't at risk of facing a manslaughter charge, Alice thought with a shudder. She was glad his memory was intact. She wanted him to remember what he'd done forever.

'We shouldn't need anything further from you,' the policeman had said to her. His parting words. 'You can go back to living your life now, Miss McClaren. You had a lucky escape. But the worst is pretty much over.'

A nurse who had entered the room as they were leaving tutted over her shoulder at them.

'Pretty much over,' she echoed. Her thick Irish accent filled the room. 'I'm Neve, by the way. That man is an idiot, if you don't mind me saying.' She was checking the monitors, refilling bags of medicine and hooking and unhooking wires. Alice felt a bit like a machine, and it got a bit awkward when she emptied her catheter. 'You have a long road ahead of you before you feel normal, and I don't sugar-coat my words.'

'I noticed,' Alice muttered back. 'I feel like I've been through a spin dryer. What does my face look like?'

The nurse stopped her ministrations. 'Do you want to see?'

'I don't know,' Alice realised. 'Do I want to see it?'

Neve pulled a silver and cream compact out of her uniform pocket. It had a watercolour drawing of a brown bunny on the back.

She opened it, turning it till she was satisfied that Alice could see herself.

'Now, we did the best we could with your hair. We washed the blood out. Brushed it a little.' Alice was just happy her hair was still there. She had expected to look like some kind of extra from a horror movie. She had part of her head still bandaged up. Neve told her it was to heal the recovery, protect it from infection. She refuted her claim it made her head look like a giant white marshmallow with a loud ripple of laughter. Apparently, that was still the drugs she was coming off.

Her face was scratched up, a couple of stitched areas still visible on her lower forehead. A deep gash on her right cheek at one time, she could tell from the angry skin around it.

'Was this from the glass?'

Neve nodded, continuing to move Alice's body slowly as she washed the areas uncovered. Alice watched her passively, one eye still on the mirror in her hand. Her lips were pale, a tiny little mark on the bow of her lip, but everything looked like it would heal well enough.

'The plastic surgeon came to assess while you were asleep. He stitched you up. You should have a small scar, if that. He's pretty good.' She lifted her right arm, and Alice took in the thick welt of light rainbow bruises she still had.

'I must have been a mess, if my bruises still look that bad.'

Neve nodded, making a note on the chart at the bottom of the bed. 'The bruising was black, thick. You did well. You'll heal. You have been lucky, and I don't say that lightly. We'll get the catheter taken out in the morning hopefully. The doctors are keen to get you back on your feet, get your mobility going. Your muscles will take time to build back up. A little bird told me that you used to run, though?'

Alice scrunched her eyes up. 'A little bird called Callum?'

Neve grinned. 'Got it in one. That will help, you being on the athletic side. You'll get back to where you were, it just won't be overnight.'

Alice sighed heavily. 'Great.'

'I know, pet.' Neve shot her a sympathetic glance. 'Can I get you anything before you turn in for the night?'

Alice narrowed her eyes. 'Yeah, did you nurse me when I was... you know.'

'Asleep? Yes, love. What do you want to know?'

'The man. Callum. He's been here a lot. You've seen him, with me?'

Neve smoothed down the edge of her blanket, flashing her a wide-toothed grin.

'Since the minute you got here, he's been here, in your room. He drove the doctors mad, so he did. He's a stubborn one. It's cute to see. Of course, I'm terminally single with my hours. Everyone on the dating sites just ask about the uniform when I tell them what I do. Not like your bloke. The nurses here have been swooning over him a bit,' she confided, warming to her theme now. 'He's never given any of them a second glance. You've got a good one there.'

'Oh, right,' Alice muttered back. 'Thanks.' Neve took her leave, taking the stuff away with her and turning down the lights in her room before she left.

'Sleep well, Alice.'

Left alone, Alice ran through what Neve had told her. The fact that she was that to him now: so important that he'd sat by her bed day after day. Talking to the doctors, her parents. Her dad's voice came into her head. *He's part of the family. You rather like him.* She thought of him cussing out the doctors when she'd first woken up. How scared and desperate he'd sounded. Everything he'd given her a glimpse of in that kiss. Could she really be Callum's true love? She wasn't sure she even believed in that, not really. It was out there she knew, but rare. Not everyone got that in life. Thinking of Callum, scrunched in that chair night after night, it warmed her heart to think about it. About him, and how she was going to play this. What if she never remembered him? What then? What would she say to a man who sat beside her bedside, kicking off with the doctors in his fear? Living with her? It sounded so... permanent. She tried again to recall anything. A tiny glimmer of anything she could pull from the time she'd lost. Something about Callum that wasn't from when she loved to spar with him. Nothing came. Just the twinge of an oncoming headache.

She didn't even have her phone. It was smashed up in the crash. She wanted to go through it, to see the life she had for herself. See her own texts, her own social media posts. *Oh God, I'll probably be in the paper. Better avoid Google.* Not that she had her laptop either. She was stuck in this bed, half unable to move.

Apparently tomorrow that would change; she would be moved out of bed. Small steps, maybe to sit in the chair. Her muscles had already wasted away while she was asleep, and the physio was keen to get her mobility up again. So was she. She needed to get back to her life. Hopefully she would jog her memory back into place. If she could just remember...

6

CALLUM

Callum sat on the front step of the house he shared with Alice, sipping a beer and watching the quiet street at night. The skip, half full of rubble from the old rockery out back he'd been digging up, sat on the drive. An empty bag of plaster, partly weighed down by rocks, flapped in the evening wind. It pierced the silence of the night. Flap. Flap. Flap. So quiet, and so dark. It was inky black, the sky. It held so few stars he could count them on one hand. The breeze caressed his jaw, making his freshly shaved skin tingle.

He'd sat here many nights before, with Alice. The pair of them knackered after working on the house, usually covered in some kind of dust or paint flecks. Her sipping her own bottle next to him, snuggled into his side. That ratty poncho she chose to wear on cold nights tickling his nose as he pulled her in for a kiss. He could never stop kissing that woman. Even then, when she'd been his. It was like he needed to constantly remind himself of that fact, and her. Not that he did. She was as besotted with him as he was with her. He knew that. *Had known* that. It felt like that was gone now. It was like her heart had died, and the pieces of him entwined within didn't survive when she was brought back to life.

Her eyes were the worst. When she'd looked at him in the hospital room, he'd never seen her look so devoid of... anything. Those deep-green eyes, so... vacant. She didn't even recognise him at first, and he'd been spending his days memorising every tiny detail of hers for months. Years. *Decades.*

He knew even before the doctor worked it out. He could tell something was badly wrong. What he wasn't banking on was the fact that her brain would be stuck on the second worst night of his life. The night he'd got too drunk, and his emotion had spilled over. He'd made such a dick of himself, and she'd been so mad. Not a great start to charm a woman waking from a three-month nap.

He'd gone right round to her house the next day, sunk to his knees on this very step, and begged her to forgive him. She had, in the end. Not at first. What she actually did was scream at him for waking her up on her only day off and slam the door right in his face. When he returned an hour later with bacon sandwiches, coffee and doughnuts, she'd relented and let him in.

She didn't remember any of that, though. She didn't remember how much he'd tried to win her over. God, she had been so hard to date in the beginning. Fiercely independent. There was just something there, under his skin, that knew it would be worth it. They'd been so bloody happy, so close to everything coming together, and then the accident had happened. He thought he'd lost her.

That was the first worst night of his life. A pole position memory. Her scream on the phone, the grind of metal, the sound of glass. Callum had run straight out of the door and headed to where she'd said she'd been in the taxi. His chest still burned at the thought of that run. The whole way there, his feet getting cut because he hadn't stopped for shoes. Every large step he took, he just kept thinking the same thing. *Not her. Not now. Please.* She was streets away from home, but it felt like he ran forever.

They wouldn't let him ride in the ambulance with her. The

doors had slammed shut, his last image the chest compressions that had shook her body on the gurney. A passer-by had offered to drive him, but he couldn't remember the ride, or the good Samaritan. He'd shouted his thanks and ran to be by her side.

At the hospital, he was told her heart had stopped on the journey. It was as if when it restarted, the memory of him had been booted right out of every aorta. He had her back, but he didn't have *her*. *His* Alice.

Callum headed back indoors, slamming the wooden door just a little bit too hard. He felt like he could pull a full-on Hulk and throw the bloody thing into outer space.

The way she looked at me.

Callum had forgotten the way she used to scowl at him. He'd thrived on it once upon a time. It had given him joy to wind her up. It was so easy. He didn't even need to try most of the time. Something, well, everything about him seemed to irritate her from the off. He'd soon developed a taste for it. Winding up his best friend's little sister. Juvenile, sure, but fun. He found he was a little addicted to making her squirm. The buzz he felt from her perfect little brows furrowing, her button nose scrunching up in disgust. Her hand coming up to swat at him, as though he was an irritating horsefly, buzzing around her.

Which, one time, he did pretend to be. She ran to the kitchen in response, coming after him moments later brandishing a big plastic fly swatter. They'd ended up in the garden after twenty minutes of her chasing him, cursing his very existence, while her brother and his girlfriend laughed in the background. Callum was busy making fly noises and giving her body jolts as he jabbed his fingers into her sides, making her yip in surprise and swat him harder. Her face would be contorted up, her frustration giving way to reluctant laughter, as it sometimes did. She was always so expressive; he knew just how to read her. That had never changed. Till now.

She would remember that day, he guessed. He could ask her if she remembered, but what good would it do? She'd hated him then. She was single, and not even looking to date when that had happened. He didn't need her to remember those times, the horse play. He needed her to remember how far they'd come. How much they adored each other *now*. She'd looked at him like he was her brother's annoying best friend. It crushed him utterly. He couldn't, wouldn't go back to chasing her around the garden again in an excuse to touch her. To be close. He knew the saying. The opposite of love wasn't hate. It was indifference. Even being hated by her was preferable than not being anything to her.

He'd reasoned this fact with himself so many times over the years. It was why he teased her. Connection. Being detested by her was better than her not thinking of him at all. If he couldn't touch her soft skin, at least he could get under it. That had been enough, till the night when his emotions and beer had got the better of him. She'd looked beautiful that night, and she had no shortage of men looking in her direction.

Lewis was engaged to Migs, and they had been sucking face in the corner of the room, their relationship as vomit inducing and as solid as ever. Callum had arrived late; the job he was working on hadn't gone to plan. One of his builders had drilled right through a water pipe, causing a flood and meaning they'd all had to scramble to repair the damage. It had written his day off, and he was looking at a headache the day after. If it had been any other engagement party, he wouldn't have gone.

The second he'd set eyes on Alice, he was glad he'd bothered. Just being near her gave him a high. Recharged him. She'd looked stunning that night, and it had evolved from there. A night of watching her from afar just didn't cut it any more. He was feeling every inch the lonely bachelor and he had to try, right? But his beer and whisky-soaked thoughts had gotten the better of him. She'd been so mad, slapping him and getting into the taxi. All he'd gained from her that night was the bird, when she flipped him off on her departure.

But it had been the night that started everything. The only trouble was, that was where her damn memory ended. Right where it had all begun for them. As he headed up to bed to get a few hours' sleep before he headed back to the hospital, he wondered how life could be so cruel. He'd got her back, sure, but she felt further away from him than ever before.

7

ALICE

The trolley the cleaning staff used had a squeaky wheel. It sounded like a cat being trod on every few yards. Over the course of the last few days, Alice had learned to despise it. She'd just get used to the peace of it being gone, and then somebody would wheel the ruddy thing back out again. She'd wondered to herself many times whether it was an emergency one, for spills and stuff. She was on the intensive care ward though. Many of the people on here were asleep or sedated. So not spillages then, just a regular cleaning trolley.

As she sat in the boxy, plastic-coated chair next to her bed, all she could do was listen for the squeak. Even if she tried not to, her ears seemed to be tuned into its frequency. There was no real discernible timetable to it either. She knew that things were cleaned every few hours; she'd seen a cleaning time clock-in list on her bathroom wall. She saw the cleaners come into her room, but the trolley was left outside each time. Alice couldn't tell whether the trolley that specific cleaner used was the offender. She was too annoyed with herself to ask either. She didn't want people to think she was going mad. It was driving her barmy, the mystery of the squeaky wheel, but she didn't *want* people to know it was. She didn't quite trust them not to lock her up in some kind of rehab centre.

She'd heard the doctors discussing her health outside her room, and she knew that they were talking about her going home. As in, her being discharged and leaving the hospital. Which is what was stressing her out. Well, that and the damn trolley. She had to go home, but she wouldn't go home without knowing irrefutably what that noise was. As she'd said to her dad on the phone the first day she'd refused visitors, she had her priorities straight. She knew what was important.

It was the first thing she wanted to ask Callum when he arrived. About the trolley.

He'd left late the night before. After breaking through the barrier. In more ways than one.

Okay, so for three days after Callum had kissed her goodbye, she'd shunned everyone. She wasn't necessarily proud of herself, but the minute the nurse had left, when she'd seen her face in the mirror, she'd fallen apart. It was a lot. Things were moving fast. Too fast. She found herself wanting to throw any spanner in the works, just to give herself a minute to think.

She asked for the doctors to come back in, to test her knowledge, to ask her questions. She binge-watched the news channel. She was stunned at the state of the world, the enormity of the events of the last couple of years, but then again, she had felt like that since before the coma.

She'd been tired, she remembered. The last memory, her going home, she'd analysed it over and over. Every moment with Callum. How'd she felt. What he'd said. How she'd felt about her life. She'd been happy, but not all the time. Not outright depressed. Jaded, maybe.

She had been working hard. Lewis and Migs's engagement

party was supposed to make her feel better too, a hit of love and family after the long week of trying to run her business and organise contractors for her house. She'd seen a total of fifteen by then. Six were over budget, three of them had asked her where her husband was, nixing them from the list immediately. Some were okay, but she didn't feel like they were the right fit. Two of them had ogled her openly. One had even asked her out, then taken a phone call outside where he didn't think Alice could hear. Telling his wife he would of course bring home some milk. And nappies. She'd locked the front door on him and ignored him till he went away. She'd felt overwhelmed. Almost wishing she *did* have a husband, who could tell gits like that off and take some of the stress on his shoulders. She just never thought too hard about whose shoulders they might be.

She remembered thinking to herself that night, earlier, before the kiss attempt from Callum, that she needed to change. Work a bit less, or at least try to have a bit more of a social life, rather than just existing to run through a to-do list every day. She never thought it would actually happen. She'd lied to herself before that she'd work less, but the next day she was right back at it. Steadfastly single and working her arse off. The knowledge that she did in fact, get a life and had no recollection of any of it was ironic at best.

Now she felt different. Not cheated so much, but angry that someone decided to do a stupid thing. A stupid, drunken thing that affected her and stole two years of her life to boot.

Two eventful years. From the little she'd heard, she'd been a busy little bee herself. She'd needed a minute, so she did what she would have done before she went for her little nap. She took charge. Banned all visitors till she found out what state she was in, emotionally and physically. Hunkered down to draw on her own strength.

Physically, she wasn't too bad. She looked like the grungiest colours of the rainbow; she had some little scratches which must have started out as big scratches. She didn't have the clothes from that night; they'd been cut off her by paramedics and then taken by the police. Not that she wanted them back. Or to see them.

In her locker was a selection of new clothes. All her size. Different to what she might usually have worn. These were a bit more confident. The underwear was all lacy and very sexy. It made her blush when the nurse told her that Callum had brought the bag in for her. He'd seen her underwear.

Then, she realised that he'd seen more than that. Probably a lot of times too, which sounded so absurd in her own head that she giggled out loud. If the teenage girl she once had been had known that little fact, she would have probably done more than laugh. When she thought of his goodbye kiss, her cheeks flamed with warmth. *He only gave me a chaste little kiss, and I'm already wanting to do it again.* Whatever her body was dealing with, it sure recognised the touch of Callum on her skin. She needed to get her head straight and figure out what the heck she was going to do. She knew one thing for certain. She couldn't just go back to the house with Callum. Not after that kiss. It was too much. She didn't trust herself right now, especially around him.

When she'd finished talking to the doctors, and hiding in her room, she'd got herself dressed in a comfortable pair of grey sweatpants and a fitted T-shirt. Over the next two-and-three-quarter days, she'd gotten to know her body again. She could walk, slowly at first, and with help, but although her limbs still felt weak and fuzzy at times, and it made her despair, the nurses spurred her on. Her physio was impressed so far, but she just wanted to get out of there. The coma had given her body time to heal, and her runner body was weakened, but present. By the end of the third day, she felt like she was back in her own skin, and her thoughts turned back to Callum.

Getting better meant going home. Where she lived with her brother's best friend. The kid turned man who had scowled at her for half her life and was just always... there.

At the end of the third day of enforced isolated therapy, all she could think about was how Callum still stayed. That first day, she had been so cross with him, but he'd stayed. Answered her questions. The comment he'd made about being forgotten had stayed with her too. She did care about him. She knew that, even with the coma and the brain fog still swirling around in her head. The kiss had confirmed it for her. She just didn't know what those feelings were. Did her body remember the man, or still pine for the boy? She couldn't be sure, but the look of sadness on his face was not one she wanted to see again. Especially if she was the cause. She tried to put herself in his shoes, but couldn't imagine how she'd cope. Being with her was hurting him, and she could not tolerate that.

She'd shut him right out after that night. She'd shut everyone out. Stopped taking calls, especially from Callum. She'd had to. It was just too confusing to think about right at that moment. She'd found herself going through her past with him, what she could remember of it. All pre-relationship of course, which was entirely unhelpful. She was getting to grips with her body again, but the revelation that she'd been in a crash and woken up with a live-in boyfriend? Even though it was Callum, someone she knew, it was still crazy. Bat-shit totally crazy.

Her past was full of him, but not much of it gave her any clue as to how they got from being irritated by each other to shacking up. He'd said he liked her, but one confession didn't add up to all this. The fact their lives were so entwined.

She needed some of the dots to connect before she saw him again. Seeing him was the problem, though. She'd had more than a mental reaction to the news. She'd had a rather embarrassing physical one even before that. Seeing him there, in her hospital room, concerned, all alpha...

Could that be it? The growling, moody eyes, the brooding nature.

'Oh God,' she said aloud to the empty room. 'I still fancy him.'

Great. Her brain had wiped their relationship, but seemingly left a lick of lust behind. More than a lick, she corrected her own thoughts, and thinking of him as a kid only added to that. Something about the broody nature, the attention he'd given her. It reminded her of when they were younger.

She tried to make the pieces fit but got nothing but a headache to add to the one she'd had since waking up. The hospital staff had told her to expect that, but whenever she pushed the old grey matter, it prodded back. Keeping him away was necessary. Self-preservation even. He'd looked so hurt; she didn't want to add to that by giving him mixed signals.

The nurses had made a few comments about him not being on the ward. Alice wasn't to know that he normally brought a box of doughnuts in for them every morning. No visits, no doughnuts. She'd been in the doghouse with them all since. Every time he called the ward, asking to speak to her, she declined. The nurses passed on his messages in huffy tones. Guilt-inducing looks. Eye rolls when she declined the offer of a phone to call him back. Her parents only rang twice, but they hadn't changed a bit. Well, they were a little older and the worried looks were new, but they were still the same, and she understood the people who had raised her. She knew they were trying to take things in too. She wondered if they were talking to Callum about her. She hated the thought of that. As the baby of the family, everyone had always tried to shield her. Well, Callum not so much. Thinking back, he had treated her more like an adult than anyone else who lived under the roof of her childhood home.

And she'd gone right back to thinking about Callum again. They were together. So whatever had happened between them, after that night, had been fast. They'd said she'd lived with him for eighteen months. So that meant, from drunken slob-kiss-gate, to when he moved in, the whole thing had taken six months. Pretty fast, some would say. Given that Alice had only dated a few men in her life, and been in a relationship no longer than three months, she knew it must mean something. She hadn't been a zombie during that time, she had been herself. Her usual bossy, opinion-ated and relationship-doubting self. Which she had thought no man would ever break through. But by the way Callum had looked at her when she'd woken up, she knew they'd been in love.

She could see it on his face and that's what had freaked her out. The fact that he was looking at her like he was really seeing her, and what he saw, he adored. It was a lot of pressure for a freshly thawed ice queen. Especially since she'd felt... something melt. Lust and something else. Recognition, but not at first. When she'd first looked at him, all crumpled up and shaggy, dishevelled, the look on his face when his eyes locked with hers had stirred her. Deep inside, she knew him. She couldn't explain it, but she felt out of her depth.

Of course, she knew him; she'd reasoned that he'd probably spent half her childhood under her family's roof. He was ever present. She'd tried to reason that this was the key, but when she'd seen her parents, her body didn't have the same response. Maybe when she saw Lewis. Her brother always made her react, they were like silly teens half the time and best mates the rest. He'd be mad, having his visits blocked. Maybe she should call him, allow just him to visit. Swear him to secrecy. Maybe seeing him would help. She needed her big brother.

A nurse sorted it out for her without comment. She'd come back to the room half an hour later. He was on his way.

She'd gussied herself up the best she could, finding a make-up bag amongst the things Callum had left for her. She was waiting for him when the commotion started at the ward door.

'What the hell?' One of the nurses ran over, and Alice could make out two heads, smashed up against the two glass slats in the door. The door was opening and shutting in quick succession, a few inches at a time. Bang. Bang. Bang. The nurse pulled the handle, and two men spilled into the room.

'Lew? Callum?' Alice took the two men in, marvelling at the sight of Lewis and his fresh-looking split lip. Blood was trickling down his chin, matching a smear of red on the glass of the door. Hmm, some things never changed. The two of them were always scuffling, she remembered with a flash that made her headache intensify. Lewis was wearing a smart suit, and she clocked his Tweety Pie belt buckle. He thought the little touches of individuality gave him an edge over the other carbon copy suit wearers in his rather formal law firm. He had lots of quirky belt adornments, but Tweety was always her favourite. Oddly, even though all of the nurses were looking at them, and the two of them had obviously just fought each other outside, it was the sight of that silly buckle that made her break. She laughed. Not just laughed, she brayed like a donkey.

'Is she all right?' Lewis asked, his mouth open halfway, directed towards Callum. Clean-shaven Callum. The beard had gone. He looked even hotter without it. *Damn him*. He shrugged, an odd smile on his face. He looked less dishevelled, his dark locks out of place the only sign of struggle.

'She's still in there,' he muttered. 'Hi, Ali.'

'Hey, sis.' Lewis beamed, putting his arms out in front of him.

It was that comment that sent her racing to his arms. Callum lifted his arms the second she started moving. She didn't realise till after she'd already passed him what he'd thought. She pulled herself away from her brother's shoulder to smile at him.

'Sorry,' she whispered. He nodded, his face blank. There it was again, that hurt look. That-cut-me-deep-but-pretending-it-didn't look. She squeezed her brother tighter, turning away. 'Thanks for coming.'

'Try to stop me,' they both said in unison. Behind them, one of the student nurses gasped, nudging her mate, who was stood gawping at her side.

'I get it now; she's got another fella on the side!' It was meant to be a whisper, but the comment echoed around the space. A couple of titters started up, but a growling voice cut them dead.

'He's her brother.' Callum's voice was unsteady, shaky. 'I'm her... I'm with her.' She eyeballed him over the crook of Lewis's arm. He looked furious.

'How come you're here?' she thought to ask belatedly. It only darkened his features further. 'I mean, I'm glad you are... but I said no visitors.'

Callum shrugged, the frown never leaving his face, and some-thing made her think of her childhood again. That day by the fridge. He'd had that look that day. When Lewis had said she'd never be caught dead with Callum.

'You try and stop him. He was here when I arrived.' Lewis pulled away from her and gave her his usual dazzling smile. Tucking her under his shoulder, he looked down the corridor. The nurses took this opportunity to suddenly look busy, and she walked with him, back to her temporary digs. She could hear Callum's footsteps behind them. The minute they were in the room, he strode over to his chair, sitting back in it and looking tired. Lewis ushered her back over to the chair she'd been sitting in by the window, at the other side of the bed. He sat on the bed, plonking himself down on her pillows.

'Feet,' Callum half snarled, and Lewis took his feet off the bed.

'Grumpy,' he said to his friend, before turning back fully to her. 'So, how are you feeling?'

'Good, mostly.' She pointed to her head. 'Aside from the missing two years.'

'Yeah.' Lewis nodded, as usual as calm and honest as ever. 'Well, the world is still crazy. You met up with our folks again already, so that's the same. Worried about you, obviously, but still as normal and boring as ever. I got married.'

'What!' She reached forward and slapped him on the arm. 'How dare you!'

'You were there,' Lewis replied. A look crossed his face. 'Wow, this is really real, huh.'

Alice digested the news. Tried to look through the filing cabinets in her mind for something, anything. Zip. She'd been so excited about seeing her brother get married. So happy for them both. Another thing Barry had ripped away from her. Another precious moment she could never get back.

'Yeah. It is.' She bit on her lip. She could feel Callum's eyes on her, but she didn't look anywhere near his direction. 'Tell me about it then. The wedding.'

'Now?' Lewis's quizzical brow made her smile.

'Now.'

Lewis drew a breath and looked across at Callum. 'Should I?'

A look passed between the two of them.

'Stop it.' Alice felt her anger rise to the surface of her already jangling nerves. 'Stop acting as if I'm not capable of coping.'

'It's not that—' Callum began, but her words cut through his like a hot knife through butter. It was out of her mouth before she could think.

'Listen to me, both of you. I get out of here tomorrow.'

The nurses had told her earlier. There was no more hiding. On the late rounds, the doctor had signed off. She had to come back for some physio to make sure her muscles were all waking up nicely, etc., and more brain work would be needed. More checks. But the real test, the doctors had told her, would be getting back to her real life, having skipped so much. They had healed her as much as they could. The rest would either come back or be lost forever. The only things Dr B kept repeating was that the brain was a complex part of science. The medical profession was still learning more about how trauma and injuries played their part on memory, cognition.

Given that she could remember almost everything – how to walk, how to do her job – and she had family support, Doctor B was keen to get her out of there and back home. But a huge part of Alice knew that the medical team that had saved her life were still not sure about whether her memories would come back. Ever. They'd told her about some cases they'd dealt with, nothing confidential, but the outcomes were so varied. Some people got parts of their past back. Remembered people, events. Others never did. That part of themselves was lost to them forever, and Alice feared that outcome more than anything else. At the time of her last memory, she'd been steadfastly single. Not even looking for that special someone. Now, she had Callum – what if she never remembered their journey? Her teenage heart would have been there; it still beat in her chest now. What if she'd missed the best part? Falling in love with the boy she'd known for years. The way he looked at her, the crease in his brow. He was in this. Committed. That kind of love wasn't something people walked away from. Even with her cynicism on full alert, she couldn't cancel out the feeling she'd forgotten a once-in-a-lifetime experience. Falling in love with him. What if he was it for her? She was just supposed to fill in the blanks along the way, never feel that again? Even Sleeping Beauty didn't have to go through this shit. It felt so... unfair. Like she'd gone to the toilet when the movie was playing and missed the best parts. Of all the years she could have lost, it sucked beyond belief the years with Callum were the ones that had fallen out of her head. Fate wasn't just a cruel mistress; it was a vindictive bitch.

Her family seemed so sure that she would recover fully. Her mother had been leaving positive messages with the nurses, telling her that she had every faith in her recovery. It was a lot of pressure.

She'd been hiding, she knew it. They knew it, but that time was over. She was being booted out, and she got the feeling that everyone around her were holding their breath, waiting for her to reboot to the Alice she had been before the crash. It didn't sit well with Alice one bit, nor did it help when they constantly looked to Callum for the right way to proceed.

'Tomorrow?' Callum echoed. She ignored him. She needed to get this out. Needed to exert some control before she left the sanctity of her hospital room. Set her stall out, before she got lost in all the things she didn't recall.

'Tomorrow. I'm going to check into a hotel.' She kept her voice down, not wanting a passing nurse to hear. She had only been discharged on the basis of the support she so obviously had. The fact that Callum had told them he was off work and would be ready to be there with her full time. It was a done deal, but no one had thought to ask her what she wanted to do.

'What?' Lewis said. 'Alice, no.'

'Hell no! Not happening, Ali.' Callum looked panicked, his head rapidly shaking from side to side.

The two men in her life piped up, but she shushed them both with a finger.

'Hey. Coma card. I speak first. I will check into a hotel—'

She jabbed her finger in the direction of Callum when he protested again. 'For God's sake, Callum, this is what I am talking about. I am always seen as the baby round you lot, all of you do it.'

'I don't,' Callum retorted, the resentment clear in his voice.

She looked him square in the eye. 'No, you don't. Normally. But when I fell into the – fell asleep.' She sighed. Trying to unscramble the jumbled events was exhausting. 'The last thing I remember is that we were friends, you were my brother's best friend, and I'd just turned you down. *For a date*,' she emphasised. 'I can't and won't expect you to stop working and upend your whole life any longer. You can't babysit me forever, especially if I don't remember us.'

His jaw clenched. 'You didn't ask me to, but it's happening, Ali. Whether you remember us or not, I do, and you belong at home, with me. It's your house. You need to come home.'

There it was again. That steely belief that they belonged together. She could hear it in his voice, see the emotion on his face. *What if I never feel that again, Callum? What then?* It was so unfair.

You belong with me. This man loves me. No, it's not love. It's more than that. End game. She could feel it from him, had since she'd woken up. Even when she had no idea who he was. It wasn't just some relationship. It was Callum. She knew the difference between a relationship and soulmates. Every time she saw him, she knew, and the fear of taking that away from him, not feeling it herself, scared her more than waking in that hospital bed. It wasn't just her life any more. He would never walk away. When he said things like that, making her feel like she was his everything, she couldn't help but feel grateful. Loved. And back to feeling frustrated when her memories threw up nothing but a big, empty void.

God, I wish I could remember something. Anything. Callum spoke as though his world revolved around her. Isn't that what every girl wanted? One crash, and it was lost to her. She felt stupid, desperate even. He was saying all the right things, and all she could do was look at him. They seemed to do that a lot, look at each other. She wished that was all it took to break this spell. Lewis did it for them, and she focused back on her worries.

'I agree, Callum's right. You can't stay in a hotel on your own. What if you get confused?'

'Confused about what? I remember where I live, Lew. I'm not stupid. I can still look after myself. I have memory loss, not paralysis.' She turned to Callum. 'What if I freak out on you, eh? I can't even think about you being in my house.' He flinched, and she rushed to correct herself. 'Our home – house! Our house I mean, whatever. I don't need anyone wiping my arse, least of all you.'

Lewis sniggered, but she got a slap in this time.

'Shut up, Lewis.' Her eyes had stayed on Callum's, and she saw them crinkle with warmth at her defence. 'I don't want to not go home, but I can't bear you all mollycoddling me. I'm still here. I'm still me. You've been through a lot already, and I don't want Callum to be caught up in all this crap.' Wow. She did feel protective of him. It was weird. She was always a little protective of him, she remembered. Growing up, she'd chased a couple of unsuitable girls away from him in secret over the years. She used to tell them he had lice, but as they matured, it turned to some kind of nasty sounding STI. It worked and it had been for his own good. Just like now. 'I don't want to be some burden. If I come home, I don't want to be wrapped up in cotton wool. I mean it.'

She could do this, but on her terms.

Callum leaned closer, resting his elbows on his knees. 'If you come home, I'll play this however you want. But no hotels. Or going to your parents,' he added as Lewis started to pipe up about their offer. Alice had already decided that going back to her parents was the last thing she wanted. 'You come home with me, and I promise I will do anything I can to help you.' His eyes, so dark, the passion of his statement lighting his face up. She noticed him twirling the ring on his finger again, and she looked away. No green tinge yet, worse luck. 'We're in this together, sparrow. I'm not going anywhere.'

Looking back at him, brows raised so high on her forehead that her cuts stung, she realised she believed him. She'd never seen him looking so determined. So sure that everything would be okay. Like if they were together, nothing bad would happen. It felt strange, and she knew she should be more freaked out, but it was Callum. She knew him. More importantly, her body seemed to recognise him too. What else was she going to do? Live in a hotel forever? Hurt him all over again?

'Okay,' she uttered. Lewis's face lit up. But Callum didn't move a muscle, just kept his dark-brown eyes utterly focused on hers. 'I'll come home. For now.' She had to get back to her life. Hope for the best. When she saw Callum's lips turn up, the ghost of a relieved smile on his features, she hoped with everything she had that she was doing the right thing. For them both. She had loved her life before; sharing it full time with a man was a lot to take in. Callum was far from a stranger, but right now, she wasn't sure what he was. Or would be.

8

CALLUM

She was letting him in. God, he thought the coma was bad. But after their kiss, she'd frozen him out for nearly three days and that was almost worse than the coma. Knowing that she was awake, in hospital – not wanting to let him anywhere near her. He'd been desperate to be there, talk to her. He'd hung around the hospital foyer, drinking far too much coffee and spending a fortune on parking, just to be nearby. When he'd seen Lewis walking through the doors, he'd taken his chance. He'd been so happy to see her; had held his breath when she came to him. His arms were out in an instant, desperate to have her in them again. Wondering if seeing him again had finally set something free.

And she ran straight past. To Lewis. Of course. 2020 Ali would have done that too, and probably given him the finger as she scampered past. The loss of what was never in his arms anyway almost broke him, but for the fact that she was up and about, and able to get to her brother. The look on Lewis's face when he cuddled his sister. Losing her would have smashed them all apart. Seeing her standing there, it made him so happy, it counteracted the sting of rejection he felt when he was around her. Almost. He felt like a bit of a stage five clinger. It made him think of the girls that had always seemed to follow him growing up. How oblivious he'd tried to be, and annoyed he'd really been inside by their constant attentions. He'd become one of them.

She'd obviously improved leaps and bounds in the couple of days she'd kept him away from her. Not only that, but she also looked more like herself and was back in her own clothes. He had to admit, maybe the time on her own had done her good. Even if it had half killed him. It had given her time to think, he guessed. Space to digest what was going on in her head. *The life with me she doesn't remember*, he thought with a pang. It was like they'd regressed back to their childhood relationship, not even the adult sparring partners they were in her head right now, before her memory conked out on her and blocked out every good moment they'd shared. At least she wasn't looking at him like he was some kind of stranger today. Not as much, anyway.

'Perfect.' He tried not to sound too eager. He didn't want to scare her off. 'I'll be here to take you.'

Lewis got up off the bed, making a 'weeeeeellll' sound as he headed towards the door.

'I'm going to go grab a coffee, anyone want one?'

'Me, please,' Alice replied. She was still staring across the room at Callum. He stared right back.

'Robbo, coffee?' Lewis asked. Callum just kept looking at her, his lips pressed together. She broke contact when she heard Lewis chuckle, making Callum curse under his breath. 'I'll just get your usual.' He finger-gunned in Callum's direction.

'Thanks,' Callum said gruffly. The second his pal had shut the door; the words were out of his mouth.

'Keep going. I know you want to say something else.' He knew what she was thinking before she did. He always could. *Till now*, he thought with a jolt that made his anger rise again. Drunk driver

Barry was lucky he was in jail. If he'd have gotten to him first that night, Callum would probably be sitting in his place. But that night, all his attention had been on the woman in front of him. His attention was always on Alice. 'Keep going. I want you home, back in your life, Ali. Tell me how you want to do this.'

She'd been looking at the door, as if realising that they were alone for the first time in a while. He watched her for signs of panic, but she faced him. He saw the fire in her then, and it warmed him. She was still in there. He just needed to unlock how she felt about *him*. She needed control, to feel like she was in charge of her own life. He would never take that from her, as much as the caveman in him seemed to have reared its head. It had always been there, the protective streak towards her. First as his best friend's little sister, then his friend, then his everything.

Well, they were never actually normal friends. A friend of sorts, even though they regularly wound each other up. Their friends just thought it was hilarious. It was a running joke that they sparred with each other on nights out. Anything from drinking contests (which he let her win every time; he didn't like her being tipsy without him to take her home safely), to dancing and rival karaoke. The karaoke made him think of something, and his mind started to whir as she sighed and drew a long breath.

'I need to take this slow.' She gripped the arm of her chair tight, and Callum watched her fingers flex across the wood. Her hand was still bruised from the cannulas. He wanted to kiss it better, and the fact he couldn't tore him apart every time.

'Okay.' He nodded, swallowing. 'And?'

She pursed her lips, gazing off out of the window before speaking again with a shrug.

'That's all. It's an adjustment, but the doctors have said that this memory loss is damage from the crash. It might not come back, and...'

'I know. I think it will.'

'It might not. Then what?'

'Then we deal with it.'

'The doctor says I can do stuff, just nothing you know, heavy. He says I'm one of his miracle patients. Going home so early. I don't feel like a miracle.'

'You're alive. Up and about. That's a miracle. You slept and got better. You're a fighter, Ali. Some things just move quicker than others.'

'So you'd be okay with it? If I never got it back?'

'Yes. I wouldn't care.' He flexed the fists resting on his thighs and stood. Lifting the chair up, he brought it so he sat an inch from hers, facing her. 'I didn't mean that. That was a lie, and we don't do that. We're always upfront. Brutally honest sometimes.' He smiled. Her frown told him she wondered what he'd just remembered that had made him smile. What memory her grey matter didn't twig. 'Of course, I care. I meant it doesn't change anything for me. I just... I will do whatever you need. You just need to understand that it might take me a minute sometimes.'

'That's what I wanted to talk about.' Her palms were tapping on the arms of her chair, and he moved his to still them. Kept them there, flexed on top of hers. He wanted to show her comfort. That she was safe with him. That she used to feel safe with him.

'Keep going,' he urged. Not moving. It was oddly intimate. He knew she could feel the heat from his palms on the backs of hers, gentle but all-encompassing.

'I've always liked your hands,' she said, not thinking. He could tell by her face she'd done what she often did – spoken her thoughts out loud. It was about the five-hundredth thing he loved about her. Her little tell. It had served him well over the years. It worked when she was mad too. She told him what was bothering her half the time, without meaning to. She did it more around him, especially when he was trying to distract her, which made for cute thing 501.

He was leaning in close. He didn't know when that had happened. She'd leaned too. 'It's true,' she thought out loud again. It made his heart clench. 'Have I ever told you that?'

She saw him swallow. Heard it. He watched her and she knew. So close to his face now. Were they both moving to the other?

'Yes.' He breathed it. Huskily. His voice was giving him away.

'When?' she asked. Was she pushing for the answer she thought might be true, or the one she dreaded? His heart was in his mouth, but he knew this woman. He knew how to communicate with her. Be truthful. 'Different places. More than once.'

'Okay.' He wanted her to ask more.

He filled the silence when she didn't. 'Normally, when I had my hands on you, then you'd tell me.' He drew a steady breath, trying to keep his focus on the conversation and not on taking her in his arms. Kissing her like she *had* to damn well remember him. For now, he took heart from the blush on her cheeks. He was getting through to her, showing her what they were about. The story of them, piece by piece. 'Keep telling me what you wanted to say. I don't want you to run off to a hotel by yourself, so we need to make this happen.'

She blinked at him for a few seconds, and he rubbed his thumbs along the backs of her hands. He raised a brow. 'Alice?'

'Right.' She nodded. 'You distracted me. I need it to be on my terms. Slow.'

'We can take this as slow as you want. I promise. Do I distract you a lot?' he teased, curious about the answer.

'I don't know. Do you?' Her brow was furrowed now, and he leaned in and kissed it without thinking.

'Shit.' He felt her tense. 'Sorry, sparrow.' He pulled back, just enough to give her space. 'Habit.'

'I know. I get it. You don't have to be sorry. This is what I mean, Callum. It's complicated. And what's with the sparrow thing?'

'You spit out what you're trying to say, and I'll tell you.'

'Fine,' she huffed. She made a show of moving her hands as if she was pulling them away but looked relieved when he moaned. She liked his touch. She knew she'd made him aware of that. More than once. She turned her hands, putting them into the cradle of each of his. He linked his fingers through hers, looking down at them both. He leaned closer but stopped himself short of kissing them.

'Huh.' She gazed at their linked hands. 'This doesn't feel as weird as I thought it would. I don't know if it will work, ever. The memory-jogging thing, going back to normal life, it's not guaranteed. Doctor Berkovich was vague enough on that one for a man who deals with impossible-sounding brain parts all day. I can't ask you to stop your life for that.'

He said the most honest thing he could. 'Neither do I, but I want to try. You are my life, as much as that might freak you out.'

'It doesn't,' she started.

He shook his head, feeling the smile try and fail to pull at his lips. 'It does, I can see it.'

'It's not you, I just—'

Callum cut in. 'You just woke up to a life you didn't understand. You need control.'

'I'm scared of making the wrong move,' she admitted.

Callum smiled. 'Baby, every move you make from here is forward. I'm here. I'm not going anywhere…'

'So…?'

'So tell me what you want for us to try. Tell me what you want, Ali. We can go from there.'

She took a deep breath. Callum was still watching her, his eyes roving over her face. She was overthinking. He could read her like a book, even now, when she had pages missing from her story. 'Sparrow?' The minute she heard that, he knew what she was going to do. Her eyes sparked. *Come back, baby. That's it. I'm here.* He held his breath.

'You're right. I do want to go home. Live my life, find my way back. I do want that. I just don't want to be lied to. Sugar-coating a turd doesn't stop it being a turd.'

God, she was funny. He'd missed her little ways of thinking. She was still there. Everything he loved and adored was still ingrained in her. In him now too.

'Okay.' He tried to keep it together, even though on the inside he wanted to scoop her up and head for the hills. 'Done. What else?'

'I hate it when you all look at each other, over my head. It makes me feel invisible. When you think I'm not looking. I don't want to be thought of as some medical experiment. I am still me; I just need to catch up. I want to know everything, good and bad. Okay?'

'Fine. That it?'

'No.' He felt her thumb rub along his and waited for her to speak, and for his tingling nerve endings to quieten down. 'About us.' *Shit.*

'Us?' he uttered.

'Yeah, us.' She had leaned in again to match him, but he made sure he didn't cross the gap. 'I keep upsetting you, I think. I thought maybe a hotel might be the answer for you too.'

'No,' he uttered involuntarily. His brain fired the word out like a bullet. 'I don't want that.'

'I thought maybe just till we spend some time together. I keep flinching when you go to touch me, you get upset. I thought maybe we could trade off. Me at the house one night, you the ot—'

'I can cope with all that, no hotel. I promise. I get it. That's not your life, Ali.' God, he sounded so bossy. He kept waiting for her to raise her guard even further. Dig her heels in. 'It's not my decision, sorry. I don't like it, but this is your pace.'

She didn't look convinced. What could he say to convince her?

'We live together. It's... that's your life.' He didn't want to say it was the best chance of triggering some memory; she'd had that hammered into her by the doctors. He wanted her to come home with him because she wanted to be there. To work on this together. 'I'll be at work some of the time, during the day. You could explore the house then, and I won't crowd you. Hotels are expensive, plus you'd be on your own.'

'Hotels are pretty safe,' she rebuffed.

He knew he looked as miserable as he felt. He couldn't stop the corners of his mouth from turning down like a toddler about to cry. 'If you really want that, I'll do it.' He was pacing around the room now but stopped dead. His head was spinning with things he could say to her, but he knew she wouldn't remember. Every little moment they'd shared was locked away from her. From them. He couldn't access them, or her. He always knew what to say when it came to Alice. He had spent years learning the code of her. Recognising what thrilled her. Scared her. Made her get out of bed in that adorable grouchy way on a morning, begging for coffee and silence and scowling at anyone who dared to engage with her before the first lick of caffeine hit. He was going to have to start at the beginning. *The beginning... that's it. That's the key to this.*

Whirling around, he pushed himself back into the chair. Set his eyes on hers again, locking in as they always did. Settled in, like he was about to watch his favourite movie. He never understood why people said staring at people was weird. He couldn't get enough of seeing Alice. Seeing her eyes gaze upon him, eyes that he'd thought would never open again. His body knew her. She knew him the same way, surely? Maybe somewhere in that muscle memory, his touch was recorded on her skin. She was his and vice versa. He'd belonged to her the minute he'd seen her as more than Lewis's little sis. He could push this for the both of them. He could love, fight, cling on to them – all on his own if he had to. Till she didn't want to any more.

'I don't want us to be separated like that, but I get it. I want you to feel comfortable, but we've known each other for ever. I've slept under the same roof as you for half my life.'

'I know, but not like this!' she said, putting her hands on his chest. He felt afraid for a second that his pounding heart would bounce her hand right off. 'I feel weird around you.' He felt her fingers move, caressing him. She didn't acknowledge the movement, so neither did he. Even as her fingertips were making the skin under his clothing sing with the pleasure of being near her. 'When we get close, like this,' her gaze dropped to his lips, and he prayed to the gods of patience to boost him up, 'I feel weird. That's something, right?'

'Yeah, it's something. Weird how?'

'Well.' Her head tilt really delivered the blow. 'I don't want to punch your face in or swat you with a newspaper.'

'Progress,' he rumbled. 'That's good. Doc was right about you.'

Her cheeks were flushed. 'Waking up was something. Getting back on my feet. Yeah, it felt good, but that's not the end of it. I feel like I fell asleep one day tragically single, and the next morning my story has been written, but I missed some chapters. I hate it. I feel... a kind of way about you, but I can't fill in the blanks.' Her eyes fell onto her fingers, and her hands stilled. 'See? I'm touching you like I do it every day. That's not us.'

'It bloody is.' Callum put his hands over hers. 'We are close. Alice, you know we are. Without the romance stuff. I've known you my whole life, everything I remember has you in it.'

'We tolerated each other. Had a laugh. I mostly wanted to punch you.' She didn't add the lusty stuff.

'No, I fancied you rotten. We got past that, because I came to you the day after that stupid fight. The night you last remember. We talked and made a deal.'

'This gets worse. Am I also secretly married to a gentleman looking for a green card or something? Is he outside too?'

He squeezed her hands.

'Only me.' He didn't mean his voice to have a possessive edge to it, but it creeped into his tone anyway. 'You just forgot me.'

Her mouth slammed shut at his comment, but he didn't take it back. He couldn't help but feel the hurt and want to let it show in some way. He was committed to her, but the weight of everything she didn't remember was crushing him under its sheer heft. Their last conversation together, before the crash. His mind kept going back to that. How his whole life had seemed complete in that second, during that phone call. The security of knowing he was with the right person, living the life he'd always wanted to. Those ten seconds of elation, them both being so happy – her voice as she squealed down the phone, telling him she loved him so much. Answering his question over and over. It felt like that was the summit now, not the start of a whole new chapter in their joint lives as they looked down from the lofty top. It was gone. The screams and twisting of metal had burned all that elation away. He'd get it back or die trying. Just like last time.

'You want to take this slow, right? Go back to your life, not rush? Be treated like you?' She took his words in, nodding slowly. 'And you want those two years back. To try and get the memories loose.'

'Yeah.'

His face broke into a grin. *Gotcha, baby.*

'Do me a deal then.' *God, I sound like a gameshow host.* 'The same deal I made with you before. That day when I came to apologise, I asked you how many dates it would take for you to consider being with me. I dared you. To give me a figure. How many it would take to prove that we were meant to be together.'

'What did I say?' She was intrigued. *Come on, baby. I dare you not to fall back in love with me.*

'You told me if I couldn't do it in ten, I'd lose.'

'I never did.' She laughed. 'Although it does sound like me. You always did get under my skin. Got me riled up.' She threw him a cheeky look. He winked back.

'I still do. You want to see what else I do? It will cost you ten dates.'

'Ten dates.' She echoed him, he could see she was trying to connect something in her mind to what he was saying.

'Yeah. Ten whole dates, planned by me. You agree to come with me, see what happens. Some things we can't do exactly the same, but I'll work around it. You move back home. Let me take care of you while you recover. I'll keep my distance, give you your space. Keep your parents away if needed. I know your mum fusses. And I get to live at home. Full time. I'll look after you.'

'I don't need looking after.' Alice looked around her, at the debris of her stay here. How tired she looked after even a day out of her bed. 'Much.' She bit her bottom lip hard. He wanted to reach forward, release it from its ivory prison. He tightened his grip on her instead, her hands in his making him feel braver. Stronger.

'What if it doesn't work?' she murmured. He wasn't sure this time whether it was a spoken thought or a statement.

'You mean if you don't fall in love me again by the end of it?' He wanted to be the one to say it. He could see she was struggling with this, and he had no intention of losing, or toning down their relationship to make her feel more comfortable. She didn't sleepwalk through their time together. She had been right there, with him. He needed her to be again. 'Then if you want me to leave, I'll leave. We can come to an agreement about the house.'

She didn't say anything for the longest time. Callum thought he might burst, but she broke the silence of the room with a question.

'What was the forfeit last time? We always had a forfeit before.'

Well, it wasn't a no. *Keep coming closer, sparrow. I'm right here.*

'You hired me that day. To work on the house. Your builders were shit, some crew you hired let you down the first day. I came to your house just at the right time.' He couldn't resist smiling, remembering how elated he'd been when she'd agreed the first time. Almost as much as when he'd asked her another question. The answer to that had been his greatest moment in life. *Which turned into the worst*, he reminded himself. Pushing the thought away. Locking it in a drawer, just like the other half to what he always carried with him. He needed her to say yes to this. He was going to put it all on the line again. Readily.

'The deal was, I got ten dates, and if at the end of it we weren't together, you didn't pay me for any of my labour on the house. Just costs.' It added to thousands, being such a huge project. It still wasn't finished. The crash had set the home reno back, for obvious reasons.

Her jaw dropped, just as it did the last time he'd challenged her. He knew she was doing the maths. He wanted to punch the air.

'Seriously?'

'Seriously.' He lifted their hands, flexing his palms so they were both in the air, palms flat to each other's. 'Same deal this time. You let me do those ten dates, again. If at the end of it, you want out? I'll... agree.' He sounded too much like he was quoting a job on one of his construction sites, but he couldn't say the words *let you go*. *If she'd stayed in that coma, you might have had to.* He never wanted to say those words to her. Not ever.

'Just dating,' she checked. 'In line with the past when we dated?' She was smiling. She kept trying to stop, but it spread across her face like wildfire. 'It sounds like something we would have done before. Like a dare, a big challenge. Could it work? I mean, it makes it less awkward, right?'

He sighed. 'I don't feel awkward, but if it makes you feel better, yeah.'

'You'd do that?'

'Date you again? Yes. Forever if needed? Yeah. *The Notebook* has nothing on me. Ryan Gosling sucks anyway. Say yes?'

She laughed. 'How many times have I made you watch that film since we got together?'

'About as many times as you made me watch it growing up. You still cry. Quit not answering my question.' She grinned at him, just as Lewis threw his massive clod-hopping size elevens into the room and ruined the bloody moment.

'Coffee!' he trilled, laughing as they sprang apart. 'Oh, hello. I see nothing changes that much then.'

Callum wanted to tip that coffee straight down Lewis's crotch, but he took the two cups from him and threw him a dirty look instead.

'What do you mean?' Alice poked him as Lewis walked past the two of them and plonked himself back onto her bed.

She smiled at him when he gave her the coffee. He nearly dropped his cup. *Was she going to say yes?*

Lewis was drinking some kind of new piss-coloured energy drink, and he spilled some on the bed sheets when he landed. 'Oi! Get off, you scruffy berk!' She gave his arm a yank, which did nothing. The next minute, Lewis was on his feet, and the can was in Callum's hand. Half a second later, it was in the bin.

'Hey!' Lewis protested, but Callum ignored him. He didn't even feel himself move or grab his best friend. He just reacted when it came to Alice. It had always been the same. 'Dick.'

'Takes one to know one.' He couldn't stop himself from having the last word. It was the same when they were kids. Worse when it involved Lewis *and* his sister.

'Jesus, you two haven't changed at all. Calm down, Kevin Costner.'

Callum stuck his tongue out at her, which made her laugh like a fourteen-year-old. *Dear God, why did she always regress in his presence? It was freaking adorable.*

'Lewis,' Alice belatedly thought to ask, 'what did you mean when you came in?'

9

ALICE

Lewis had ended up standing quite contrite in front of her, where Callum had plonked him before returning to her side like some kind of bodyguard. It was strange, but when he'd picked Lewis up like he was a bag full of air, a memory had sparked. She couldn't stop thinking about it.

'I meant that you two were always like that, together. In the corner, chatting or whatever.' Her brother looked sad for a second, checking out the pattern on the floor for a long time before meeting her eye again. 'It's nice, that's all. I missed it. We missed you. You scared the shit out of me.'

Alice didn't trust herself to speak, so she just nodded. Once, barely. The air in the room had changed. As if a layer of ash had settled on them all. The embers from the past, the pieces of them that had been seemingly burned away from them. She felt a wave of responsibility. Her accident, her memory loss, but they had all suffered around her. While she slept, they'd worried. Memories were about connection when it came to her family. What was the point if one family member couldn't recall a thing? It was so cruel, whatever the reason for the severing. It closed down conversations that could have taken place. They had no roots now from which to shoot from.

She looked across at Callum and couldn't help but think of him crumpled up, sleeping next to her bed all those days and nights. Dishevelled and bearded, his life on hold till she woke up. Not knowing if she would. Who she'd be if she did. She wondered if he'd ever considered a scenario like this. He said he wanted to stay, but would he? What if she got attached? Or didn't feel it and crushed him on date ten, or sooner? She didn't like the responsibility of it all. For another person. She would die for family. For him too. He was part of that. Or, what if she fell in love with him, but he stopped loving her?

He must have considered all this. Three months sitting in a hospital room was a lot of thinking time. But he was still here. Battle worn but still ready to fight. He thought they were worth it, and she wasn't blind. She was attracted to him; she knew him. Well. She knew his ways. She could trust him to look after her, explain things. Be honest. Not sugar-coat the turds. But it was still such a risk. She could get hurt too. Then how would she cope? A break-up, the family all upset. Suddenly, she wanted to cry. She pinched her thumb between her fingers to stop the sting behind her eyes erupting.

'I'm sorry you went through that, sis. I really am.' She felt her brother wrap her in his arms, and she stopped her overthinking to sink into him. She felt Callum's hand take the coffee cup from her, felt the brush of his fingers along hers, just a moment longer than needed.

'You still smell like you,' she said, breathing him in.

Lewis chuckled. 'I hope that's a good thing.'

She laughed, but it turned into a bit of a watery sob. 'It's your goofy aftershave. You still wear the same from when you were seventeen.' She sobbed again. 'Wild Man, it was called. I can still remember the stupid blue bottle. I can remember the name of your aftershave, but I can't remember your wedding.'

'I know.' Her brother held her that bit tighter. 'You were there though, and we have so many photos, you won't feel like you missed a thing. A wedding video too. I'll drop it off if you like. Give you time to settle back in. We'll talk more then.' He was speaking fast now, the old Lewis coming back. The fixer. He and Callum were both like that. Alice had always thought it was what connected them so strongly for so long. They were opposites in most other ways. 'You can get through this, Alice. That bastard driving that cab won't win. We're all here.' She could feel him smile against the top of her head. She tried not to think about how they had changed. What else she'd missed.

'I know,' she agreed, pulling away from him to wipe the tears silently trickling down her face. 'Send everyone my love, won't you?'

'Of course I will. When you get a new phone, I'm sure they'll be blowing it up. I'd better go, get home.'

'I'll see you out.' Callum followed him, but turned to her at the last minute. 'I'll come back.'

'No, you should go home too, get some rest.' He looked so tired in the light from the corridor's brighter strip lighting. She felt an overwhelming urge to go hug him, look after him. She tried to conjure up some kind of memory. Some sign of her taking care of him in the past. She wasn't so naive to think that he would be this loving if she'd been a cold-hearted bachelorette bitch. She got nothing, but the feeling didn't stop. The need to care for this man was there, deep under her skin. 'You look tired. Don't drive yourself ho... back. Get a ride with Lew.'

He shook his head, a little smile dancing across his features for a fleeting moment. 'My truck's in the car park, Ali. I won't be long. We need to finish our conversation.' Something about his look told her he wouldn't be leaving without one.

She watched him go, heard him and her brother talk outside the door, hushed, deep rumbles that met her ear as nothing but muffled tones. She could hear them embrace, their usual back slapping bro-hug audible in the corridor. She settled herself into bed, feeling tired and ever so slightly drained. The door opened again with a hush, and he was back.

'Hi,' he said, coming back to claim his chair, setting it close to her bedside. 'You really feeling okay?'

'Tired,' she admitted. 'The headaches are still there. Makes it worse when I push it.'

His lips tightened. 'I hate that this happened to you. I should have been with you. Work kept me back, and—'

'Hey,' she put her hand on the bed rail, and he claimed it. 'It wasn't your fault. I blame Barry.'

He laughed then. 'I hate Barry.'

'Me too,' she laughed. 'Stupid Barry.'

'He is stupid!' Callum countered. 'Who's called Barry these days anyway? He sounds like a fruit and veg seller on a soap.'

They were both laughing together. 'Yeah. We should form a We Hate Barry Club.'

Callum pointed his finger at her. 'Definitely. You can design the posters.' Alice creased up.

'Why is this funny?' She held her side, which still felt tender.

He laughed again, but his eyes watched her clutch her body with a wince of his own. 'It's not, really. I do hate him though. If I could have got my hands on him that night...'

'You were there?'

His eyes slid to the window. 'We were talking on the phone; you were on your way home, to me. We were really happy.' He swallowed. 'I ran to you.' His eyes went dark. 'Saw him being pulled out.'

It was her turn to swallow now. 'You saw me, too?' His face told her he was choosing his words carefully. 'I was a mess, eh?' He shook his head, but it wasn't a movement filled with conviction.

'You were hurt, sparrow. I'd rather not put this into your head before I leave, okay?' His teeth worried at his lip. 'It will never happen again. Do we have a deal?'

She'd already decided, but him talking about running to be by her side had tipped her over the edge. She'd always liked the protective side of him, even though she would be loath to admit it to a living soul. She'd kept him away for three days. Tried to forget him, but he'd been there the whole time. She had to know what their relationship was like. She had to go home. She was very rational about that; she had things to get back to. What she didn't want to admit was the pull of him – Callum Roberts. She could feel it, between them. More than they were before. It was something she needed to see through. For them both.

He wasn't just some random person; it was Callum. His photos were all over her parents' house, just like her and Lewis's. Her independent, slightly stroppy shield was still there within her, and it had clanged up the second she woke up. The fact that he'd already broken through all that once, and was still here, looking like he adored her, even now? He was fighting for something she didn't remember, and the bottom line was, it made her want to fight too. If only to see what he was fighting so hard for herself. People changed; she knew that. More than most, given the week she was having. Maybe seeing her life would help her to wake up.

Either way, the house was where she lived. All her stuff was there, her business. He said he wouldn't push her, would even keep her sometimes over affectionate family at bay. Most of all though, she had to admit to herself that she was desperate to get answers herself. To see her life, and how she fitted back into it. Especially given this very handsome new addition.

She was pretty sure that he knew now that she'd secretly

fancied him as a kid. There was no way it hadn't come up at least once in the two years she'd missed. Which was soooo embarrassing now. She couldn't even feel out if she *had* told him, because then she'd play that hand anyway. God. It was so annoying. She was arguing with herself in her own stupid brain. She needed to get answers. Looking at Callum, seeing him look at her that way, it looked like he was desperate for her answer. Like he really needed this for him too. Maybe he did. She'd never had someone love her and then forget her completely. It must suck. Although, given that her previous longest relationship (the one she remembered from her dating history) had been a very short-lived car crash with an unfaithful pond-sucking amoeba aka Ashley, maybe she would have liked it. It she could erase Ashley sodding Peterson from her dating history, she would *Spotless Mind* that stuff in a heartbeat. Locking eyes with Callum, she decided to try. Roll the dice. Try not to overthink, and leap in. Avoid the nagging feeling that she might never feel it again and could break the man in front of her. *Oh God. I really could break him.* He wasn't Ashley. He wasn't some short chapter of her life. He was the best parts of her childhood. Even when they were winding each other up, she thrived on it. Every day she would seek that moody little look of his. Now though, he was an adult. They both were. Linked together intrinsically. Feelings were on show for all to see. So much pressure. She felt like she was holding his raw, beating heart in her hands, and everyone was surrounding them, waiting to see if she could squish it between her fingers or put it back in his chest.

'Sparrow,' he muttered softly. 'You haven't spoken for a while. I need to know, baby. Will you come home with me tomorrow?' This was it. Squish or stick.

'Yeah, I will.'

She watched his face light up, saw him go to hug her but pull back at the last moment.

'Wait!' She yelled. 'It's a deal, but we do it slow. Okay? No pressure. And you can't look at me like I shot your puppy if I say something wrong.'

She meant it in a light-hearted way, but she saw his smile fade. 'Like that. I don't want to upset you, but I don't...'

'Love me,' he completed for her. He spat the word out like it was the worst thing that could happen. 'I know, Alice. But you did once, and there's no fucking way you won't again. It's still part of you, Ali. I know it. We just need time.'

Wow. Hearing him talk to her like this was... new. Hot. Nice. She could see how pre-coma her had been tempted. Well, she'd always known she'd felt like this around him. It had crept up on her even when she'd tried to squash it down.

His dark-brown eyes closed, cutting his gaze off from hers. She wanted to hug him, make him feel better, but that would just confuse him. She was the one hurting him. Alice realised she was totally out of her depth. She just couldn't navigate this, being out of control. She needed a bloody cheat sheet, some kind of spoiler alert on her life. Like the ones she hated on the internet, spoiling her favourite shows before she had a chance to watch it herself. *A spoiler or two would be nice right about now,* she thought to herself futilely.

'I wasn't going to say that. I was going to say that I don't want to upset you when I don't remember things, but I'll try. The ten dates thing.'

'No hotels.' His expression was stony.

'No hotels,' she nodded. 'Just... space.'

'Good,' he ran his free hand through his dark hair. 'Now you've said yes, I'm going to have to stay over at Lewis and Migs tomorrow. I hate the thought of that but needs must.' His grip tightened around hers, and she looked at their interlinked fingers. 'Our first date was at the house, the night after I tried to kiss you. It was a really chilled night. I think it could work as a homecoming and not be too much. We made the deal, and that night I came back over. We hung out a while.' He leaned in close. 'I want to do this right, so since your memory ended just before that, we'll start the day after all over again. It's almost poetic.'

Alice could do nothing but gaze at him. He sounded like he had it all planned. He was smiling his head off, holding her hand tight in his like it was the most natural thing in the world. If that wasn't enough to top her week off, tomorrow, she was going on a first date with her live-in boyfriend.

'I don't know about poetic,' she retorted. 'Crazy, maybe.'

'Oh, you'll see, sparrow.' He stood up, taking her hand with him and dropping a kiss on it. 'Leave it to me. Tomorrow, I'll take you home. You can shower, go to bed, rest, whatever. I'll take care of everything else.' He laughed when she gave him a sour look. 'I forgot how stubborn you were,' his lips quirked with each word. 'Feisty.' She yawned, and he huffed with laughter again. 'Feisty, tired sparrow.' He stood by her side, putting his arm under hers. 'Come on Aurora. Lie down, get some rest.'

She didn't argue with him as he pulled the blanket and sheet over her. She was shattered. The persistent dull headache was getting better, but it still drained her battery.

'Are you going to tell me what that nickname is about?' She yawned again. Something was digging in her back. He saw her frown, lifting her forward and straightening everything up.

'You keep asking me that.'

'Because you keep not telling me.'

He plumped her pillow in silence, brushing her hair away from her face and smiling as she snuggled down. 'It feels weird when you touch me like that.' Her filter was off again. His brows knitted together.

'In a bad way?'

She was fighting to keep her lids open now, the fatigue pulling her under quicker than she expected.

'No,' she murmured. 'Not bad. Strange, I guess. We used to rough house and stuff, but you never held my hand or touched my hair.'

'I wanted to.' She heard him say, just as her stinging eyes closed shut. 'I always wanted that, sparrow.'

10

CALLUM

'I know you bought me this, Callum Roberts, and it's not funny.'

Even in a wheelchair, she was hopping mad as he rolled her down the corridor. The large stuffed gorilla sat on her lap, while he pushed her chair and carried the many bags of clothes and other gifts she'd had in her room. He'd bring something every day, he'd promised himself, and he'd stuck to it. Just to feel like he was doing something other than staring at her bedside. He'd known she'd get mad at the gorilla, but at the time, he didn't know how much it would mean to *him* to have her mad at him. It had broken the tension he'd felt when he'd first arrived at the hospital to take her home. Put them back to where they were. Even if it was as sparring friends. That was the plan, right? Ten dates to win her heart again. To show her there was nothing better than them together.

'I think it's hilarious. I knew you'd like it.' He leaned forward and patted the gorilla on the head. 'He's pretty cute. I think he'll love his new home with us.'

'I hate gorillas, remember?'

'I remember everything, my love. I was present when your hatred of the species was born.'

She half screeched with indignation. 'Well! Those primates scarred me for life! Awful crap-throwing thugs.' She slapped the toy gorilla on the side of the head. A man walking with his wife in the opposite direction threw them a surprised look. Callum chuckled and kept walking to his car. 'I've never been to a zoo since.' She pouted.

'I know,' he laughed. 'You were watching them get it on though.' She twirled in her chair, and he stopped, wanting to lean in closer. 'I think any ape would have thrown doo-doo at a twelve-year-old watching them have sex.'

'I was eleven, not twelve! You ask Lewis, I didn't know what they were doing, did I? God, I will never live that down! You didn't even see it happen; you were off with Dad watching the crocodiles. Lew said that they were wrestling, and to keep watching! When that turd hit the glass, I thought my number was up. I forgot the glass was even there.'

She was laughing herself now, and he picked up his pace. He got to the flatbed at the back of his truck and unlocked the boot. He couldn't wait to shove her stuff in there and get her into the passenger seat and out of that chair. He wanted to wash away every trace of the hospital from her.

She'd rang him that morning, telling him that she could come home at 10 a.m. She didn't want a big song and dance, with her parents and Lewis, so she'd asked him to come in secret. She'd said she wanted to see her house first, adjust slowly, but Callum knew she was feeling out of control. He knew her so well. She was so fierce, so strong, but her confidence had been knocked out of her. She was always sure-footed, and now all he wanted was to hold her up till she could do it herself. He wanted her to himself, selfishly. He wanted them to be together at home, like before. He felt like he couldn't breathe as they left the hospital and wheeled out into the fresh air.

'This isn't your truck.' She was eyeing the writing on the side. 'Where did the white truck go?'

He shrugged, not knowing how much to tell her. He didn't want her freaking out in the parking lot. 'I upgraded when business went well, I needed more space for my tools. You started complaining about them taking over the house.' Plus, he'd sold his place. Signed up for half the mortgage on the house they lived in. Used the difference to grow, expand. It had been her idea at the time, but right now, something told him it wasn't the time to point it out.

'That doesn't sound like me, complaining,' she retorted sarcastically. She was mouthing the wording on the side panel, silver block lettering on the sleek black surface. '"Callum Roberts Construction", wow. You've moved up in the world.'

He shut the boot, opened the passenger door and strode over to where she sat in the chair watching him.

'Couldn't have been much worse. My first van had gaffer tape holding the back doors shut.'

'No, that was the second one,' she said absently. 'The first one smelled like...'

'Cheese! God yeah. I forgot about the cheese-mobile.' He could see one of the porters coming for the chair, so he took the chance. He leaned in close, and she gasped in a breath. *Good*, he thought. *She still feels something.* He knew it. He'd seen enough little gasps over the years to know that even when she found him to be the most insufferable man on the planet, she still thought he was hot. Still reacted to him. 'Ready?' he said, tucking his arms beneath her.

'For what? Oh!'

He lifted her easily from the chair, gently. He hated that her body was still healing. He wanted to check out every little mark for himself. It felt like her body was estranged to him, as well as her mind. Altered forever. He held her a little closer.

'Callum, I can walk! No babying, you promised. Put me down, the porter's laughing.'

When Callum looked, the porter was indeed belly-laughing as Alice squirmed in his arms. Behind him, there was a small congregation of nurses, all giggling spectators. He turned to them, taking a bow.

Alice groaned, wiggling harder, but still failed to get out of his firm grip. 'God, you are the worst!'

'Nope.' He tucked her into his truck, resisting the urge to strap in her seat belt for her like he would a toddler. 'I've been waiting for this day. I promised myself that I would take you home and spoil you. I'll rein it in, but just indulge me for now, okay?'

'Fine,' she said. 'Wave to your groupies.'

She pointed out the window at the nurses, who all gave her a wave. She blushed, waving back and ducking her head down.

God, she's cute when she gets jealous. Little did she know he couldn't have picked one of those nurses out of a line-up right now, even after the months he'd spent in the place.

'Buckle up.' He pointed to the strap before he put the key in the ignition. She rolled her eyes but did it. 'You ready?'

She was looking out of the front windshield as if she'd never seen people before.

'Yeah, I think so. Thanks for keeping this quiet. I wanted to get home first, before anything else.'

He nodded and reached for the hand in her lap automatically. He stopped himself, gripping the gear stick instead. It felt a bit too much after carrying her to the car. She kept telling him to slow down, but it was hard not to reach for her.

'Oh, I forgot. I got this for you on the way.' He pulled the plastic bag from the footwell. 'I got the closest to your model, but it's a new number. I figured you might want to ease back into all that. We can get it switched over when you're ready.'

She pulled the box out of the bag, staring at the mobile phone. 'Right, er... thanks.'

'No problem,' he said easily. 'The cloud should log everything in for you, so the numbers should transfer too. I figured you might have to reset your passwords, but—'

She was rubbing at her head, so he stopped. 'Too much?'

'A bit,' she admitted, shutting the phone back in its box. 'Thanks for this.'

'Sure, sparrow.' He turned the radio off. It had been playing low in the background. 'When can you take some pills for your head?'

She shrugged. 'It's written down in the medication bag. To be honest, even with the meds, the headache is still there. They did say it could last a while. Tell me where sparrow came from.'

Callum sighed. 'If I tell you, you might freak.'

'So, tell me anyway. No babying, remember? I've already guessed it's a pet name.' Her brow raised the challenge issued in her voice like a flag. He focused back on the road.

'Fine. I call you sparrow because of Monty.'

He gave her a minute, knowing those beautiful little cogs in her head were turning double fast.

'Monty,' she repeated, in awe. 'Wow, I forgot about him.'

Years ago, they'd had a day out in the park. The sun had brought them out, looking for something to do. They'd headed to the park, the four of them as ever. Callum had brought a cricket set, and a stray ball had careened through tree branches, bringing a little bird down with it. They could see the little thing, motionless on the ground. Migs crying, Callum running close behind Alice. She'd screeched at her brother, run to see if the unlucky bird had survived. 'Poor little Monty the sparrow. Hit in the face with a cricket ball. Lewis was such a bad shot.'

'Still is.' The pair of them shared a smirk. 'You were so cute that day, rescuing him like that. Helping him get better. I said it in my head.' He took a deep breath. 'It stuck from then, I guess.' There was no guessing; it was exactly the reason why. He risked a glance at her profile as he made the final turn to their street.

'It's from back then? Monty?'

He nodded, holding his breath as he pulled his truck in alongside the full skip. The driveway faced the garage, and the bay window of the living room was covered with newspaper.

'Yep.' He turned to face her, killing the engine. 'I didn't tell you about it till we dated.'

A smile sprang across his lips at the memory. She watched him.

'What's the smile for?'

He wanted to tell her. Should he? They were parked on the driveway now. He'd gotten her this far. She trusted him, had chosen him over her parents and Lew to bring her home. He knew she felt it, but he constantly flip-flopped between shocking her with the truth and playing it safe. He knew she was as skittish as a colt. He knew two-years-ago Alice by heart. He loved every version of her with each beat of it.

'Truth?'

'Always,' she replied boldly. 'Please.'

'I let it slip, the first time we...'

She looked at him blankly, and for a second he wondered if he'd gone too far.

'First time we?'

Oh God. She doesn't get it. He could feel his face pale, his mouth opening and closing like a floundering fish. A second later, she laughed her head off.

'Sorry! I just got it.' She was laughing hysterically. 'Oh God, I'm sorry.' She spoke between peals of laughter. 'I didn't get it at first, but... oh.' She pulled herself together, wiping a tear of laughter from her cheek.

'You know, a man could take that the wrong way.'

She flashed him a guilty look. 'Oh, I didn't mean it like that. It's just... weird.'

Weird. Being naked with me is weird to her now. Great.

'Again.' He tried to look amused. Not dejected and broken, like he'd felt pretty much for the last quarter-year. 'Not great for the ego.'

'Sorry.' She nodded. 'I know.' She looked out of the front windshield, and he saw her take in the house properly for the first time. 'Callum?' she breathed.

'Yeah?' She was looking at the house, her eyes running over every facet. Not for the first time, he wished he could read her thoughts. Did she even like the house, what they had been working on for so long?

'The house.' She sniffed in, her chest rising. Turning to him with tears in her eyes, she looked more like her than she had since leaving the hospital. 'It's... it's... beautiful.'

11

ALICE

It was nothing like she'd planned. She took in the large brick front of the house, the bay window changed from the old rotten-looking wood to grey glazed. She couldn't see much through the covered windows. The skip on the driveway was filled with plastering materials, old bricks.

'It's still a work in progress in places. Hall's just been finished,' Callum told her nervously as he opened her door, keys in hand. 'Don't freak out, okay? I'll carry you in.'

His arms were around her so quick, protest would have been futile, but she didn't bother protesting this time. It had been quite nice the last time, she recalled. His arms around her, the scent of his aftershave enveloping her like a spicy caress. Her legs felt like jelly. All she could do was cling around his neck as he strode up the pathway. He'd kicked the truck door shut behind him, and she felt the thud in her head. Her brain was working overtime, overlaying the house she remembered to what she was seeing now.

'It's so... different.'

Callum stopped at the front doorstep.

'You love it, I promise. Hold tight,' he said close to her ear, and she shivered at the contact. She knew he'd have felt it. She felt him unlock the key with the hand he moved from beneath her. His grip so tight, she never wavered in his grasp. When the lock slid into its housing, he turned the thick metal doorknob. 'Welcome home, Ali.'

She barely noticed him walking into the house. They'd locked eyes as he crossed the threshold, and something slammed into her. Harder than the truck. A memory. She didn't even register her surroundings as her eyes widened.

They'd been out... somewhere. Were coming home. He'd picked her up. She'd had a suitcase with her, she remembered. The details were fuzzy. It was more the feeling of him. Not the particulars. He'd chased her up the driveway. She remembered getting the key into the lock before his arms were around her, lifting her up in his thick, muscular arms.

'Put me down, ya big lummox,' she'd said, kissing him hard. 'I was gone one night! You're like a co-dependent Labrador.'

He woofed, opened their front door effortlessly, tucking her closer. Dipping to kiss her like a man starved. When he finally pulled his lips from hers, his smile was triumphant.

'One night's too much,' he'd whined. 'Welcome home, sparrow.'

'You did this before. I remember, I think. Yeah. I called you a "big lummox",' she told him. Callum's grip faltered, stuttered for a second before he gripped her tighter. His face was the epitome of shock and hope.

'Yeah?' he said, his brows knitting together. 'You remember?'

She nodded at him, wide eyed. Eager to tell him the details, to check what her brain was telling her was true. She needed to know, because in his arms right now, she sure felt it the same.

'I'd been away for a night. You picked me up, I was laughing.'

His face slowly filled up with his smile.

'You went on a conference, an expo for work. I had to work, couldn't get away. You really remember that?' His grin was contagious. She grinned right back. It was a true memory. It happened.

'You really remember that!' His excitement grew, and he spun her around in the hallway. It knocked her dizzy, but she was too busy laughing to care. They both were.

'You remember me!' he yelled, twirling and stopping dead to pull her closer. 'I can't believe it.' He said it with reverence, awe. 'I knew you would beat this. What else do you remember?'

She was tucked tight in his embrace, the heat of him all around her. The memory of them was swirling around in her brain, but how she'd felt in that moment was the freakiest thing of all. She'd felt... so happy. Loved. He was still watching her, his face close to hers. The scent of him all around them. She needed more. The snippet was like pure gold, but that was it. A small slice of time. She needed more. Wanted more.

'You carried me, called me sparrow.' She closed her eyes. She couldn't bring herself to mention the kiss. 'Welcomed me home.' *And what a welcome it was.*

'Anything else?' he pressed, and she watched his tongue poke out, slide across his bottom lip. 'After that?' His nose brushed along the length of hers. Slowly, before he met her gaze with eyes she'd never seen a darker shade in. It was intoxicating. She couldn't have been prised from his grasp for all the design jobs in the world. 'Ali, tell me.'

Callum's pocket started to vibrate. He cursed under his breath, and she took the opportunity to wriggle out of his grasp. She'd been so close to kissing him, and that was nuts. She'd been out of the hospital what, an hour? Dry humping on the doorstep wasn't part of her plan. He ignored the phone after checking the screen, turning back to her with an air of regret emanating from him.

'It's just work.'

'It's fine, go call them back. I should rest.'

He clenched his phone-free hand and stopped when he saw her looking.

'Alice, we—'

'You must have a lot to do.' She motioned towards the staircase. 'You can't have gotten much work done lately with everything. I think I'll go lie down.'

He nodded, heading towards the staircase. 'I'll see you up. Get your things from the car in a bit.' He didn't look at her as he passed, and she felt the sting of rejection coming from his stance. The staircase was on the left side of the hallway, and he turned at the bottom. Reached for her hand.

She took it and followed him up. She barely took it all in, the rooms and all her changes. Her bedroom was tidy, clean. Welcoming. The bed was new, bigger. It called to her.

She could see his things on one side of the bed, her least favourite side. A paperback thriller on the nightstand, a lamp. A photo of the pair of them, their faces smushed together, sweaty. Medallions around their necks from a charity run she remembered saying she wanted to take part in. His arms were around her in the photo, her back pressed to his chest as they both beamed out of the frame.

'Do you want anything? Food? A drink? Shower?'

She shook her head. 'I just want to sleep, to be honest.' She wanted to get a minute away from him to process everything, but she was bone tired. Everything seemed to take a great effort these days. 'I'll be fine for tonight.'

She'd sat on the end of the bed, and he came to sit next to her. A palm's distance apart.

'I'll cancel the date. It was too much too soon anyway. I'll go get your stuff; let you settle back in.'

He went to leave, but she covered his hand with hers on the sheet. Took it away a half-second later. Left it hanging somewhere in between.

'Don't cancel it. It's working. I've already had a memory.' It was true, and she needed it to happen again. Before the end of their deal, when she had to make a decision. It still shocked her that while so much of her life had stayed the same, her existence had been so different from what she had remembered. She still had her house, which was now seemingly on the way to being completed. She still had her job to go back to. She had family, who were still all happy, healthy. Nothing had really changed, other than her. And Callum. He was the piece that didn't fit, yet he seemed so at ease here. With her. With the conviction in his heart of the power of their relationship. What if that memory was nothing at all? A blip? What if at the end of all this, she couldn't see herself in this life with him? What then? The pressure of needing control, of the thirst for answers drained her battery far quicker than any of the physio she'd endured so far.

'I need to do this, Callum. Everything else makes sense, almost. I can just about cope with what I've missed if I don't try to dwell, but I don't want to mess up.'

He shook his head, almost angrily. 'You won't mess this up. I told you, no pressure. I get how hard this is.' He ran his bird-ringed hand down his scruff. 'But I know how good things are between us. I'm willing to fight for that. More than. I just don't want your pity, okay? The truth, remember?'

She nodded, turning over his words in her head.

'I still want the date. You said it was here, right? Low-key? I'll be fine after some sleep.'

He went to make her a cup of tea, and she rummaged through drawers in her dresser till she found something to sleep in. An over-sized T-shirt with Elmo making a rude gesture on the front. It made her laugh as she put it on. Opening the next drawer, she saw rows of neat socks, all thick, manly knit in dark tones. The one under that was full of boxer briefs. She fingered through the rows until she heard a cough behind her. She jumped, almost slamming her fingertip in the drawer in her haste.

'Cup of tea.' He smirked, bringing it over to her bedside and tucking the covers around her when she slid into bed. 'I have to nip out, see a client, get the stuff ready for tonight. Were you just perving in my drawers, by the way?'

She ducked her head, hiding her eyes in her hair. Slurped her tea, trying not to look guilty. 'Accidental. Coma brain, remember?'

He chuckled to himself, heading for the door.

'Of course, how could I forget? I'll be back soon. Rest up. I turned the landline ringer off, but it's the button on the side if you need it.' She eyed the phone on her bedside table. She might call Migs. She needed a friend's perspective on all this.

Maybe tomorrow. *God, I wish I was the type of girl to keep a diary. I would have speed-read that thing by now.*

He popped his head back round the door, just as her head sank to the pillows. 'Ali?'

'Yeah?'

'I am glad you're home. Don't go anywhere, okay? I won't be long.'

Her eyes were already closing.

'I'll be here.' She wriggled under the covers, relishing the feel of being in her own bed. Even if she didn't remember being in this one before, it felt amazing to be back here. 'Bye.'

She could feel him still there. She opened one eye and saw him looking at her from the doorway.

'You're still here.'

'I know, I'm going.' His whole face seemed to melt. 'It's just hit me that you're home, that's all. Sleep tight, sparrow.'

She heard him close the front door behind him and was out like a light before his truck left the street.

* * *

One good thing about being home with little memory of the house you live in? The fact she'd planned the layout herself. As she hid in her now-finished walk-in closet, dialling a number on the landline, clad in only a towel, she was thrilled she'd decided to bother with it. She wasn't a total girly girl but having somewhere to hide right now was worth every penny.

'Please have the same number, please have the same... Migs! It's me!'

She could hear Callum downstairs. She'd woken up earlier, found a sandwich wrapped up at the side of her bed. A Post-it note declaring *Eat Me* stuck on top of the foil-wrapped plate. She'd polished off the lot, and the bottle of water, before showering. Callum had come running up the stairs when he heard the water running. It was going to take some getting used to having him here. Navigating around him, figuring where she'd put her own shit in the house she'd forgotten too. Noticing his stuff.

'Alice! Oh my God are you okay, where's Callum?'

Alice took the phone away from her ear to dull the screech.

'Shush! My head. He's downstairs, getting ready. Listen, I know we have a lot to talk about, but I don't have time! Did Lewis tell you about the dating?'

'About the date, yeah! It's so romantic, I can't. Are you really okay? God, we've missed you so much, I thought—'

Her voice was getting a little sobby in tone now, and Alice was on the clock.

'Migs, listen. I know we have to catch up, but please, I need help.'

'Anything. Lewis! Lewis, come here!'

'No, no!' she shouted down the phone, trying to hide in the back of the closet, under the racks of clothing. She wrapped a long, winter, berry-coloured coat over her face to muffle the noise of her voice. 'Don't get Lewis! Ooh, nice coat. I didn't know I had... oh never mind, listen! Don't get Lewis, I'm fine. I just need...' She sighed, pulling the phone closer to her ear. 'I need to know what to wear for this date. Callum's being weird, but not weird – cos we're together, but I don't remember him. So I don't love him, but he loves me. And I fancy him, but I can't tell him that – cos...' She tried to think of why again, but it was all a swirl of wanting to run and wanting to jump back into his strong arms and kiss the ever-loving hell out of him. Damn the consequences. 'Cos I am a bloody chicken when it comes to this crap, and it seems the coma didn't see fit to lose that part of me. I don't want to upset everybody, Migs. Shit. What am I doing?'

The line was quiet for so long Alice thought she'd missed the click of the call disconnecting. 'Hello? Migs?'

'I'm here,' she said softly. 'That was a lot. I don't know how you're managing all this.'

'I'm not, really,' she admitted. 'I had a memory though.'

'You did? About what?'

'Callum,' she murmured, poking her head out of the corner of the door to check he wasn't in earshot. 'He called me sparrow, carried me. Into our house. I'd been away for work. I got a glimmer, but it was really vivid.'

'Wow,' she exclaimed. 'Did you tell your parents? What did the doctors say?'

'It was a ten second memory I had six hours ago. I'm hardly fixed. I didn't tell them yet. I remember Callum though, Migs. Boyfriend version.'

'Good.' Migs sounded relieved. 'We've been so worried about you, both of you. Callum's been a total wreck. He never left your side.'

'Ali?' He called her name.

'Shit,' she whispered into the phone. 'He's coming up here, I've got to go. I'm hiding in the closet.'

Migs laughed, and it sounded so like her, it gave Alice a pang to hear.

'Well, sounds like you two are doing just fine. Jeans and a top, honey. You can't go wrong with that. Come see us, soon? I miss you so much.'

'Ali?' He sounded amused. 'Are you in the closet?'

'Yeah, promise. Bye.' She rushed off the call, just managing to stand and shove the phone behind her back as Callum walked in. He took her in, her coat half wrapped around her, hair wild, face flushed.

'Whatcha doing in here then? Digging an escape route?'

He lifted his hands and made a burrowing motion. She went to slap him, but he swerved with an easy dodge.

'No, I was just deciding what to wear.' His eyes were full of mischief as he took in the room. Half of everything she owned was on the floor, metal hangers sitting in a thick pile like scrap.

'And talking to yourself?' He went to look behind her arm, but she moved it to the other before chucking it down onto a pile of clothes behind her. 'You know what they say about people talking to themselves in wardrobes.'

'Even if I did, I probably forgot,' she quipped back. 'Can I help you with something?'

'No.' He smiled, running his hand along a white silky top she hadn't noticed before. Sleeveless with a shimmer to the fabric. 'Just telling you I will be back at seven. For our date. And don't go into the living room till then. It's all set up.'

Given that she hadn't ventured further than the bathroom, she was good with that for today.

'I love this on you.' He rubbed the fabric between his fingers before stepping back. He cleared his throat with an awkward huff. 'I put my number into your phone, and it's asterisk two on speed dial. You'll be okay for a while?'

She was already frowning at him, his hands already raising in surrender.

'Sorry, I know. I know.' He kissed her on the cheek and was gone. The scent of him lingered in the small room, surrounding her. She looked at the rail opposite hers. Full of men's clothing. Suits, work boots. Sexy shirts that looked fitted, tight. She wondered what he would be wearing tonight. Remembering the silky number he'd looked at, she reached up and pulled it off the hanger.

* * *

She was ready by six thirty. She would have been at least half an hour quicker, but she'd spent a lot of time looking for stuff she needed. Finding things she didn't know she'd ever needed. Looking around her house for where things were.

She'd watched loads of those design makeover shows over the years. The ones where the residents of the house flitted off to a hotel for a few days while the TV crew moved in. It felt a bit like that. Like she'd discussed her wants for the house and had returned to see the end result. Callum had been vague about the details, but she knew from the skip, the plaster bags in the hallway, that work was progressing. What she was worried about was paying the bills going forward.

She needed to get back into the world, she realised. Ring a few people, if only to tell them she was moving around again. In the land of the living. She sat on her bed, wondering whether wearing heels was a stupid idea, given that they weren't leaving the house. She put them on anyway, if only to dress up her outfit. She sat on the bed, threading the leather strap into the buckle, and looked around her in the silence.

The bedroom was huge, the largest room in the three-bedroomed house she'd sunk every penny into. In the master, the walls were now freshly plastered. The house had a chimney stack running through it, and she'd elected to remove the whole thing. Go more eco-friendly, showcase her creative talents while being cost-effective and future-proof. The stack was gone, and it had opened up the room just like she'd imagined it would. The soft tones in the dove-grey walls made it look fresh, modern. Her furniture was here, most of the pieces she'd remembered ordering. Putting on hold in the local shops around her, making use of the local handcrafted talent they had on the doorstep. It was better than she'd expected. Wood panelling along the wall where the headboard rested that she'd never even thought of.

It was neat, tidy. Functional but homely. She couldn't help feeling a surge of pride as she looked around her. It was comforting, knowing that the woman she'd lost for those two years hadn't changed completely. She'd been living her dream. Sure, things with Callum were...

She stood, frustrated at the inability to be able to articulate her own feelings for him, even to herself. Her heels sank into the thick cream carpeting as she spied the ajar closet door.

Pushing into the room, she looked again at the closet. The lighting that was so perfect. She noticed for the first time that the panelling came through here too, matching the room outside. She ran her hand over the smoothly sanded top edge, her hands stilling when it arrived at Callum's rail.

She felt her heart quicken, taking in the oh-so cute couple's closet. Her clothing, brighter and more daring than before. His, so familiar, and yet so alien being across the way from hers. She ran her hand along his rail. V-neck T-shirts that she knew would cling to his skin. A stack of work trousers, sewn with many pockets, a built-in tool caddy around the waist. Thick boots sat underneath the rail, jostling for space against running sneakers, wellies, trainers. Smart dress shoes that matched the suits above them. She wondered how often he wore these. How long he spent wearing the grey sweatpants he kept several pairs of. He lived here. When she'd known him last, he'd had his own place. Bought it young. Younger than all of the other friends they'd grown up with. He seemed to want to put roots down the second he could. Given that his own parents hadn't been the best, she'd understood him completely at the time. Wanting to have a space of his own. He was like her. He wanted to be in control, not at the whim of anyone else. Nothing wrong with that. Now, there was no talk of his place. His clothes in the closet, his book on the nightstand. This was a man who was happy here. Contented enough to snuggle down under the covers and read.

She pushed the closet door closed behind her, spotting some perfume by the side of her bed. Her usual brand. She smiled at the discovery, daubing herself with it as she noticed the small stack of paperbacks next to her own bedside table. One of them, a romance, had a bookmark wedged halfway through it. Picking it up, she didn't recognise the cover.

'Damn it,' she cursed to herself in dismay, pushing the book back onto the pile. Her favourite author. 'I've missed two in the series now.' She kicked out in frustration, regretting it when her Bambi heel-wearing toes connected with the hard wood. 'Son of a bitch!' She felt herself start to shake, the pent-up exhaustion and shock of the last few days screaming down at her. She wouldn't remember the sodding series anyway. She'd read most of it in the blank space of time she'd lost. Her memory was a fair few books behind the one taunting her from across the room. It was so annoying. Heart-breaking. Frustrating.

All that... stuff. Laughs with her parents, nights out. Weddings. She couldn't remember Lew's wedding, and it was the one thing she was looking forward to when it came to the M word. Watching her brother wed his sweetheart, after being together for so long. They'd all been in a crowd, growing up. Now she felt like Tom Hanks in *Big*. Like everyone on the planet had moved on, evolved. She was just a girl in a woman's body, wondering why the hell she didn't know anything. Feeling like she was one big burden, when everything in her screamed, *stand on your own two feet*. She felt the sting of tears again and ran for the phone.

'Hello?'

'Lew, put Migs on. I need her.'

'Alice? You okay?'

'Yes! Put Migs on, quick! It's nearly seven o'clock!'

'What? Where's Callum... oh... the date! Migs! The date's starting!'

'Lewis,' Alice growled through gritted teeth. 'Stop being a dick and put her on!'

'Jeez,' her brother retorted. 'I think the coma made you meaner!'

'Lewis!' She let her little sister voice whine through.

'Okay, okay! She's here!' Alice was sure she could hear a slapping sound, then Migs came on the line.

'Alice? What's wrong?'

'My brother is an immature idiot.'

'Preach, sister. I slapped him for you.'

'Not hard enough.'

She heard Lewis laugh before she heard more distortion down the phone as the pair of them started to scuffle with each other. 'Come here, woman. Crush me under your weight!'

'Eugh!' Alice took the phone from her ear and yelled again. Louder. 'Eww! Lewis, put my friend down and ruddy well sod off!' One look at the clock had her terror rising. It was four minutes to the hour. She went to the mirror, checking that she looked okay in her outfit.

'I'm back. What's wrong? Did you not find anything to wear?'

Alice frowned at her jean and top combo. 'Yeah, but I'm freaking out! I agreed to have ten dates, but I don't remember any of the dates!'

Migs's voice was deadpan. 'Kind of the point though, right? To get to know each other again.'

'I know but, it's Callum! He chased me with a frog when I was six. I chased him back with a hammer I'd swiped off my dad's work-bench. I remember a lot about him. Just not this.'

'I've always said you two were like Tom and Jerry, but sheesh. I didn't even know you'd done that!'

'Before your time,' Alice quipped. 'I feel like I'm chasing him with the hammer again.' She drew the phone closer to her mouth as she heard an engine outside. 'Shit, I think he's here. I hear the truck.' The rumbling of the engine shut out. A second later, she heard the slam of the truck door. 'What am I going to do?'

Migs's voice was a strong contraction to her shaky tones.

'Don't panic. You just got home. Everything doesn't have to click into place today. You know Callum really well. You just need the blanks filling in, that's all.'

There was a knock on the front door, and Migs, hearing it, squealed along with Alice.

'Why is he knocking?' she stage-whispered into the phone.

Migs sounded like she was about to swoon. 'Oh wow. He's doing it right down to the little details, honey.'

Alice twigged. 'He's knocking, because when we first did this, he didn't live here.'

'Exactly. Go with this, Alice. Don't get too in your head, okay? Have fun, even!'

'Have fun? I can't do this, Migs. Two years is more than a blank. I basically fell asleep and pushed him out of my head. What if it doesn't work? Any of this? What then?' She lowered her voice as the knock came again. 'His clothes are all in my closet, Migs. He has a pants drawer, and he reads in bed, apparently... and he runs too? Did you know that?' She didn't wait for an answer. Of course she knew; she was the idiot fumbling around in the dark here. 'I don't know what the hell I'm doing!' She was half yelling now, and the knock was harder this time. 'I'm freaking out that I'm going to cock this up.'

'Why?' Migs cut in. 'If you don't remember him, and from what Lewis said, that last time you do remember, you slapped him. Right?'

'Yeah.' She flushed, heading out of the bedroom and loitering on the stairway. She could see his shape in the hallway window by the door. She leaned down the staircase, ogling further, but then his face appeared at the glass. She ducked her head quicker than a Tory dodges taxation. '*So?*'

'So,' Migs sang back, 'you care. Somewhere. There must be something to this, or you wouldn't be so worked up.'

There it was. Her jaw dropped just as Callum hammered on the door again.

'You're right,' she breathed. 'I do care. Shit. I have to go.'

'Okay, have fun! Call me tomorrow!'

'Migs.' She dashed her phone back to her ear as she bounded down the stairs as fast as her still clunky body could carry her. 'One last thing... on this date, the first one. I mean the first, first one – did we... you know?'

Migs's laughter mocked her as she slid the chain off the front door. Reached for the handle.

'Don't worry,' she teased. 'You were a classy girl.'

'Eugh!' She heard Lewis retch in the background. 'I forgot how gross this is.'

Alice cut the call off on their laughter, grabbing the handle and finally opening the door.

'Hi,' he said, holding a bunch of flowers, a bottle of champagne. The dusky night his backdrop, his smile lit up her porch. She wasn't entirely sure it was down to the flash new lighting installed either.

'Hi,' she echoed back, taking in the sky-blue shirt he was wearing. Open at the collar, she could see the top of his chest. The cut of the fit as the material around his torso poured effortlessly beneath the thick leather belt. His buckle was small, silver. She could just make out a heart strewn through with arrows painted on the enamel surface. He looked so good. Hot. His dark eyes were taking her in too, she knew. Could feel him appraise her right there on the doorstep. The night air seemed to crackle around them as they surveyed each other. She realised she was still holding the phone in her hand and whipped her hands behind her back. His lip twitched.

'Took you a while.' He leaned down, dropping a kiss onto her cheek. 'What happened? Did your escape route have a cave-in?'

* * *

'I nearly did escape, you know, earlier.'

'Oh I know. I had a pack of dogs sit out the back in case you jumped the fence.' He reached for another slice of pizza after offering her the box first. She'd waved him off with the dough ball she brandished. 'I couldn't, I'm stuffed.'

He looked at the multitude of primary-coloured boxes spread out on the sheets laid out at their feet. There was enough to feed a small pack of dogs, as it went. He noticed her take in the feast.

'Yeah, I was a bit worried you'd forget what type of pizza you liked best, so I took a shot.'

She laughed, till clocking his serious expression. 'Oh. You meant that, didn't you. I didn't forget everything, dufus.'

'Dufus! Wow!' He hit the palm of his hand against his forehead. 'Forgot that one. Better than skip rat.'

They'd just been talking about all the nicknames she'd had for him throughout the years. Dufus. Dur brain was another favourite for a while. Penis breath ran for a good long time, till skip rat took over. She'd called him that because he'd actually dived into a skip when Sharon Jones had chucked Alice's backpack in there; Lewis was too busy laughing to help, but Callum had jumped straight in.

'Skip rat was a bit much. Sorry. You did come to my rescue.' He was sitting cross-legged, opposite her. She was leaning against the kidney-shaped sofa. It dug into her back. 'You know, when I first fell in love with this couch, I didn't realise it was so...'

'Like a slab of concrete?' He guessed at the ending of her sentence, and she had to agree. 'It's the worst. You were adamant we had to get this, to match the room, but I wanted a huge fabric corner sofa.' He laughed to himself. 'We had a bit of a disagreement in the shop, so much so that the guy knocked 10 per cent off the sofa to get rid of us. Just be grateful you don't have to sleep on it.'

'Why would you...?' She felt her brain click. 'Oh, no spare room, right?' She looked around the room. 'I can't believe I don't know my own house.' She rubbed at her forehead, and felt his hand pull it away.

'Don't panic,' he said. He looked at her hand in his and released his grip slowly. 'It's your home, Ali. Every bit of it is you.'

She thought back to the bedroom closet. 'Not everything. I love the panelling in the bedroom, but that's not me.'

He smiled. A slow, easy smile. 'Ah well, that was down to the builder.'

'Right.' She thought for a moment, then it clicked. The Deal. 'You,' she breathed. 'You won the bet, right? You did all that?'

'Of course,' he replied, wiping his mouth on a napkin and opening the champagne. It popped loudly in the room, and he filled two flutes he'd brought from the kitchen. 'Although I am regretting not having a spare room now. From tomorrow, I have to sleep on that torture device.' He nodded behind her at the couch.

'Sorry,' she said, feeling awkward. His face fell.

'No, no. I'm joking, honestly. I don't mind.' He passed her a flute. 'You can have one, I already checked with the hospital. I'm just happy you're home.'

She didn't know how to respond, but he was already cleaning up some of the empty boxes. Making himself busy as she wiped her mouth and hands.

The room was just like she'd envisioned. A thick chunk of reclaimed wood had been turned into a TV wall, the television in the centre of the console. Surrounding it were books, some she recognised as old favourites. Others were obviously Callum's. She could see in every inch of the room their relationship laid out before her. The photos on the bay window, next to the vase of fresh blooms he'd brought. The whole TV wall was covered over in sheets, giving it the cosy look of an exotic tent. He'd lit candles in hurricane glass holders around the corners of the room. Recreating the blank, torn-down canvas that the living room had been on that first date. The attention to detail made her wonder just how much he'd put into this the first time. To do it all over again two years later. It made her feel... special. On the spot, but special.

In the corner, resting on the side table next to the couch, was something covered in a sheet. Boxy. She heard him in the kitchen, opening drawers, before coming back into the room with a tub of ice cream and two spoons.

He saw her raise a brow at him, and he came to sit next to her on the sofa, dragging a couple of oversized cushions from it to shield their backs.

'Here.' He passed her one of the spoons, and the open tub. 'Your favourite, still I hope.'

'"Cherry Garcia",' she read from the tub. 'Perfect, thank you.' His shoulders relaxed; she could feel the tension leave him as he pushed the side of his body against hers. As if reassuring himself that she was there. Like her touch soothed him. As his body heat warmed her, she was surprised to realise that she felt the same. It *was* comforting. Like a muscle memory of wrapping up in a warm blanket. They sat for a while, eating spoonfuls of the dessert in an easy silence.

'Tell me about our first date,' she said suddenly. She found that she wanted to know more. She waved her hands around the room. 'I get the decorations. This room was a mess when I first moved in. What did we do?' He pushed another spoonful into his mouth, and she found herself watching his lips curl around the spoon. 'I mean, on the date.' She swallowed and looked away from the feelings his actions were provoking in her. God, she felt like a bloody teenager again.

'We talked about the house. You showed me the plans, what you wanted to do. You'd already agreed to the date.' Another grin flashed across his features, and she wondered how she could ever have forgotten him. Sitting here now, feeling the warmth of him next to her, she couldn't fathom out how anyone would let that leave their brain. She pushed the feelings of panic and dread away, not wanting to dwell too long on the thought of everything she'd lost. 'We ordered pizzas and ate ice cream. Your TV wasn't even unpacked. We ended up watching some action thriller on your tablet, squashed together amongst the dust sheets.'

She blushed to think of it. 'Sounds like I really showed you a good time,' she quipped, trying to lighten the mood when nothing in her brain sparked. *Don't force it,* she tried to remind herself. *One day at a time.* 'Pizza, dust and free labour.'

He shook his head. 'I loved every minute, Alice. You were so happy, so excited about the house. Your plans, they were infectious.

I wanted to make this house a home, for you.' He locked those chocolate-brown eyes right on hers. 'I fell in love with you a little bit more, just from that night.'

Hearing him say that so easily dropped her breath away. 'You did?'

He moved closer, and she focused on the very centre of his pupils. They were so dark she almost fell in. 'Totally,' he murmured, and she felt the rumble of his low tone all around her. 'Took you a bit longer, as always.' He raised his hand as though to brush her cheek, but booped her on the nose instead. 'No action thrillers tonight. We hated it the first time, so I got something better.' He stood up, and leaning over the boxy shape on the couch, he pulled the sheet free and clicked a button.

The projector that had been hidden under the sheet whirred to life, and the sheeted area in front of the TV wall lit up with a bright, warm creamy-coloured light.

'A projector?' She half shrilled, a mixture of panic and excitement flowing through her simultaneously. 'Oh my God, I've not seen one of these since school!'

He settled back in next to her, a little black remote control in his hand.

'I know, right? Thought it would be more romantic than a tablet. You ready?'

He fluffed the cushion behind her before doing the same to his and settled down lower. She felt his arm come around her shoulders, and she snuggled into him a little closer.

'I think so.'

He squeezed the top of her shoulder, his thumb rough against her soft skin. 'I'm right here,' he half whispered to her soothingly. 'I'm glad you chose the top I love. You look amazing.' He reached his fingers up, running them once against the strap of material on her shoulder. 'You always do.'

She could do nothing but look at him, staring into the eyes she knew so well. All while he touched her skin, something she didn't know, but really bloody liked. A lot.

'You're not so bad yourself.' It was out of her mouth before she could filter it, but it was true. His eyes widened a little when she parted her dry lips. The ice cream was melting in the tub in her hand, but she could do nothing but let it drip from the carton onto her jeans. Short sharp drops of cold brought her out of her stupor.

'So,' she said, louder than necessary. 'What are we watching?'

She wiped at the spots on her jeans, filling her spoon with enough Cherry Garcia to stop her mouth from doing something impetuous. Like licking him from head to foot, for example. Snogging his face off against her utterly trendy torture rack of a couch.

He waggled the remote at her. 'Ah well, my little forgetful one.' He pressed a button, and the machine behind them whirred into action. 'This is the wedding of the year.'

'What?' Alice breathed, as an intro slide came onto the projector wall.

The Wedding of Lewis and Migs

She turned to Callum. 'Thank you,' she said, smiling even as her eyes filled with tears.

He gave her a wink. 'Don't cry, sparrow.' He pointed to the screen, and she felt his arms come around her. 'Is this too much?'

His free hand hovered on the remote control.

'No,' she said, taking in the screen as it filled with the outside of the wedding venue. 'No, I want to see it.'

The video had it all. The run-up to the vows, Migs getting ready with her bridesmaids. She could see herself on the screen, dressed up and make-up done, laughing with the others while they watched Migs transform into the perfect bride.

'She looked beautiful. Didn't she look perfect?'

Callum kept his eyes on the screen. 'She did. To be honest, I was too busy checking out my date. I thought you were the most beautiful woman there.'

As if on cue, the scene changed to the pair of them at the altar, Lewis teary eyed as he declared his love. Alice watched intently, but she wasn't looking at the pair getting married. She was looking at Callum, who was standing over the groom's shoulder, his eyes fixed on the bridesmaid at the back of Migs. If the look of love on the groom's face wasn't emotional enough, Callum's expression surpassed it by miles. She watched him on the screen, gazing at the screen version of her in adoration. She risked looking at him, and he wasn't watching the wedding. He was watching her. His face was so close to hers; she could see little flecks of hazel around his pupils.

'You loved me, didn't you?'

She saw the flecks dance when his eyes widened.

'I still love you, sparrow.'

'No.' She pointed to the screen, where the room had erupted into cheers as Lewis kissed his new wife. She watched the pair of them link arms, half running back down the aisle as the whole wedding party celebrated around them. Callum headed straight to her side, and she watched as he took her into his arms. Saying something that made her laugh out loud, before holding her to him and kissing her. 'I mean then, at the wedding.'

He said nothing at first, his gaze flicking to the screen. 'Yes,' he said eventually, and she felt his arm tighten around her. 'I never know how much to say, when you ask me things like that.'

She got what he meant. As much as she was curious, and feeling things, she still pushed him away when she felt panicked.

'This must be pretty exhausting for you,' she half whispered. 'I want to know though.' She looked back at the screen, where the video was showing the wedding breakfast. The pair of them were sat together, drinking and laughing at the speech from Migs's dad. 'We look happy.'

'We were. Are,' he corrected, but it had less conviction in the tone. 'I loved you then, I love you now, Ali. I think I've always loved you, even before I really understood what it meant.'

His thumb was moving in small circles on her shoulder, and the little movement was so intoxicating she forgot to worry about the future. Here, with him, she felt like things finally made sense somehow.

'Of course,' his tone turned playful, 'it took you a little bit longer to see it.'

She couldn't help but roll her eyes. 'Doesn't sound like me.'

He chuckled, turning back to the screen.

'That's how I know that we'll be okay,' he murmured, breaking out into a grin at a funny part of the wedding video. Lewis trying to take off Migs's garter with his teeth while she sat red-faced on a chair in the middle of the dance floor.

'What, because I'm stubborn? Blind to the truth?'

His eyes found hers again. 'No, sparrow. Because we were meant to be together. A love like ours doesn't just disappear.' His jaw flexed. 'No matter how much is stacked against us.'

Alice had forgotten all about the video. She was too absorbed listening to him talk.

'You really think so? That doing this ten dates thing will work? What about—'

He took her hand in his. 'I know so, and when I know what I want, I'll spin the damn Earth on its axis to get it.' He leaned forward, and she held her breath, waiting for his lips to touch hers. She felt them brush against her forehead, before he leaned his against hers. His eyes were so close she could barely focus. 'I just want you to trust me; can you do that?'

'Yes,' she said as his fingers stroked along the back of her hand. The feeling of him touching her skin was addictive. She wanted more every time. A little bit more, each day. If her mind was unsure, it seemed more and more that her body wasn't. She wanted him close. The teenage part of her would be sat giggling up her sleeve now if she saw them sitting here like this. 'Yes, I trust you, Callum. I always trusted you.'

'Even when you wanted to strangle me?' he laughed.

'Even then.'

He pulled away, just a little.

'Good to know. Maybe you can do one more thing for me.'

'What's that?' she asked, wondering – no, hoping – that he would ask for a kiss. She couldn't help herself. Yes it was weird, but this was her life. She was trying to get it back, wasn't she? The teenager in her rolled her eyes, but the spicy scent of him was flooding her senses. She didn't love him, but she wasn't made of stone either. She felt the tension between them. Knew from his dilated pupils that he felt it too. 'What do you want me to do?'

He squeezed her hand. 'Walk me out.'

Her libido crashed to the soles of her feet. 'Oh, okay,' she said, practically jumping up to avoid the rush of embarrassment she felt. 'Sure.'

He put his shoes on at the door, pulling on the blue denim jacket she'd grown to love on him. He took her hand, followed her out of the front door. She stood in the doorway, still wondering whether she'd misread the situation. Confusion was becoming a very unwelcome bedfellow.

'Thanks for tonight,' Callum said, squeezing her fingers in his, pulling her over the threshold and onto the front porch. 'I had a good time.'

'Me too. Thanks for bringing the wedding video. It almost makes up for not remembering it in the first place.' It had been amazing, a real insight into the missing months, but most of all, into their relationship. It gave her hope that things might just be okay. 'You're staying at Lew's tonight, right?'

He nodded. 'I'll be back tomorrow. I think it will be good for you to have a night here, on your own.' He looked up at the house, as if asking it to look after her for him. 'I had a great night. It was nice, just us.'

She nodded, feeling like she should agree out loud, say something else, but for some reason all she could think about was pulling him back into the house. She wasn't afraid of being alone – all her memories of her place before now was her living there alone – but tonight had made her feel a little differently.

'Nice that we didn't spend the night taking the piss out of each other, like the old days.'

He laughed, pulling her into his arms. 'Oh, we still do that.'

'We do?'

His beautiful eyes focused on hers.

'You'll see,' he promised. 'We'll be like that again. For now, I need to show you how our first date ended.'

His eyes dropped to her lips, and his arms came up around her. Wrapping his warmth around her tightly. When he went in to kiss her, his eyes closed. She could see the long dark lashes framing his lids before she closed her own. When their lips met, she felt a jolt. A spark so big that she thought she might ignite. *Was it always like this?* she wanted to ask, but she felt like she already knew the answer.

He kissed her gently at first, tentatively. When her lips parted, the tempo changed. His tongue met hers, tasting her and deepening the kiss to something she felt throughout her whole body. Her nerve endings were tingling as he kissed her senseless. She was pushed against the house now, his body solid, flush against hers. So tight, a passer-by wouldn't have been able to push a sheet of paper between them. Her hands were in his hair, his holding her so tight to him, she wanted to lift her legs, wrap them around him to pull them even closer together. Absorb him into her.

'Alice,' he breathed when he finally broke the contact.

'Uh-huh,' she replied, dazed. Her damn lips were on fire, her whole body igniting from the touch of him. The feel of his body pressed up against hers, the spicy scent of him practically steam-rolling her senses. For a girl recovering from a car crash *and* a coma, she felt pretty darn great right about now. He dropped a kiss onto the tip of her nose.

'Thank you for a lovely evening,' he murmured gruffly, and then he was gone. He held her fingers till the last moment, till his feet hit the stone path. The heat from his body still lingered as she watched him just walk away. Get into his truck and drive away. She caught the little smile on his face through the window as he pulled away from the house.

'Well,' she said to no one as she sagged back against the wall. 'That was...' Her fingers came up to her lips, as if she could tangibly feel the touch of him still on her. The spice of his scent hung in the air around her. 'Interesting.' *And friggin' hot as hell.*

When she managed to coherently tell her legs to move, she headed back inside. The living room was still set up, the projector screen blank. She sat down, folding her legs underneath her, and pressed play on the remote. The wedding video started up again, and this time, instead of focusing on the bride and groom, she looked at the couple clearly besotted with each other. She watched every detail, every movement. The best man dipping the maid of honour during a slow dance. The way their eyes looked for the other always, lighting up when they spotted each other across the room. Callum's speech about everlasting love, adoration that didn't falter or fall away in the tough times. A deep, unabating passion that met every bump in the road, adapted and learned to overcome the trials of life. As the video came to a close again, her eyes wet with tears, she found herself torn. Torn between fighting to get every single moment back and fearing that she never would. That *they* never would be the couple in that video again. For a woman who never believed in true love, she went to bed feeling pretty pissed that she'd had it, all of it. Only to forget it entirely.

Before she finally closed her eyes, wrapped under the covers in the bed they'd shared, she had two thoughts. The first one was the goodbye kiss. The recreation of that first date kiss had felt much more than a replica. She was guessing the heat between them was not something he was trying to infer. You couldn't infer that kiss. Hell, she'd almost dry-humped the man on the front porch. The best second first date kiss of her entire life.

The second thought, the one that turned her lust to rage, was that if she ever got to meet Barry, she would take great pleasure in beating the ever-loving shit out of him. Barry took her life, and she wanted it back.

12

CALLUM

'Tell me you're not pinning everything on this. A dare? Callum!'
The minute he'd reluctantly left home to go to Lewis and Migs's for
the night, they were on him. He was in a mood already having to
leave her, but for the plan to work, and work well, he needed to
leave her there. Like he had done that first time, after snogging her
face off on the doorstep. He'd nursed an erection the whole car
journey. *God, she'd felt good. It felt even better than the first time.* When
he'd finally pulled away, leaving her breathless, he could see the
night apart would be worth it. She was under no illusions now
about what heat the two of them could spark within the other. So
far, so good. Migs continued to earbash him, talking about all the
things that could go wrong. 'You know how stubborn she is. Was. Is!
She's Alice 2020 version, remember? What if it freaks her out too
much? Oh my days I need a drink.'

'Not a chance, sorry.' Lewis shot his wife an apologetic look. She
flipped him off. 'She's got a point, Cal. I know my sis. She's like a
hedgehog when she feels threatened.'

'I had to do something! She wanted to check into a hotel. You just said how stubborn she gets; how prickly she is when she thinks she's being managed. I needed her to stay with me, with us!'

Migs tried to haul herself off the large, overstuffed cream leather sofa, but gave up, reaching for the family-sized bar of chocolate instead. 'I know, but, Callum, that's madness. What if it doesn't work?'

'Yes!' Lewis, who had been stuttering and pacing, clambered onto his wife's point, sitting down on the arm of the sofa and dropping a kiss on her head. The beer bottle he was swinging around fizzed up, and a shower of foamy beer sprang up over his fingers.

'Yes! My beautiful wife is right! What if it doesn't work?' Lewis's face paled. 'You can't move in here! We've got enough on our plate.'

'Lewis!' Migs slapped him. 'Of course he could live here, but he doesn't need to. He lives with Alice, where he belongs.' She pointed a long finger at Callum, who was wearing a line into her hearth rug. He couldn't help it. His mind was working overtime after that kiss goodbye. He wished he was there now. Leaving her alone in that big house, when she didn't remember half of the stuff in it, worried him. It felt alien for him not to be there. Nowhere had ever quite felt like home, till that house. With her.

'It's going to work, but I think you're mad. It's a big deal if this doesn't work, Cal.'

'Yeah.' Lewis took another swig of beer, his face dropping when he saw it was near empty. 'Beer?'

'Yeah,' he said, not caring either way. *I'd rather be back in my own house, my own bed. With my girl, swigging champagne in bed. Messing about under the covers.* He kept pacing, one way, then the other.

'Cal, honey... er... can you sit?' Migs's voice sounded pained. 'I feel like I'm at a tennis match.'

He plonked himself down on the armchair in the corner. The first time he'd sat down since driving round to Lewis's house in a kiss-drunk stupor. She broke off a piece of chocolate and threw it at him. 'Eat that.'

'I just ate.'

'It's to shut your mouth up while I talk.' He rolled his eyes and sucked on it with a scowl. 'Good.' Migs smiled. 'It's date one, right?' Her eyes scrunched up. 'I remember this; you kissed her on the doorstep?' Her face lit up. 'That's it, I really get the plan now! You're trying to recreate it for her! It's so cute!' She clapped her hands together before slapping Lewis on the arm. 'You'd never do anything like that for me! Jerk.' She turned back to Callum. 'It's so romantic, helping recreate your love story.' She was happy, her tone of voice and her smiling face emulated that. The tears rolling down her face were a new development. She saw the two men eyeballing her with concern, Lewis rubbing his arm. 'Sorry. Hormones!' She laughed, before shoving another slab of chocolate in her mouth. 'So did it work?' She leaned forward, her eyes widening. 'So you kissed her on the doorstep, like last time? It worked?'

Callum nodded, feeling like he was still fighting the urge to grab his keys at any moment and race the truck back to her. He kept sucking on the chocolate to keep his restless feet from moving. He needed to stick to the plan, as painful as it was to take it slow. He already didn't know how he was going to get through a whole twenty-four hours before he got to see her again. 'Yeah, and she kissed me back.' A daft grin erupted unbidden on his chops. 'It was so good. Us. She makes this little comfort sigh when I—'

'Lalalalalalalalala!' Lewis chanted loudly, sticking his fingers in his ears. Migs tutted loudly, and he stopped.

Migs was hooked. She was gripping Lewis by the forearm now. Lewis whimpered but she ignored him. 'And...? What did she say?'

Callum nodded. 'I think she was too shocked to speak properly.' His face softened when he thought of Alice, staring at him from their front doorstep as he'd pulled the truck away. Bee-stung lips, swollen from his eager kisses. Her top off one shoulder a little, where he'd tousled it. Her hair, a little wilder than before, from his roving fingers. And her expression. That mix of curiosity, shock and lust. He'd seen it before. On the first first date they'd had. 'It was even better than before. She's still in there, Migs. I can feel it, feel her.'

'Steady,' Lewis warned, just before an ornamental pillow twatted him in the forehead. Callum's hand landed back on his lap, playing with his bird ring like he couldn't stop himself. Migs made an approving sound and focused on her friend.

'I'm telling you, Callum, she's still that same person. I've heard it. On the phone, she was nervous. Worried about what to wear. She's definitely not gone. I know that as well as you do. You said yourself, she didn't have a personality transplant. She loved her life; she didn't want to change it. I have to have faith in that...'

'I bloody hope so.' Callum thought of how lonely he'd felt, by her hospital bed. Not able to talk to her, laugh like they did. He wanted to moan to her about the squeaky trolley that kept him up nightly. He'd begun to grind his teeth when it passed the corridors outside her room. It would have annoyed her, too. He knew. She'd have demanded they find it, oil every trolley in the hospital if they had to. Her tenacity was never-ending, and he hoped for their sake, she'd use it. Fight with him to get their lives together back again. It was so disjointed now. He felt like the teen boy he used to be, moody around her because he couldn't stand the thought of another day without her being his. They had so much history, which he clung to now, while he mourned everything they'd lost. All those little in-jokes, anecdotes. Gone. And the saddest thing of all, the fact that on that phone, seconds before the crash, another moment had happened. Another first lost. A first that when done right, had no need of being redone at all. It was gone. Another answer. Immediately lost, deep down in her beautiful head. He wanted to have that moment again or die trying.

'I can't lose her again,' he said, the wretched feeling coating his words, making them sound sad, low. 'I'll make her remember. Make her love me if I have to.'

Lewis had leaned closer into Migs while he spoke, and he saw the look that passed between them.

'What?' he asked, when neither spoke. 'You know what I mean. She's still the same person. She can't just...' His thoughts trailed off, faster than his words. Jumped on them, ensured that they wouldn't be spoken. 'Walk away.' *She can. Shit. She can. She could not remember me ever again. Not want this life or feel any connection to it. A great kiss is not a relationship.* He thought of her own fears about hurting him; her caution at the ripple effect her accident was having on them all. *She'll walk away, to avoid hurting me. Her family.* The thought killed him and dulled the progress of the night.

'She won't,' Migs said after an age of silence. 'Alice does love you, Callum. It's not just about the family stuff; she's just shocked. We just want you both to be okay. It's a lot for you, both of you. Give it time,' she said, and Callum knew full well that was what he didn't have. He had to cram eighteen months of pure fucking bliss into ten moments that were strong enough to help him keep the love of his life. The one he'd already waited half his life for. It was like running up a slide with his hands tied behind his back, desperate for another ride. He might never get back to the top. Might never see that view again, the joy of it all. It made him want to put his fist through something.

He clenched his hands as he lifted his tired behind out of the chair. 'I'm not sure I'll have enough of it.' He flashed them an optimistic smile he didn't feel. 'I'm going to bed. I have to get to work tomorrow; stuff's really piling up, and I don't want to be late for Alice.'

Lewis gave him a sympathetic look. 'Hang in there, man. I'm driving her over to our parents in the morning. Mum offered to make her lunch, but I think she just wants to fuss.'

Callum slapped Lewis on the shoulder in their usual brotherly way. 'Good, that's good. Maybe it will help.'

Lewis raised a pessimistic brow. 'You do remember my folks, right?'

Callum chuckled at the thought of Alice being fussed over by her mum and dad. She'd hate it, he knew. He couldn't help the chuckle that escaped him. 'Well, even better. One day with that, and she might not freak out about co-habiting with me.'

Lewis pulled a face. 'Eugh, bro.'

Callum punched him on the arm, hard. 'Quit that! It's not new to you, is it? I'll be on the couch anyway.'

'Good,' Lewis bit back, rubbing his arm. 'My arms can't take much more of this.'

Migs cracked out laughing, and Callum watched the pair of them settle back on the couch. He had to look away. It felt weird, just the three of them.

'Night, guys.'

He headed up the stairs after resisting Lewis's offer of another beer, to his bed in the spare room. He'd slept here some nights, while she was in the hospital. A few hours here and there, when Lewis and Migs forced him to come to theirs for food and enforced rest. He hated being back here. When she'd woken up, it had been the miracle he'd been praying for. He'd even been to the chapel to pray for her. To beg a deity he wasn't sure he believed in, to give him back *his* reason for living. The way Callum saw it, if there was a god listening, giving one life back had to better than ending two.

Then she'd woken up, groggy but such a sight for sore eyes. His prayers had been answered. Till she'd looked at him. Really looked at him, and that was when he knew.

Collapsing into bed with a sigh, he knew that it wasn't just the deal he was chasing, he was running too. Running as far away from that look on her face, as far as he could get. It had felt like his soul had slammed back into his teenage body, and he couldn't endure that again. She had to be his, totally his again, or all was lost. He'd have to let her go, and that was unthinkable. He just hoped that with all his hard work, all the risks he was taking, she would feel the same once more.

13

ALICE

'Morning, sis!'

Lewis's energy normally took her at least two coffees to cope with on a morning. She remembered that, but today it wouldn't be a problem. She was already two down, and the third was clutched in her hand. She resisted the urge to chuck it at the grinning idiot on her doorstep. It *was* red hot. More importantly, she was loath to waste the caffeine.

She'd put her big coat on already, but looking out at the rather warm April day, she wondered if she'd need it. She felt weird enough wearing clothes she didn't recognise. They were growing on her, though. She liked the colours better over her usual darker outfits. The coat she'd decided on was a long puffy affair, cream padding clad around her body.

'You ready?' Lewis thumbed over his shoulder to a car she didn't recognise.

'That yours?' It was flasher than the one she remembered. 'Poser.'

Lewis watched as she locked up, and she caught him keenly

observing her put her keys in her purse. She narrowed her eyes to slits in his direction.

'Knock it off. I'm not senile, Lew. I checked the oven, I didn't leave the bath running and I can manage to look after my own keys.' He looked sheepish. 'I called you a poser, and you didn't even bite back!' She huffed her way down the path.

'Sorry,' he said, reaching over to give her a hug once they were in the car. Alice was well and truly regretting the coat now. She felt like the Michelin Man. She managed to raise her arms high enough to hug him back. 'I'll stop, knobhead.'

Alice grinned at him, settling her handbag on her lap. 'That's more like it.'

He pulled out of her street, taking the familiar route to their parents' house on the other side of town. A loud chirp rang out.

'You got your phone back!'

'What?' Alice jumped. 'Oh, yeah, Callum got me one. I forgot. I thought it was yours.' She rummaged in her bag, took out the phone and opened the text message:

Morning. I miss you. Hope you slept well. I'll bring dinner home at six. Say hi to your folks for me.

She'd just read the message when it beeped again.

This is Callum, by the way.

And another.

Your boyfriend.

It beeped again. A photo. She clicked on it, and an image of Callum leaning on some scaffolding came up. His dark brown eyes were hard to spot amongst the hi-vis. It was quite a manly shot, she thought to herself. She'd always kind of liked him in his work gear.

Underneath, three dots bounced across the screen.

Just in case you needed a reminder. LU.

LU? She thought for a moment, her face heating up when she deciphered it. Love you.

'Idiot,' she muttered under her breath. Her finger traced his face absently.

'Callum?' She nodded at her brother, showing him the snap.

'Yep.' She hit reply. 'I think he might be bored at work.'

She tapped away a response.

I know. I will do.

No, that won't do. Bit cold. She deleted and started again.

I slept awful.

Nope.

Miss you too.

Hell no. So what if she'd lingered in the doorway, long after his truck had driven off? It was just a kiss. In fact, it had been a bloody fantastic kiss. Her teenage heart had almost exploded within her at the thought of his lips on hers. Her back against the brick as he devoured her in the porchway. No wonder she'd continued with the deal. She knew herself well enough to know that when she experienced this the first time, she was probably about as open as she was now. Maybe even less guarded than post-coma Alice.

She'd always been the same, and he'd changed all that. On the strength of that kiss, she now had more of an inkling as to why. She had missed him, that morning. Waking in the house alone, it was a surprise to feel that way. After all, she'd bought the house and lived in it for a couple of months before their date. She wasn't scared of a solitary existence that way. The thing was, when she'd opened her eyes, she'd done what she'd done most of the night. Thought about Callum.

'How was he, this morning?' she finally caved and asked.

Lewis turned down the song he'd been humming along to while her head was in her phone.

'Cal? I didn't see him. His truck was already gone when I woke up.'

'Right.' She nodded. 'Does he always go to work early?'

Her brother kept his eyes on the road, but she caught his shifty look. 'What? What did I say?'

Lewis sighed. 'I don't think I should be telling you this, but he's not been working much, with the hospital and everything. He has a team of people under him, but the new jobs haven't been coming in without him to drive them. He pretty much ignored his phone the first week. He fielded a few calls, delegated what he couldn't avoid, but the business, I dunno. He lost heart, I think.'

Alice was worrying at her lip, nibbling it between her teeth. Another layer of pressure added to her chest. 'Oh, right. He never said. That's my fault too, isn't it?'

Lewis shook his head vehemently. 'Don't ever say that. He wouldn't hear of it either. None of this is down to you, Alice. Callum knows what he's doing. He's got a few jobs to quote today, a few sites to look in on.' Alice took the news in. It added another layer to Callum. The worry he must had had with work on top of everything else. He was the sole earner, she reasoned. Coma victims didn't tend to work much.

'How bad is it?'

Lewis flicked his eyes to hers, her pinched face giving her away.

'The truth, Lew. You promised.'

He sighed heavily. 'I know. Fine. It's not that bad. The money's still coming in, but he needs to get back to it sooner rather than later. Most of the time he's on the road, in the day. Running things. He just needs to catch up, is all.'

'I'm guessing my work stopped when I did,' she digested. Among her things from the hospital was her handbag contents. Minus her phone, which had been in her hand at the time of impact. She'd gone through the paper diary she'd found, grateful once again for being a Luddite pen-pusher and note-taker in the modern electronic age. There were some bookings in it, but the meetings were all in the past. The diary just kind of stopped after March. April's bookings were all crossed through. 'I haven't even contacted my clients.'

'Callum did.' Lewis clicked the radio off. 'He rang everyone. He made time for that. Most of your projects you worked on one at a time, and with the house, you were both eager to get it finished. Don't worry.' He patted her hand. 'Callum's business is strong. Don't be worrying about money and all that yet.' The driveway of their parents' bungalow came into view, and they both went quiet. 'You have better things to focus that fretting on,' he added with a sarcastic grin.

'What. The. Hell.'

Her parents' house looked pretty much the same. Some cosmetic changes. A few different plants in ornamental tubs on the borders of the front lawn. Her dad had painted the wooden trims on the rose trellises a soft pink. It was comforting, for the most part. It was the ruddy great sign that was different.

Above the door, painted in Dad's characteristic hand, was a

huge sheet, strewn across the side of the house. Lewis pulled onto the drive, and the front door was yanked open.

'Lew,' Alice whimpered as they went to meet them. 'I am so not ready for this.'

'Welcome home!' Their parents jumped out, Alice not seeing the huge phallus-shaped and very shiny confetti cannons till the last minute. 'Woo-hoo!'

They both set their weapons off at the same time, and Lewis and Alice were pelted by multicoloured confetti and a huge blast of air as they rounded the front of Lew's car. Alice jumped two feet in the air and ended up sprawled across the bonnet. Lewis cursed under his breath, and Alice heard their mother tell him off as he righted her back on her feet.

'Really?' Lewis sounded quite angry. Alice looked up and saw the thunder on his face. 'What are you doing, trying to kill her off?'

Dad dropped the cannon at his feet, and their mother was already apologising as she hooked both of them in her arms and squeezed them together.

'Sorry! We're just excited. Hey, the local news called.' Her mum's eyes were popping out of her head. 'We could be on the telly! Come in, I've made some sandwiches, you know. Picky bits. We can have a good chat!' She started to usher their dad into the house. 'Quick, Gerry. Pour the Prosecco.'

'Lewis, take me home.' Alice tried to run to the passenger side door, but he held her fast.

'Nope. You need to get in there, spark some memories. Callum would kill me if I took you back now.'

'Don't make me!' she protested. Her parents were already halfway indoors. 'I'm not up to this.'

'Don't worry.' He picked her up easily and half dragged her in the crook of his arm up the drive. 'Callum's already filled everyone in on the deal, okay? The dating, and definitely no mollycoddling.'

'Oh.' She'd have to text him later, thank him. 'Right. The sign's still shit though.'

Lewis yanked her over the threshold when she tried to rip it down on her way in.

It read, in slightly drippy and unevenly painted lettering the words,

SORRY YOUR BRAIN BROKE, WE LOVE YOU!

Just underneath that was a crudely drawn version of what she assumed was meant to represent her grey matter. It had a big crack running through it, like a broken heart. Covering the cracks was a gloopy box, which Alice took to be a drawing of a plaster.

She was still fuming as Lewis pushed her through to the living room.

'Lewis, if you don't take that down, I'll—'

He deposited her on the armchair next to Dad in his chair, shouting, 'On it,' as he headed back to the doorway, Mum snapping at his heels. A minute later, Alice heard the satisfying sound of something ripping, and her mum's indignant protests. They now appeared to be wrestling on the front lawn. Alice listened, hoping that Lewis would win and get the abomination of a poster into the recycling bin. Hell, if he had to stuff their mother in there too, to shut her up, Alice was good with it.

'I told you she'd hate it, Louisa!' her dad half shouted towards the open door. 'She means well, love,' her dad patted her on the arm, like he always used to when she sat in the adjoining chair. 'How are you, with all this?' He thumbed in the direction of the door, where the two quarrellers could be heard scuffling about in the front garden.

'Lewis Gerald McClaren, if you don't get out of my way!'

'Mum, it's ripped. You are not putting that back up!'

'You watch me! Oi! Get off! You're not too big to go over my knee, lad!'

'Mum, I'm over six foot, and you shrank an inch last month! I will take you down!'

'Try it!' Her mother was screaming like a prop forward now, and her dad shut them out by closing the living room door.

'We won't have long,' her dad said solemnly, taking his seat back on his throne. 'I wanted to say more, at the hospital, but you know...' She did know. She probably wouldn't have taken it in anyway. 'I just worry about you, Alice. It's a big change.'

No shit, her brain spat out at her. 'Yeah.' She nodded dumbly instead. 'It is. I'm sorry to put you all through this.'

'Hey, we'll be having none of that. All right? I blame Barry bloody Evans.'

Alice felt her lips twitch. 'I hate Bazza,' she laughed.

Her dad pounded his fist once on the arm of his chair. 'So do I! My mates down the pub even wrote his name on the dartboard.' He mimed throwing a dart aggressively. 'I've had bullseye every Friday night since. How's things going at yours?'

She thought of her house, a big smile coming across her features. When she thought of the porch, it widened even more. *Maybe I should leave that bit out.* 'It's good. Weird, but good. I think Callum's doing a really good job, from what I can see. He's going to give me a proper tour tomorrow. He didn't want me getting over-whelmed with everything.'

'Good,' her dad managed to get out before the living room door opened, shattering their peace. 'Callum loves you, my girl. Trust him, okay? I know what you're like.'

'What?' she asked. 'What am I like?'

Her dad eye rolled his answer. 'Stubborn, independent. I know all this will be driving you mad, having to rely on people. It was hard enough for you to even get a boyfriend, and then Callum came along, and that was that.'

'What was what?' her mother said, looking flustered and red faced. Lewis was right behind her, and she saw a grass stain on his sweater. 'Your brother ruined our banner!'

Lewis giggled at the side of her, and she landed a blow to his gut, cutting the laughter off with a tight 'huff' escaping Lew. 'I warned you, son!' The formidable force that was her mother sat awkwardly in between the two chairs, resting one butt cheek on each arm. 'Now come on, let's go have some lunch. I've laid it out in the dining room.' She half hoisted Dad out of his chair before he could get a word out. 'Come on, or the sandwiches will curl up. I want to hear all about your big first date with Callum!'

The rest of the day was pretty much the same. Which is why, just as the sky was getting dark, she was hiding in a different closet.

Her old bedroom was just as she remembered leaving it, which was oddly comforting to her. It smelled of her. Every item she saw had a memory she could remember attached to it. She was sitting cross-legged, under and hidden by the rows of clothes. Her mother used the closet as extra space now, but the items in the boxes underneath were all hers.

Lunch had been nice, on the whole. Her mother asked far too many questions, kept telling her about things like she'd remember, and then get upset or infuriated when Alice reminded her about the coma. Lewis was on good form, but he'd escaped back to work after lunch. Alice had run off upstairs as soon as her mother had donned the Marigolds. Dad had already fallen asleep in his chair. Probably his way of escaping his wife when she was on one.

It's nice in here, she thought. *Cosy, like a childhood den.* She used to sit in here for hours, as a kid. Drawing pictures, reading books. It was always her little space when she needed a minute. Her mother had told her to spend some time in there before she went back to her own house. Her optimistic face is what had sent her running to her own little Narnia. She was tired of being observed by her family. She felt like she was constantly upsetting them, half the time not even realising it.

She pulled one of the boxes closer. It was full of photos, all loose. Pictures of all of them over the years. Birthday cakes at home, or at restaurant tables, carried by waiters. Snapshots of the nights out they'd had. Stock car racing, bowling, camping under the stars. The beach.

She pulled one out, taken on the coastal beach her parents ferried them to over the years. She remembered it like it was yesterday. Migs and her had been trying to sunbathe. She'd pulled out her camera to snap a shot of the two of them, and Callum and Lewis had been caught, right in the back of the frame, buckets in hand. The second she'd hit the shutter button, the pair of them had launched their buckets of freezing cold ice water. The shot was a perfect flash of time. Migs screaming, Alice looking like she was about to commit murder. Callum had his arms wrapped around her; Lewis caught in mid-air, his head back, laughing hard. She remembered it so well, she could almost feel the sand beneath her, smell the sea. Callum was looking down at her, her face scowling back at him. She'd seen the snap so many times. At one point she'd kept a pinboard above her desk, all of the photos in this box formerly being on display.

'What?' she murmured, looking at the two of them closer. 'How have I never noticed?'

It was the expression on Callum's face. The look he was giving her in the photo. His arms were tight around her. His stance, like he was shielding her rather than trying to stop her from getting him back. The look on his face. He was looking at her like she was precious. Like he loved her. She looked at her face again. The scowl, the hunched over body, coiled to strike if needed. She'd seen the same look on his face every day, since she woke up. She couldn't stop looking at the photo.

Pulling out her phone, she took a photo of it and sent it to Callum. Her phone chirped almost instantly.

WOW. Blast from the past. I loved that day. Lewis bringing you home soon?

Home. Well, that would never not be weird.

No, he had to get back to work. I know, we were so young! What happened?

Speak for yourself, Sleeping Beauty. I'm still hot. I'll come get you. Nearly done with work. You hungry?

She laughed.

You don't have to do that. And no, Mum made enough to feed the whole hospital. She put some in Tupperware to bring back.

Score! Love your mum's cooking. You really okay? Why the photo?

Alice looked at the faces again before replying.

Seeing what jogs something, I guess. I look feral.

Ha ha. You wanted to take my head off. All I could think was how good you looked. I could smell the ocean in your hair that day. Bring it with you, for me? Be there before six.

You want the photo?

The reply was instantaneous.

When it comes to you, always. See you soon. Miss you.

I'll bring it, see you soon x

She'd debated the kiss, but she needed to add something. Did she miss him? She seemed to like having him around. She knew that, missing him was... different. She had found herself missing their usual banter, but that was coming back. She felt comfortable with him.

Xx

He'd sent two kisses back. Acknowledging hers. Her stomach flipped. This was all new to her; even pre-coma, she hated dating. Now she was trying to date a man she already lived with. Knew inside out, or thought she did, anyway. The slightly gorgeous, scowling protective boy had seemingly turned into a protective, hot as hell, happy man. A man who was even bigger than she remembered. Muscles doubled, it seemed. *And now I'm thinking about his body again.*

'Alice? You coming down? Your dad thought it might be nice to watch a film before you go.'

Alice froze in place. Then she remembered she wasn't a guilty teenager, hiding in her closet mooning over photos of Callum. She was a grown ass woman... mooning over photos of Callum. 'Coming, Mum!' she shouted, making sure everything was back in place, bar the photo she'd tucked into her purse. That was for Callum. She took a last look around her old bedroom and headed downstairs.

14

CALLUM

Callum's phone buzzed across the coffee table, jerking him awake from the twelve minutes' sleep he'd managed to get on this attempt.

'Nnnggg?' He growled, reaching for the phone. He hit the green button and threw a throaty hello down the line.

'It's me. Did I get you up? It's past eight!'

'What? Who?'

Lewis's voice became louder. Callum pulled his aching, pretzel-shaped body off the couch, standing to pop his bones back in place. 'I said, it's past eight. You never sleep in. Alice okay?'

Callum went to listen at the bottom of the stairs. Nothing.

'She's still sleeping. Listen, can I call you back? I need to get going.'

'I know, the second date? Dad told me.'

Callum rolled his eyes. Last time around, the dating had been more of a solitary thing. A wooing, carefully constructed to win the girl he'd always wanted to be his. This time, it was more like a *Carry On* caper, with a little team of meddlers at his disposal. Whether he wanted it or not. They were family though, had always been.

This time though there was even more on the line. Callum

could feel the pressure from those around him, everyone desperately hoping it would work. The fracture would be great if it failed. He wasn't just thinking about his heart, either.

'Listen, Lew,' he started, 'I don't want everyone to be focused too much on this. It might not work.' He didn't believe the words, but he did fear the meaning. *It had to be work. Do or die.* 'She's still pretty tired. Coping with a lot.'

'I know, Mum said she fell asleep at hers.'

Callum tried to hold in the sigh he felt. 'Yeah, she didn't wake up. I put her straight to bed.' He eyed the couch, one of the reasons why he'd had about an hour's sleep overall. The woman asleep upstairs in their bed was the other. 'I'm not sure she'll be up to today.'

'Well, listen. That's why I'm calling. The dating. One of them was at my wedding, right?' Callum gnawed at his lip.

'Yep. I've been wondering how to get round that one.' Of course, he had an idea, but he couldn't spring *that* on her. He was trying to keep her forever, not make her run for the hills. He wanted her to be there with him because of the present, the future. Not the past. Even if she never got that back, he wanted to spend the rest of his life making it right. Showering her with so much love and happiness that it would make up for what she'd lost, and then some. 'None of our friends are getting hitched.'

'I know,' Lewis said breathily, excitement flowing through his words. 'But Mum and Dad are.'

'*What!*' He thought he heard a noise from upstairs, but his ears didn't detect anything else. 'What?' he said again, half whispering.

'I know, it was Dad's idea. We were talking about the dates, and something sparked. It's their thirty-fifth year of marriage this time. Mum's been begging him for years, so he thought he'd kill two birds with one stone. And Migs said she didn't mind them using the same venue as ours. Help recreate it.'

'Seriously?' Callum had been sweating about date nine. Date nine was the night everything cemented. The best day and night ever. Weddings, especially those in country hotels, were not easy to recreate. 'They'd do this?'

'Yep.' Lewis sounded excited. 'I mean, the olds remarrying is a bit naff, but it's a whole new memory you know, in the same place. I think it could work. So does Migs. Migs needs to see Alice too, you know. I think we should tell her. It's getting harder to keep the two of them apart.'

Callum nodded. He'd thought as much. She needed her friend. Finding them talking on the phone in the closet the other day had only confirmed it. 'I'll tell her today.'

'Good.' Lewis sounded relieved. 'So, ring Mum when you can, eh? They're already firing on all cylinders. They've got a date from the hotel, a cancellation. It's not long away.'

Callum nodded again.

'Cal?'

'I'm nodding. I'll sort it. Let you know. Tell your parents I owe them big time.'

He rang off, eyeing the couch with a disdainful look before heading for the shower. He needed to wake himself up. Wake up his sleeping princess and try to make her day special.

The hot spray from the power shower they'd fitted licked at his bones, reawakening them and unknotting some of the damage from the couch. Turning off the water he applied some eye gel he'd found in the bathroom cabinet under his dark-brown eyes. He looked shattered.

'Nice,' he moaned to the mirror. 'You look rough, lad.'

He winked at his reflection, smoothing some deodorant stick under his arms before wrapping his lower half in a towel and heading to get dressed. He was humming to himself as he walked through the bedroom to the closet. His hand snaked up to the edge of his towel, and whipping it off, he threw it into the open laundry basket.

'Er...' He jumped at the voice and turned to face her. Full on. 'Good morning!' The 'ning' part came up high pitched, squeaky. Alice was lying in bed, her face hidden by the duvet cover bar for her very, very wide green eyes. That were currently looking straight at him. *Shit. He'd forgotten.* He put his hands over his nether regions.

'Sorry! Sorry! Habit, I swear.' He almost lunged into the closet to grab some kecks, but the look on her face stopped him. Her eyes weren't on his face any more. They were significantly lower. He let her gaze rove over him. She stopped back at his eyes, and he kept his smile hidden when he saw her cheeks fill with colour. He chuckled when she tried to whip the duvet over her head, making sure he walked slowly enough into the closet to give her a good view of his backside too. His whole back side. He counted to three in his head as he grabbed some old sweats for the date. On the count of two, she erupted.

'You have a tattoo of my name!?'

He pulled his sweatpants over his boxers, tugging the T-shirt over his head as he headed back to her. She was sitting bolt upright in bed now, the duvet bunched around her raised knees. She patted herself down. 'Do I have one of you?'

She moved her shoulder forward, pulling the baggy black V-neck T-shirt she was wearing back so she could check the skin on her shoulder. He sat down on the bed next to her, stilling her hand.

'No. Just me. I got it for our one-year anniversary. It was a surprise.'

'You're not kidding.'

'Want to see it again?' He said it playfully, but the breath stilled in his chest when she said yes. Leaning forward, closer to her without touching, he waited. She took his cue, and her hand lifted the T-shirt. He felt himself shudder when her fingertips brushed his skin. He wanted more. He pulled it off, over his head. Looked over his shoulder at the tattoo. At her. It was a simple, elegant script, 'Alice' written across his skin in black, curling letters. A bird outline flew over the name, the wings dark, the small bird caught in flight.

She ran her hand along it, tracing each letter. He felt her brush her name onto his body, and it gave him the balls to pull her closer. To cut through the old tension that surrounded them anew now. 'You always did that.'

It was true. Many a night she'd lulled herself to sleep, tracing her name. On the few nights he'd not caged her with his body, the best little spoon on the face of the earth. 'I know things are weird, but we've done this before.' He made sure she locked eyes with his before he spoke again. 'I know you liked me, growing up. You told me, and you know I know now, right?'

She looked a little panicked but nodded. 'Do you feel it now?' he asked, as she pulled her hand away. The word complete. Another nod made his heart soar. 'Good.' He reached for her hand, pulling it to his lips and kissing the back. 'It's agreed then. We both know we fancy each other like mad. Have for years.' He got up from the bed, throwing her a wink. 'We can work with that.' He was absurdly pleased that her lips formed a pout when his T-shirt went back on. 'Come on then!'

He clapped his hands together, more eager than ever to get the date on the road. He also planned to mainline coffee till she got downstairs. He needed his energy, and the lack of sleep was making him foggy. 'You get dressed, think practical. Warm, and nothing you don't mind spoiling.'

'Well, that's easily done. I don't remember most of my clothes.'

'You have some decorating clothes. Bottom shelf. I'll get breakfast on the go. House tour first, then we have a little project to do.'

He went automatically to kiss her, not stopping himself when he realised. Just diverting the destination. He laid a quick peck on the scar on her forehead. The one he'd kissed whenever he could in the hospital. He felt her lean a little closer, or maybe it was just a trick of his euphoria.

'Project?' she called after him. 'What was date two?'

He turned in the doorway. 'Date two was right here, at your house.' He flashed her a devilish grin. The one that always turned her to mush. 'We got down and dirty.' The flash in her eyes told him he'd hit the mark. 'We worked on the kitchen, back then.' The kitchen was finished now. They both loved it. Even more because they'd made it together. 'So today, I thought we'd work on the garden plans. It's where we're at. You'll see.'

'The garden?' She pulled the covers off, her excited face lighting up. 'You're on.' She looked down, as though she was spotting her legs were bare for the first time. She squeaked and pulled the covers back over herself. 'Callum.'

He leaned against the door jamb. 'Yes?'

'Did you bring me home last night?' Her brows knitted together, and Callum waited till she pieced last night together in her head. 'I fell asleep at my parents', didn't I?'

'I brought you home,' he confirmed, knowing where this was going full well. 'You didn't wake up. Your mum said you'd had a long day. I put you to bed.'

She pincered the long T-shirt she was wearing between index and thumb. 'And undressed me. This is...?'

'My T-shirt.' He found himself shrugging. 'You normally sleep in them, and I wanted you to be comfy.' The slight look of shock horror on her face faded into something warmer. 'I swear,' he lifted his hands into a Scout gesture, 'I closed my eyes the whole time.'

'The whole time?' When he opened them again, she was standing in front of him. 'Even the bra?'

He took a step closer. 'Even the bra.' She pulled a face. 'Okay, I might have peeked. Just a bit. I've seen you naked a million times, sparrow.' He ran one finger down the material of his T-shirt. 'I've taken my T-shirts off that body a hundred times. I know every inch of you.' He moved his fingers down to her hand then brought it up to rest against his chest. 'Just like you know me. You think I'm pretty hot, you know.' He meant it as a joke, to break the tension, but she tightened her fingers on his pec.

'I never said I didn't, Callum.'

She pushed her hand slowly up his chest, and when his arm came around her, she sank into him.

'Can I kiss you?' he half begged. It felt right, to ask her this time. The last time, it had been the date that called for it. This time it was all him. His need. 'Ali?'

'Yes.' She was already pushing up on her toes, claiming his mouth. He let her take the lead, and she sank into his body, his arms coming around her tighter, pulling her up into his embrace. Her lips were seeking, urgent. A quest to delve into his depths, and he welcomed it. It was a while before either of them came up for air. By that time, both of their T-shirts were crumpled. Their lips swollen from tasting each other, her bed-head hair made all the sexier by his busy hands.

'Well, that made up for the night on the death trap.' He swooped down to get another kiss before tearing himself away with a groan. 'Come on.' He slapped her on the bottom. 'Get dressed, or that garden won't be getting touched today. Ten minutes, and I'm coming back up to get you.'

He was at the top of the stairs before she stopped him.

'What did I get you?'

He turned to look at her, consciously keeping his feet on the carpet and not gravitating back her way.

'For our one-year anniversary. The tattoo was a surprise, right? For me?'

He felt himself break out into a smile. Raising his left hand, he pointed to the ring on his wedding finger. 'You bought me this. You had it made; one of your clients is a jeweller.'

'Sara?'

'That's her. You just did another one of her properties a few months ago.' He twirled the circle of white gold around on his finger.

'A sparrow,' she added. 'I thought it was from a woman, back in the hospital.'

Callum felt her protectiveness wash over him. He knew she'd taken notice of the ring. As if he would wear a trinket from anybody else.

'It was.' He turned away. 'It was from *my* woman.'

He headed downstairs to make breakfast. The April weather gods were throwing him a bone today with sunshine and dry skies. He wanted to make it all count. Grabbing the frying pan, he fired off a text to Lewis, telling him Operation Date nine was a go. Even if he had to pay for the wedding himself, it would be cheap at half the price if he got her back.

15

ALICE

By 2023, Alice had thought that things in her life would be at a certain level. She'd envisioned the house would be completed and would be a showcase for her business. A place she could work and live in, hang out with the gang in. She'd never thought much about a man in her life, but she sure was now. The fact that it was *the* man she'd secretly fancied and openly tormented for years was getting less alien to her day by day.

In fact, at this particular moment, she could really see the advantages of having a boyfriend. Especially given that she was sitting on the patio, drinking tea from a mug while he took a pickaxe to the earth, ferreting out old rockery stones and wheelbarrowing them to the skip at the front. Whenever he swung it back, she could see her name flex across his bare shoulder blade. It was very entertaining. Like a dinner and a show, she thought as she tucked into one of the doorstep Ploughman's Callum had made them for lunch.

After breakfast, he'd taken her round the house. The tour had made her feel so much better. Settled. The living room was complete, though she had to admit, the sofa was a duff pick.

Upstairs, the stairway was clean, fresh. The master bedroom she knew well enough, the panelling made by Callum's hand featuring in the other two bedrooms as well. Both offices, his and hers.

'Definitely no spare room then,' she'd observed, looking at his dark wood desk, push pins scattered on a map of their area. A year calendar on the wall, annotated and marked up with different jobs.

'Nope, I talked you into letting me have a man cave instead. We were going to extend, next year. I think you'd even started the planning. Drawings at least. Nothing concrete.'

Then he'd led her into the garden, showing her where they'd decided putting the extension to the back.

'It would come out in line with the patio, wrapping around it without blocking the sun.' He'd come to life talking about what had been their dreams, with her. She absorbed everything and could even see it as she looked at the bones of the house from the back garden. The land at the back was a good size, plenty of garden left. It was exactly how she'd plan it now, if she was do it again.

'So we'd have had what, a spare room upstairs, and then what on the ground floor?'

'We hadn't figured that out yet. You said you had an idea, but we didn't...' He trailed off, like he always did when the memory loss stood between them like a shadow. 'We just didn't get to it.' He'd shaken himself before her eyes, turning to the rockery at the back. She'd hated it since the first viewing of the house. It wasn't even a nice-looking rockery; half the succulents were dead, and there were house bricks in lieu of some of the rockery stones. It gave it the hue of a rubble heap. 'Speaking of which, since we can't remake our date in the kitchen, this is where the romance lies today.'

The work on removing the rockery was clearly underway, and Alice frowned at the analogy.

'Our romance lies in that pile of crap, eh?'

His broad shoulder pulled her to his side. 'You have a point, but we both hate this thing.' He pulled away and her side mourned his touch. Or maybe just his warmth. It was a nice day, but the break in contact plunged the temperature down a notch. 'Sometimes you have to dig deep to get what you're looking for.'

And that had been them, for a good hour. She'd picked the stones up, chucking them into the barrow. Nothing too much. It was nice, working with him. Easy. Till Alice's back had started to hurt and he noticed immediately. He'd ordered her to sit down. Fed her lunch and hot tea, and then the show had begun.

He'd gone back to the rockery with gusto, taking his sweaty T-shirt off and tucking the end into his jeans. *Je-sus.* She hadn't been able to take her eyes off him. Not for one minute. She'd tucked into the food, half wishing it was popcorn. He was watching her too, she knew. He'd give her an occasional glance over his shoulder, his dark hair wet with sweat. The sun shining on his glistening skin. See her looking back right at him. She'd kept her gaze every time, finding that she just couldn't look away. And didn't want to. She did fancy him. He knew, she knew. The kisses they'd shared had confirmed it to her. She was beyond curious now, about what came after. It scared her.

'So, what did we do on our original second date?' She told herself it was distraction, but it wasn't the entire truth.

He stabbed his shovel into the ground, coming to sit next to her in a patio chair. Again, he pulled it so the arms touched hers before sitting down.

'Sorry, bit sweaty,' he huffed.

'No, I like it.' Her eyes bulged. 'Sorry. Thought out loud.'

She rubbed at her head, as if that would stop her malfunction-ing. She always got tongue-tied around him. She'd forgotten the skill, it seemed, of keeping her cards hidden. She remembered being slicker, and at least 10 per cent less goofy.

He smirked. 'Noted.' He leaned in close, rubbing his thumb

along her jaw. 'Bit of muck,' he muttered. She rubbed at the same spot. 'We were taking the wallpaper off; you were telling me about the plans for the house.' He smiled again, wider this time. 'You told me off for ambushing you on the doorstep, kissing you.'

'I did?'

He huffed out a breath. 'Oh yes, but you kissed me again a lot more that day.' He moved closer. 'And when I'm cleaned up today, that's my plan. I'm going to kiss you a whole lot more.'

Alice felt her breath hitch. 'Okay.'

'Okay?' His brows lifted with the corners of his mouth.

'Yeah.' His hand was on his lap, and she reached out to touch the ring. 'I need to ask a couple of questions, but I don't want to discuss it.'

He lifted his hand closer, letting her fingers run over the ring the whole way around.

'How will I answer you then?' She completed her circle of caress, and he linked his fingers with hers, bringing them to her lap. 'Sorry. Go on.'

'No, you have a point. I mean I want you to answer them, but then you can't be hurt or read anything into it. I'm just figuring things out.'

His brows were shielding his eyes, his head dipped to his chest. She squeezed his hand to get him to look at her.

He was together when he finally lifted his head. Neutral was the only way she could have described his expression. 'Okay, ask me.' He kissed the back of her hand, which would have given her comfort if he hadn't followed it with a sigh.

'Remember, they are just questions.'

'Ask me. It's fine. I won't break, Ali.'

'Okay.' She nodded. 'First of all, I wondered when, on this dating... er... timeline, do we... you know...' *Don't look at him, keep talking.* 'Have sex? And! Second question was...' Her face flushed. She could feel the heat radiating from her panicked, tomato-coloured face. 'Well, that one is more delicate, but it's the one I worry about the most... what if this deal doesn't work this time? It's just that everyone knows, and people are on board, but if we... end up...you know... well.' She finally had the balls to face him again. He looked... surprisingly... okay. 'Well, it would just hurt a lot of people. And you.'

He looked back at her, and she knew that she was part of this too. More than she'd wanted to admit. Which meant that everything in her 2020 independent single-minded brain was telling her to cut and run. Sell the house from overseas, start over with a new identity. She could design beach huts somewhere, hotels maybe. Leave the pressure behind. She could make her clothes from beach debris, cut bowls out of coconut shells...

She opened her mouth to tell him as much. Her dreams of running away, starting again. Dashing back to the hospital and begging Dr Berkovich to put her under again. Let her sleep and not deal with any of it. Maybe if she went under again, the damaged part of her brain, the memory box the doctors had called it, would reset. Maybe it would buck up and get her out of this nightmare. She wanted to tell him all of this. Everything. She knew this man, and the boy inside him. He wasn't a stranger. Hell, if she'd had woken up to a stranger declaring his love for her, that would almost have been easy. People might not have so much pinning on her, and her head injury.

But his eyes stopped her from spilling her guts. She stared into them. So brown, so deep. He was holding her hand tight, and the movement of his thumb along her skin felt like lightning rolling over her. *I like him... more than a bit. I don't hate this life with him.* 'And me, at this point.' His jaw clenched. 'It would hurt me too. I do feel something, Callum. I'm just... if I never get that time back, will it be the same? Would it even work now? What if I don't... love you quick enough?'

'Babe.' Callum pushed his hair back from his forehead, smearing a streak of dirt into his damp hair. 'That's a lot of questions, but I don't want you to worry about this stuff. Why didn't you tell me?'

'How can I tell you all that?' Her mouth slammed shut. 'Well, I have now, but I felt sick about it. I'm used to teasing you, ripping the piss. Now, I have to worry about breaking your bloody heart, and my family and friends are all watching.' She had a horrible vision of herself as an arachnid. 'That's it, I'm like a black widow spider. Or one of those praying mantis things. Those females who have sex with the male, and then rip his head off and eat it.'

'I don't think that. I hate that you're panicking about all this. I'm going nowhere, Ali. I don't care if it takes twenty years. I just want you to be happy. Feel safe again in your own life.'

'Yeah,' she scoffed, a little snort coming out with the awkward laugh. 'Sure. Till I rip your head off your shoulders and use it to feed my young.'

'Well.' He smirked back, looking far more amused than he should, given what she was saying. 'They'd be my young too, right? A dad's got to provide for his kids. I'm cool with that. What's with the insect analogies, anyway?'

Cringing, she fessed up. 'I watched a lot of the Discovery Channel at the hospital one night, couldn't sleep. I'm a bit obsessed. Distraction, I think.'

In the insect life, drunken ants didn't get behind the wheel of a stolen car and mow down a load of other ants, did they? Nature is brutal, but honest. It had engaged her brain, better than any of the interior design shows she normally binged. They made her feel odd now, like she should be working. Panicking that she wasn't. The bugs didn't have any of those worries. It had soothed her. She'd been that hooked, she'd watched the rerun in the bedroom the other day. She'd always said she'd never have a TV in the master. That it was a gateway to being lazy, but she didn't hate the flatscreen. 'I'm guessing the smart TV was your addition to the bedroom?'

'You can thank me later.' He winked. He started to pack the lunch away.

'We finished?' Alice asked, knowing that there was a lot more to do. It was barely two o'clock. 'Yeah.' He nodded, not even looking at the garden. 'The rockery can wait. Come on, I think we've done enough for today.'

She looked at the small pile of rubble she'd moved, compared to his, which seemed to consist of house bricks and boulders.

'Well, you have. Sorry, it's not much of a date, is it?'

The lunch was bagged up, hanging from his arm as he held his hand out to her. She let him pull her up, aware that she was now even closer to his sweaty torso. He walked her back towards the back door.

'Ali, I'm with you. Back at our house. I don't think I could be any happier.'

He led her into the kitchen, putting the lunch stuff on the side and watching her take in the photos and invites on the fridge. The large, stainless steel, American-style fridge was crammed with magnets, appointment letters, postcards from family sent back from their holidays. A photo of Callum with his parents, all sitting smiling in their living room.

'Oh wow, your parents have been here. Do they know about the crash?'

She jumped when he answered. He was standing right behind her. She could smell his deodorant, the scent of grass and dirt mixed in with the scent of him. Spicy.

'Yeah, they send their love, but the cruise they're on was booked way in advance.' He kissed the back of her head. 'They've only been twice, here. You know my folks. I'm going to get a shower, get changed. I thought we might go out somewhere tonight. If you're up for it? Some food?'

'Is that one of the dates? Number three, right?' she asked, not thinking. She caught the look on his face as she turned to him. Disappointment.

'Er... no.' He smiled, but it fell flat. 'It was just an idea; I can cook something. We could order in. Menus are in the drawer under the coffee maker.'

'Callum, I didn't mean it like that.'

'I know.' His lips were drawn tight. 'It's okay. Not everything is a date, Ali. We live together. Eating together isn't the worst thing, right?'

He was seriously asking.

'No,' she replied, feeling silly. 'Of course not, sorry. I'm just trying to figure this out.'

He looked sad but pulled her closer. She went into his arms, not bothered by his appearance. She wrapped her arms around him, as he encircled her. *Geez, he feels good.* She was starting to be a bit of a cuddle junkie around him. The way they seemed to fit together, so natural.

'I know, sparrow. Me too. We do this together, okay? Have a look at the menus, see what you want to eat while I clean up. And if you're worrying about our next date, relax. I'll give you a clue, okay?'

'You will?'

'Yep.' He was smiling now, because she was smiling. 'That's better.' He brushed his thumb along the length of her cheek. 'I love making you smile. It's my favourite thing. Date three is at the week-end, okay? Saturday night, we're going out. No big crowds, I promise. Nothing too scary, or tiring. Just you and me. A nice smooth night. Sound good?'

'Just us? I'm not up to seeing lots of people yet.' She couldn't cope with the sensory assault around people she knew. The shock of seeing them so different to how she remembered them. Even her neighbours in the house next door had changed. She'd been expecting to see the Patels' family car out front, but they'd moved the year before. She felt sad that she didn't say goodbye to them. She probably had, but it was one of the million things her brain just hadn't stored. It was a lot to take in, and she had enough to process already. She knew what the third date meant. Usually in dating, not that she'd had much experience before Callum. 'And it's the third date.' He threw her a blank stare. 'The third, so...'

'We don't have to do everything to the timeline, sparrow.' He dropped a kiss onto each cheek, and one slow, teasing one on the lips. 'See, we didn't do that on cue. Nothing has to happen till you want it to. Third date, smird date.' He pulled away, heading to the hallway. 'Besides,' he called behind him. 'Who says you even held out till the third date?' He threw her a trout pout look. 'I'm a hot piece of ass, in case you haven't noticed. Who said it was me trying to get your pants off?'

Alice gasped.

He laughed all the way to the shower, Ali chasing after him. He slammed the bathroom door shut half a second before she got to it.

'Leave me alone, woman. I'm not a piece of meat!' he chuckled through the door. She banged her palm on it like a frustrated toddler.

'Yeah?' she called, trying not to laugh. 'Well, Mr Roberts, for that – I'll make you wait twice as long!' She turned away, but he flung open the door and grabbed her arm. He was stripped down to his boxer shorts, his skin still wet from the toil in the garden.

'Listen here, missy.' His voice was low, inviting. 'You made me work for you, believe me. We kissed it up, a lot. Early on, like this. We didn't take it further, and we had no need to. We knew what this was.' His eyes sparked with a devilish flash. 'I even stayed over most nights, in secret.' She felt a wave of desire wash over her.

'Did you?'

'Yep. I never really left. My place was covered in cobwebs within a month. It made sense, working on the house. It just... happened.'

'You make it sound like I took you in like a stray dog.'

She laughed, and his arm turned, bringing her closer with a canine channelling growl.

'Well, I always was a sucker for a belly rub. My point is, we didn't...' He rolled his eyes. 'Man, this is embarrassing. I feel embarrassed explaining our sex life to you.'

'I know.' She totally saw his point, but the thing was, she wanted to know. All about it. 'But you said you'd be truthful.'

He pursed his lips. 'You are a pain in my arse.'

She felt the smirk take over her features. 'You've told me that before, haven't you?'

His eyes bulged. 'I never said that till we dated. Do you remember that?'

She thought about it. 'Yeah.' She nodded, feeling thrilled at the realisation. 'Yes, I think I do.'

His whole face changed. Melting into something softer. 'That's great, Ali.' He frowned, letting out a little laugh. 'Why do you always remember the negative stuff?'

He didn't look mad, but she could see the hurt creeping in. 'It's not negative.' She pushed her chest to his bare one. She was muddy, but he didn't seem to notice or care. 'It's like us, I guess. The teasing, you know. Is that how we were?'

'Yes.' He wrapped his arms around her. The shower had been on a good while now, and when he closed the door shut behind them, the room quickly thickened with the steam. 'But it's so much more.' She took him in, his face inches from hers.

'Do I... still seem like me?'

There wasn't a hint of hesitation. 'Yes. You're still you, baby. I've loved you since forever. I think I love you a little more now actually. If that's possible.'

She swallowed. 'I wasn't asking cos of that.' She totally was. Her stomach was fluttering with girlish butterflies. Jesus, what was this, between them? How the hell did they ever not get together? Looking at him now, she thanked her lucky stars that she'd woken up. For the first time, she didn't feel so alone. So utterly alien to those around her.

He shook his head, a knowing smile on his face. 'Yes, you were. This truth thing goes both ways.' He turned off the shower, the silence sounding in their ears like a post-concert buzz. He took her with him to do it. Felt the flex of his muscles as he twisted his arm back to shut the water off. Then she was back, dwarfed in the comfort of his arms. He captured her chin between two fingers, lifting her eyes to his. 'I love you, and I still fancy you.' He frowned at something on her face, and dipped his head to kiss each scar. Her cheek had healed really well, her forehead too, but they were clear to see. With make-up, they'd faded to a manageable level. A level high enough for her to be okay with being seen around people. The doctors had said they'd fade, but right now, she didn't care as much. It was so nice, feeling his lips brush along each one in turn. He tucked her in closer once he'd done, his head dipped to her neck. 'I love every single part of you, sparrow. I just don't want to rush this, make you feel pressure to feel everything at the right time. That's not what the deal's for. We were close, like this.' He lifted his head, rubbing his jaw along her neckline. 'We're on track, if that's what you mean. There's no rush.'

Well, he'd obviously worked out the neck thing she had. And perfected it. Wowsers.

She didn't miss his smirk when he took in her flushed face. 'Growing on you, aren't I?'

'Ha!' It burst out of her like cannon fire. He tickled her sides, making her yelp.

'Is that a yes?'

She couldn't take being tickled. She always turned into a giggling wreck. 'Yes, yes!' she shouted.

'Ooh, haven't had that in a while.'

'Oi!'

He was laughing hysterically now, tickling her and guffawing at her attempts to take him down.

'Hey!' He scooped her up, taking her off her feet as she tried some kind of leg hold on him. She struggled for about half a second and then gave up. She was oddly satisfied by the amount of muck she'd managed to wipe onto him. He looked... earthy. Like a farmer from the Harlequin romance novels she read. 'Be careful. No more knocks to the head.' He leaned in and nuzzled her neck. She half-heartedly shrugged him off, trying to swing her leg out of his arms in the process. Her move failed.

'Knocks to the head. I feel like a cat in a tree.'

He laughed his head off, making her squirm again. His eyes snapped back to hers. 'Quit it, or this tree will put you in the shower.' She stopped squirming, eyeballing him back.

'You wouldn't.'

'Try me,' he dared. 'Done it before.'

Her eyes widened, making him laugh again. 'Honesty, baby. Now.' He put her back on her feet. 'Let me get changed, and we'll have a look through those menus.'

It took her a second to shake the thought of the pair of them in the shower, but she nodded and headed to the landing. 'Okay, I'll get changed after.'

He gave her a wink, before the door closed and she heard the shower turn back on. She was about to do what he'd suggested: try to figure out what they wanted to eat. Something that didn't involve going out. She wasn't up to it, but Saturday sounded good. She had another couple of days to get used to being home. With the hot boyfriend she had in the shower. He still loved her. She knew without a doubt where they were at. Their childhood cards were on the table, and they were dating. Talking about their past, intermingled with the dates in their future. Sounded almost easy. *Huh.*

She passed her office door and paused.

What about work? She pushed the door open and sat down at her desk. It was perfect. Everything was laid out, right where she'd planned to the last detail. A hack workspace for a coma victim. She sat down at her desk, pulling open the file cabinet in the bottom drawer.

She'd just look. She didn't have to speak to anyone. They all knew the score; Callum had covered her. Maybe just a peep into some stuff. See what jogged. The only memories she'd had so far all involved Callum. Work was still a blank void, spanning two years.

The labels sparked nothing. Addresses she was familiar with but had no recollection of working on. She kept thumbing through, till she came to an address she knew well. Hers. *Damn it, ours.*

Pulling the file out, she found plans. The ones from the architect she'd hired when she'd first bought the place. The plans for what it essentially looked like now. *Without the Callum touch*, she thought with a smile. His input was all over. She was finding more signs of his style all the time. She even liked the decor of his man cave. When she'd got over the shock of one being in her home. But then again, she had a man. He needed a cave. She could live with it if it came to it.

She kept flipping through the pages, till she came to some plans she couldn't place. It was still their house, but these designs were newer. She leaned in closer, noting the date. Three months before the crash date. Six months ago, she'd apparently made some more drawings.

Callum's name wasn't on them. Just hers. *The extension.* She looked them over: the wall jutting up to the patio, the extra rooms it would provide. Just like Callum described. The rooms were labelled up.

'What?' She read the words over and over. Turning the plans over in her hand, she read the back. She'd written a note to the architect on the back. She recognised her own writing, and the words.

TOP. SECRET.

Across the hall, the shower went off, and Alice scrambled to put the plans back into the sling. She shoved it back into the filing cabinet and was at the bottom of the stairs when the bathroom opened. She went to the kitchen, grabbing the menus she found in the drawer. She didn't register taking a breath till she was sat on her horrible bony sofa staring at a burger menu.

The labels on the rooms. The one she had thought would say guest room, said, *spare room/nursery?*

The room on the ground floor had *games/chill room/kid's playroom?* written on it. She thought over the meaning. Her plans. Her writing. Her want. Then her eyes had been drawn to the note in the corner.

Her jaw had dropped as she mouthed the words.

Our next adventure! Take your pick, sexy pants.
    LU

She'd signed it off – *Sparrow*.

Below it, she'd written four kisses.

Four freaking kisses. She didn't even write four kisses to her parents. She once did it on an email to her mortgage advisor, but that was overenthusiastic typing when he'd come through on the house.

'Shit,' she huffed, banging her elbow on the torture device masquerading as a sofa. 'I was going to dare him to have a baby?'

16

CALLUM

The drive to the cinema that Saturday was about as good as the last couple of days had been. It wasn't, at all. God knows what had happened during the length of his shower. It was big. A memory maybe? He hoped it wasn't something that had freaked her out. Too much too fast. He couldn't think what else it could be. Was he not giving her enough space? He didn't know which way was up. Whatever it was, it had an obvious effect. When he'd bounded downstairs, grinning like an idiot excited to spend a night on the horrible couch with her, he sensed it.

Oh, she was nice. She returned his kisses, held his hand. Waved him off to work every morning, ate with him every night. It just felt... awkward. He knew he'd come on too strong, but the questions she'd levelled at him, her fears and worries all came tumbling out. It had taken him by surprise, shocked and scared him. *She was worried about not falling in love with me fast enough?*

That had given him so much hope. The fact that she wanted him, wanted to spend time with him, and that was it? Sex anxiety and a timeline on their forever? He'd thought he'd silenced her fears, once and for all. He'd told her exactly how he felt, showed her. And scared the shit out of her... obviously. He'd been mentally kicking himself ever since. Every long night on the horrible couch. He'd ordered another one the night before, a desperate online shopping necessity. He'd burn the other one. It represented to him the pain of not being upstairs with her, where he should be. Where he would have been had it not been for Barry fucking Evans. How was this the way the world turned? He wanted to get off.

'You looking forward to the film?' he tried, realising that date three was underway. His chance to get over this, and he was metaphorically asleep at the wheel.

'Yeah, you seen it before?'

'Nope. It's a slasher though, just like the one we went to before.'

'Oh, first time for us both then, eh?'

'Yeah.' He swallowed hard, thinking about what other first times she'd worried about. 'Yeah. Should be good. Reviews are.'

He turned into the large car park of the twelve-screen cinema they'd gone to that same night. It was just across from the restaurant they'd gone to after. It was as close as he could get it date wise, minus the film. And it wouldn't have an idiot spoiling it this time either. He'd pointed the place out to her, half babbling to stop the impending fist clench his nerves screamed for. It gave him a minute to ground himself. Think for a minute and check his emotions. It had served him well over the years.

It needed to go well tonight. It had already started on shaky ground.

'You see La Bonita, over there?'

She looked out of the window at the restaurant. It was bright in the April night sky, lit up from within by low-hanging, copper-coloured lamps. The tables were all chunky, warm tones of wood. People sitting eating, drinking. 'We've got a table booked for after.' He pulled into a parking space away from the other cars. 'Spoiler alert. We ordered dessert, you liked mine better than yours, and ate both. So tonight, I say we get double and go to town.'

She laughed, but he didn't see it in her eyes. 'Sounds like a plan.'

She went to open her door, stalling when she saw he hadn't moved. 'You coming?'

He sighed, getting out. He met her by her door.

'I will be, when you tell me what's wrong. You've been a bit... distant. Is it your head... or something I did? Money, maybe? You can tell me.'

'No, it's not that. Nothing you did. I just wanted to get back to work, I guess. Feel things out.'

Feel things out? For the last couple of days, when he'd got home from work, she'd still been in the office. She went to bed early, her body tiring easily. He missed the progress that they'd made.

'Sorry. It's not you, honestly.'

'Truth,' he fired at her. 'Please?'

She leaned against the closed car door, and he took a step back. Giving her space.

'I saw the plans. The new plans. For the house. The extension?'

Callum frowned, his head snapping back. He wasn't expecting that.

'House plans? That's what's wrong?'

'Yes. Did you see them?'

He shook his head. 'Rough drawings you did, sure.' He sucked in a breath, but nothing sparked. 'Nothing was finished.' It had only been a few months before the crash. The drawings were as far as it had gotten.

It was strange for him to be the one to not remember something, but the extension was one thing he would happily lose anyway. He just wanted to finish the house and take it easy with Alice – if this worked between them. Extra rooms were a luxury he could easily live without. Sure, before all this, he'd dropped a few hints about a games room, somewhere to have people over, but it wasn't even on his radar now.

'You don't have to do anything with the house. You don't have to think about the extension idea, it's not important. There's plenty of space now. Our guests will probably die on that concrete slab of a sofa, but who cares? We can do it later. Or never, if you don't want to.'

She flinched.

'Okay, but did you see the plans? The ones from the architect?'

What? 'No. I didn't see them. Why?'

His worry had his feet stepping forward, claiming back the space. 'Why? Tell me, Alice.'

'There were... rooms for a... well, a baby. Did you know?'

Callum couldn't answer her, because he was still reeling. A baby. She wasn't pregnant. He knew that, though the half-second of panic before he remembered had cut him in half. They'd tested her at the hospital as protocol. She wasn't pregnant, but she'd planned for one.

'No,' he croaked, voice failing him. He licked at his lips. 'No, I didn't.'

'I didn't think so. Did we talk about it?'

A group of teenagers came running past. They'd pulled up in a car and half a dozen had climbed out like clowns.

'Get a room!' one of them shouted, the others cackling as they headed through the glass doors.

Alice put her hands on his chest, and gently pushed.

'Come on, we'll miss the film.'

'Ali, no.'

She pushed past him but took hold of his hand.

'Date three, remember? Slasher flick and a meal. No baby talk. Forget I brought it up.'

'Ali.'

He stopped just as they reached the double doors. She pulled his hand, but he didn't budge. She growled, yanking again to little effect.

'God, you infuriate me! You're like bloody Groot, with your big thick arms!' She tugged again. 'Move your tree trunks! Come on.'

'I'm not stepping in there till we sort this. I didn't know! You said you were working on them, I guess you did.' He suppressed the smile he felt. 'We both had plans, okay.'

He thought of what he was still hiding from her. She'd seen those plans and freaked.

But she told you. Tell her.

Something about the way she was acting made him hold back. Any more water, and they'd sink.

'I didn't know, but it's a good thing. We talked about everything, Al. Kids. The house, work. Marriage.'

He tried to ignore the slab of hurt that her flinch at that word caused. She was a skittish kitty all over again, and now she was picturing having a bunch of kids hanging off her. Mini people who would no doubt be natural prankers, just like their parents. Hearing her tell him about what she'd discovered gave his hope wings. He just wished it hadn't happened so soon.

'We talked about babies, but you stayed on the pill. We wanted to finish the house. Live a bit first. Enjoy life. We both agreed on that.' He drew a breath. 'But that was then. Not now.'

Callum thought of the phone call, the one where they'd been so happy, and then the twist of metal had ended it. *Far too much info for tonight.*

'None of that has to happen.' He pushed out the next words, and they tasted so bitter he almost choked. 'Not even us. I wouldn't force you to stay with me. We'd have financials to sort, I told you, but this is not a deal-breaker. I didn't know about the plans, but I'm not totally shocked. I'm glad you told me.'

She loosened her grip on his hand, and he curled his fingers around hers.

'You are?' She bit her lip. 'It sure surprised me. No offence.'

'None taken. Right now, I just want to take you on a date. Loosen up and forget all the other stuff for a while. Can we do that?'

She eyed him for a moment, and when she pulled on his hand again, he came easily.

'Deal, if you let me buy the snacks.'

* * *

The second they hit the concession stand, Callum saw him. *Ashley idiot Peterson. Fate, you are one cruel mistress.* The one guy she'd had a relationship with, pre the man she was standing with, and he was here! Tonight, as if things weren't ruddy awkward enough. Ashley had been a short-lived relationship for Alice, thankfully. Given that he wasn't ambitious, or faithful, it wasn't much of a surprise to Callum. He hated interior design and called it arty-farty. Of course, he was perfectly nice at first. She'd fallen for it, but they had never been that serious in the first place. She wasn't the marrying kind, after all, not back then. She wanted to buy the house herself, live her life. Not clean someone else's while they pursued their dreams. Callum knew the sort. A bloke-y bloke who wanted a 'little woman' at home, while he was out chasing skirt in the pubs and clubs after work.

Callum's hand tightened on Alice's and he turned her away from her ex, shielding her body as best he could in the process in the hope of blocking her view.

'Sweet, right?'

'Huh?' She was looking around her. He belatedly realised that the place had had a refit the year before, and bit back a curse. Her ears finally caught up. 'Er, yeah!' She gave him a weird double thumbs up. 'Rad!'

'I meant the popcorn. Sweet.' Her faux happy face dropped. 'I forgot they renovated, sorry.'

'Oh. Sweet's fine. Please.'

She took another look around, and that's when Ashley spotted her. Callum could see the moment his beady little eyes lit up in recognition, and felt his fists clench tight at his sides.

17

ALICE

Callum's side was pressed to hers and she felt his body lock tight half a second before she heard her name being called.

'Alice? Is that you?'

She looked over her shoulder, wishing she hadn't the second she'd done it.

'Oh, hi, Ashley. Left the swamp tonight, did you?' She smiled icily, before turning back to the server. Of all the people to bump into, her ex had to be the worst. When they'd broken up, she'd wished that he'd be hit by a random stray meteorite, or shipped off to some foreign land in a box. Obviously, her wishes hadn't come true. 'God, this is awkward,' she muttered to herself. Why did she have to remember that pillock and their car crash of a relationship, and not remember dating Callum? 'Why me, universe?' She looked up at the ceiling, waiting for some kind of ethereal answer, but as usual, she got zip.

'Are you okay?' Callum asked, but the cashier piped up with the total, and the moment to tell him was gone. He batted away her attempts to pay. 'My date, my treat.'

She saw his eyeline shift to somewhere over her shoulder, his sexy little smile disappear, and a hand tap her on the shoulder. *Oh come on, Universe? Really?*

'So, how've you been?' Ashley's voice set her teeth on edge. Had he always sounded so nasal? The cashier was still dealing with Callum, but she could tell from his hunched shoulders he wasn't happy about their date intruder.

She stepped away to stand a couple of steps from the counter. Hoping to get this over with as quickly as possible. Of all people to see. He'd been on the pub dartboard in his time too. For being a cheating, no good, lying pig.

'Yeah, fine thanks,' she said breezily. 'You?'

He looked a *lot* less attractive than the last time she'd seen him. Thank heavens for small mercies.

'No, I mean with the accident and everything.' He kept looking over his shoulder at Callum. 'I heard you lost your memory. Forgot everything.'

Jerk. He wasn't even right. 'But I remembered you, didn't I?' She narrowed her eyes. 'Have to go, film's starting.'

'Sure.' He gave her a smile that made her think of slugs. 'Listen.' He lowered his voice when he saw Callum coming. 'If you ever fancy a drink, you have my number. Be nice to see you again.' He flashed her what he obviously thought was a sexy grin. He looked like a berk. 'We used to be quite close.'

'Ashley!' Callum boomed, even though his voice was quiet. It was the force behind it. Nothing nasal about it. She felt his warmth close at her back. 'I thought I saw you. Shame I was right. No girlfriend to cheat on tonight? Ali, our seats are waiting.' He hooked his non popcorn holding arm over her shoulder, and left Ashley standing open mouthed.

'Sorry,' he muttered as they took their seats. The screen was already playing the upcoming releases. 'I shouldn't have done that, but I hate that guy.'

'No.' She shook her head. 'You were right. He tried to pick me up.'

'What?' Callum shouted, and the trailer-watching audience shushed him in stereo. He shrank down a bit further in his seat, leaning in close. 'What? Just now?'

'Yep. Knew about my memory.' She leaned her arm over his, keeping him in place in case he bolted. 'I think he genuinely thought he'd try his luck again.'

Callum's expression was murderous. It made her laugh. Loudly. Till she got shushed too. They both shrank down low, heads dipped together.

'What a dick,' they said in unison, laughing again.

It was better after that. It broke the tension, bonded them over mutual hate of the odious little worm dropping. The dark shadow that had been hanging over her was gone for a few hours.

It was still present though, like a bloody tell-tale beating heart in her desk drawer. The fact was, he'd said they could leave it there. No pressure. Which helped, for now, but each day was a day closer to date ten. Decision time.

Would they just split up? Would waiting longer be a good plan B, or just a way to flog a dead horse for longer? *My feelings for him are far from dead.* She was spinning in her own head now.

* * *

They made their way to the restaurant, her arm tucked around his. Her thoughts miles away. Walking the short distance, following the inviting smell of paella, wine, pastas.

'Table for two, Roberts, please. We have a reservation,' Callum said to the server who had a severe, tight ponytail, making her face looked pinched under the lighting.

She ran a finger across the screen on her tablet, clicking the screen.

'Wonderful, your party have already arrived. Follow me.'

She tucked two menus under her arm, speed-walking towards the back of the restaurant, where some tables were separated by discreet dividers.

'Party?' she heard Callum say. They followed her, and she spotted Lewis. And Migs.

'HI!' she shouted, so happy to see them she forgot to be mad they'd sprung this on her. 'What are you two doing here!' They were sitting down at a laid-out table for four, shielded by screens.

Lewis grinned but didn't move. 'Date three, eh? How's it going?'

The server was looking bemused at this point, putting the menus on the table and stepping back. 'I'll give you all a minute.'

'It was great, till this.' Callum's nervous energy rolled off him. 'I didn't arrange this, Al.' He turned to Lewis, his face dropping to a scowl. 'I told you I would tell her. When she was ready. What the fuck, Lew?'

Alice watched her brother's face fall. Migs was looking pretty sheepish too. A cold drip of fear ran down Alice's spine. She pulled away from Callum. He cursed under his breath. 'Alice, come on. It's not—'

'Someone had better start talking. Now.' She strode over to one of the empty chairs, sat down and poured herself a large glass of white from the bottle in front of her. Swigging it back, she levelled her gaze at her big brother. 'Spill it. What's going on?'

Callum sighed so hard behind her, she felt the wind. It was like the breeze rolling down the valley of her neck. He plonked himself in the chair next to her. 'It's nothing I did, so hold my hand and quit being weird.'

When she'd reached for his hand, Migs pushed back her chair, looking nervous. 'Just, breathe, okay.' Alice was too terrified to draw breath. 'Don't you dare go back into that coma.'

She stood up.

'Ta-da!'

Alice gasped, taking her in. 'Oh my God! You're... you're so... fat!'

Migs had been grinning like an idiot, her hands out in front of her bump, jazz hands style. She flopped down into her seat. Lewis took one look at his wife and laughed.

'Shut it,' Migs warned him. 'I'm six months pregnant, you cheeky cow!' That took Callum down, and she threw a hunk of bread at him. 'Oh knob off, Callum! You were supposed to warn her!'

'I was going to!' He pointed to the menus. 'On our date, while we had dinner. Alone.'

Lewis winced, sucking air through his teeth. 'Oops. My bad. Migs was desperate to see her.'

'You're pregnant? Really? That's a baby?' Alice reached across the table, poking her bump with one finger.

Migs picked up another piece of bread. 'Girl, one more fat jibe, and I'll bread you.'

'You're pregnant!' Alice's excitement kicked in. The server came back, but turned on her heel and fled. 'Oh my God!' She ran round the table, smushing Migs in a bear hug. 'Oh my God, I'm going to be an auntie!'

Migs laughed, throwing her arms around Alice before descending into loud floods of very wet tears.

'Oh my God, I can't believe I finally got to show you! I've been waiting so long!' She sniffed loudly, and Lewis rounded up some paper napkins. 'Sorry. Hormones.'

Alice laughed. 'It's okay, I feel like crying too! I'm so happy for you!' She pulled a grossed-out face at her brother. 'Eugh, and now

we know without a doubt you did it. I thought you'd die a virgin.'
She gave him a hug, holding him tight. 'Congratulations, bro.'

'Thanks, sis.' He squeezed her back. 'Sorry for gate-crashing,
but we just couldn't hold it in any longer.'

She went back to her seat, noticing that Callum had pulled it
closer to his. The parents-to-be were talking to themselves, the
relief in their voices evident.

'You're going to be an uncle,' she said to him in a low voice.

'I know.' The server was edging her way back to them. 'I can't
wait. Look at them.'

Alice couldn't stop looking at them. Was this the reason for her
baby fever?

'They look really happy. Did I know?'

Lewis pricked his ears up. 'No.' He filled his wine glass. 'We
didn't find out till just after.'

'Remember the Pernod and black night?' Migs prompted.

'Nope,' Alice said. 'Sorry.'

Migs slapped herself on the forehead, before jabbing her finger
towards her bump. 'Right, coma. Baby brain. Well, we hit the stuff
pretty hard one night. You were rough, I remember. Threw up all
over your front drive, you text me to tell me if you survived the
night you were going to kill me. But I didn't just throw up when I
got home. By the time the hangover properly cleared, I just figured I
was run-down.' Her eyes started to water again. 'I did try to tell you,
but you were sleeping.' Alice patted her on the hand, swallowing
the lump in her own throat down. 'This way is so much better.'

Alice nodded. What else had she missed? What else had they
said to her while she was out of it? She glanced at Callum, but he
was far away. Deep in thought.

'I think so too. Congratulations.'

The server rolled her eyes when they all started trying to hug
each other over the table.

'So, can I get anyone some food?'

Once they'd ordered, Migs headed off to the bathroom, something about the baby playing the bongos on her bladder. Lewis, seemingly sensing the mood change, muttered something about heading to the bar, and then they were alone.

'I can't believe how much I missed. I could have died never knowing. And Lewis? A dad?'

'I know, I bet he will figure out a way to expense nappies. He's already been making a spreadsheet on costs for the first five years.'

She thought of the plans. The dare of having a baby or a games room. Would Callum and her have made a spreadsheet? What if she'd have woken up and seen Migs sporting a huge bump?

'Dammit, that's why they weren't there when I woke up, isn't it?'

Callum nodded solemnly. 'Lewis didn't trust himself not to blurt it out the second he saw you, and Migs would have given the game away as soon as you saw her.'

Alice was nodding along, feeling angry and out of depth all over again.

'Do you want kids?' she blurted out. 'I mean, do you ever think about being a dad? Did we talk about it, I mean really get into it, with spreadsheets?' She was spiralling now, reaching for a glass of water to soothe her suddenly parched throat. 'Did you talk to me, while I was asleep?'

'Alice, breathe.' He went to put his hand on her leg but stopped it short. His fist clenched before he put it on his own lap. 'One question at a time, okay? We're okay.' He glared at the back of Lewis's head. 'I could kill them for hijacking you like this. I told them it would be too much.'

'I'm not a child, Roberts.' His mouth tightened at the Roberts barb. 'I can cope.'

'I know that, God only knows, I know how strong you are. Can we talk about this later?'

'No, I need to know.'

'Fine,' he spat back, grabbing his drink and draining half the contents. 'Yes, we talked about children. In the future, at some point. We talked about a lot of things. I would like to be a dad, sure. If it happens, all well and good. If it doesn't, that's fine too. We don't have to worry about any of that now.' He fixed his gaze on hers. Lewis was paying, he'd be back any minute. 'And yes, I spoke to you every day. We all did. No other bombshells, just the baby. I promise.'

Alice was worrying at her bottom lip now, so much that she could taste blood.

'Don't bite your lip, sparrow. You're safe. You're here, with me. I won't let anything happen, okay? Trust me?'

Lewis was heading back to them, a tray full of drinks in hand.

'Yes, I trust you,' she replied, and she saw his hand uncurl on his leg. 'Sorry for spinning out.'

His brown eyes were like shiny pools now. She couldn't look away.

'It's okay. I get it.'

Lewis reached their table, and the conversation stopped. A few minutes later, when Lewis was talking away about the costs of baby equipment, she reached under the table for his hand. He took it and held it closer to his body, and she finally felt her heartbeat slow.

18

ALICE

The night had gone well after that. Exhausting, but good. Normal even. Like old times, except for the fact that Callum had held her hand all night and driven her home. He'd dropped her at her bedroom door like a gentleman when they'd got home, kissing her senseless and leaving her limp and panting against the wood. It was becoming a habit.

'Goodnight,' he'd muttered against her hair. 'Love you.'

'Goodnight,' was all she could say. 'Thanks for a great date.'

He'd paused at the bottom of the stairs. 'Always, baby. Holler if you need anything.'

Then he was gone, and she was alone again. That night, her bed felt larger than usual. It took her a good while to drift off. When she did, she dreamed of him. She awoke feeling more confused than ever and decided to do what she never normally did when she had a problem: ignore it and hope the damn thing would go away.

So her Sunday had been a blur of naps, a bit of work. Hanging out with Callum while he worked on the house. As if sensing her mood, Callum didn't ask any probing questions. He talked about the house, the things they'd done. He told her about the business he ran, which had been busier than ever. He'd hired help and was doing so well with his crew that he was able to take more of a back seat. Spend more time on the house, working with her.

He was still the same Callum, exactly how she remembered him, but he seemed more determined now. He was always a workaholic, great at his job. Never afraid to get his hands dirty. She talked to him about her job. About how she was hoping to dip her toe back into something soon. A meaty little project to get her creative brain flowing again. With the pressure off, and no mention of the heavy stuff that still loomed between them, she felt herself relax. Open up. The plans could wait, she decided. That was a conversation for another time, she told herself. She just wanted to enjoy the day.

It had rained since early morning; a typical Sunday feel that she'd always liked. A guilt-free rest day. She'd gone to bed with the sunset, lulled by the rain at the window. Waking up the next morning, the sound of a truck's reverse beep pulled her from her slumber. The sun half blinded her when she drew the curtains. April weather, so contrary.

She'd not been able to stop thinking about the baby plans she'd found. When she'd first seen Migs, her burgeoning baby belly clear to see, it had made sense. Her brother was having a baby, with her best friend no less.

It tallied up in her mind, but it wasn't some baby envy she'd been feeling when she'd commissioned those plans. She knew it. She didn't know she was about to become an auntie when she'd made those drawings come into existence.

The closer she got to Callum, and she was getting close, there was no doubt in her mind about that, the more it worried her. A part of her she didn't remember had made those plans. To have a child. Plan for one at least. She'd been on the pill at the time, she knew that from the pill packets she'd found in the bathroom. The last pill removed from the packet was from the day of the crash. The Sunday pill was still sitting there in the plastic packaging. She had been in the hospital by then.

She wasn't pregnant at the time, nothing was lost. There was no baby, yet she felt so anxious about the development, her feelings were a maelstrom of disappointment mixed with panic. She needed to process it before she could even think about discussing it with Callum again.

Throwing on her robe, she looked out to see Callum heading down the drive, a tray of mugs in his hand. She got dressed quickly, heading downstairs just as the front door opened.

'Hey, sleepy head!' Callum met her at the bottom of the stairs, kissing her on the cheek.

'Hey. What's going on?'

'New couch. I've put the old one in the garage till we figure out what to do with it. Or which tip to drag it to.'

She raised a brow at him.

'Sorry, but I just couldn't hack another night. I think a torture rack would have been cosier.' The front doorbell went. 'Better dash, they're waiting to bring it in. I promise, it won't ruin the room. I got a nice charcoal grey colour, but the scatter cushions will make it match up okay, eh? With the colour accents and that?'

'Colour accents? Scatter cushions?' Alice's sarky tone was unmistakeable even to her ears. 'Been learning, eh?' Their old teasing ways kicked back in. She poked him in the chest, leaving a fingertip-sized dent on his sweater. 'You'll be talking about colour schemes next.'

He grabbed her hand, pretending to bite her finger.

'Yeah, well. What can I say?' He lifted her hand to his mouth to kiss each finger in turn. 'You rubbed off on me, sparrow. Made me all girly and shit.' He kissed her palm. 'Won't be long. Why don't you call Migs?'

'Yeah.' Alice yawned, noticing the clock. 'I will. It's half eleven? Why didn't you tell me?'

Callum had his hand on the front door handle. 'I thought you needed the sleep.' Something shifty in his look woke her up. 'Won't be long.' He looked her up and down in her slouchy satin PJs. 'You look so cute this morning. Call Migs, okay?'

He was halfway out of the door before she twigged. 'Is this about date four?'

'Might be,' he sang back, smirking as he headed back out to the delivery men. 'Call her and find out!'

* * *

'Our ride's here,' Callum pulled the living room curtains shut. He was bouncing around the room like an excited Labrador. 'Ready?'

Alice leaned in the living room doorway, tying the strap on her dark suede kitten heels.

'As I'll ever be. Why is this date such a surprise anyway?'

Alice had spent the best part of two hours in the closet, Face-Timing Migs who was sitting on her couch at home, watching daytime TV and eating pickles from a jar. They'd ended up having a whole fashion show, Migs telling her when and where some of the clothes featured in the two years of blank space in her head. Eventually, Migs had talked her into wearing the cutest little black dress Alice had ever seen. It was knee length, not too tight or flowy around her body. The material was sleek. feeling like silk against her skin. Migs had been insistent on her trying it on the second she'd unzipped the bag.

'That's the one,' she'd enthused, stabbing a pickle on her fork and waving it at the screen like an edible pointing stick. 'Stop looking immediately. It's perfect.'

'For what?' she'd asked, hoping Migs's baby brain would trip her up.

'Nice try,' Migs chided. 'Callum would kill me. I'm not his favourite person at the minute. Just have fun, okay? Don't get all in your head.'

'Oh, hardy har. A head joke.'

'You know what I mean! Just go and have some fun with Callum, okay?'

'Okay, okay! Bye!'

'Wear the dress!' Migs had shouted as the call ended. 'Listen to your best friend!'

When Callum turned from the window to look at her, Alice knew that listening to Migs had paid off.

'Wow.' He came over to her, slinging his jacket on over a winter green shirt that made his eyes stand out like a bushbaby's. His legs were encased in black slacks, dress shoes, smart and shiny. He looked gorgeous. 'You look beautiful. I love that dress.'

'Do you?' She looked down at herself self-consciously. 'I wasn't sure. Migs picked it out.' His eyes were still roving all over her.

'Well.' he pulled her close, and she inhaled the spicy scent she loved. It had started becoming a part of her day, getting a hit of his scent. 'Thank you, Migs. You ready for this?'

'Well, if I knew where we were going...'

'Sorry,' he laughed, taking her by the hand and ushering her out of the door. 'It was a surprise the first time, so you'll just have to wait and see.'

'That's not fair!' she protested as he locked up. 'I did know the surprise, but I forgot!'

'Ah, well.' Callum walked her to a waiting car, parked just off the drive. 'Barry strikes again. Now get in.'

She got in, noticing the driver. 'Lew? What are you doing here?'

'Hey, sis.' He winked at her in the rear-view mirror. 'You look nice. All right, Callum?'

Callum settled in the back seat, taking her hand like he always did. Like he had to have a hold on her, as if she would fly away without it. She was getting used to that too, she realised. It was nice to feel so looked after. The feminist in her was oddly silent as she squeezed his fingers in hers.

'Thanks for doing this, mate.' Callum patted her brother on the shoulder. When he saw Alice's face, he shrugged. 'I told you, no taxis again. Ever.' She found herself reaching towards the just visible scar on her cheek. He met her fingers with his lips. 'You look perfect,' he murmured to her before raising his voice for Lew to hear in the front. 'You know where we're going, right?'

'Oh yeah,' Lew laughed, pulling away from the house and driving off into the night. 'I got you covered.'

'How far away is this place exactly?' Alice asked ten minutes later when they drove away from the city centre, towards the more industrial part of town. Warehousing and offices loomed into view, and Alice watched for some clue of where they were going.

'Not far,' Callum replied vaguely. Lew and Callum went back to talking about work, so she let herself tune out. Till the next turn, when she could just about pick out the faint noise of music. One of the warehouses was set apart slightly from the others and looked very different. For one thing, it was lit up with a huge neon sign, and even with the car doors and windows closed and the radio on low, she could still hear someone butchering lyrics. ABBA, by the sounds. She read the sign, and her insides turn to water.

Killing Me Softly

Karaoke Bar

'No,' she breathed, looking from the sign, to Callum, and back again. 'No way.'

'Yes way, come on.'

Callum was out of his seat and on his way round to her door. She threw Lewis a desperate look.

'Quick, Lew, drive!'

Callum opened her door. 'Nice try, sparrow. Get that cute arse out of the car, we have a match to battle, and I have a score to settle.'

'A match?' Now she was scared. She wrapped her fingers around Lew's seat. 'Not a chance. I'll stay here with Lew; you go have your little match.'

Lewis peeled her fingers off his seat, just before Callum reached down into the car and scooped her out. 'Bye, sis,' he called as Callum fireman-carried her to the front doors, wrapping his jacket around her legs as he went to cover her up. 'Have fun! Call me when you want picking up, Cal!'

Callum waved over his shoulder. 'Cheers, mate! Won't be too late.'

'Heaven help me,' Alice fumed as he put her back on her heels, ushering her into the chaos. This was so far out of her comfort zone, she couldn't even see straight. 'Roberts, you better know what you're doing here.' The last thing she felt like doing was spending a rowdy night in a club. Especially given the fact that she was already feeling self-conscious with the small scars still visible on her face. *We came here for a date? In what universe?*

He turned back to her with a sly smile on his face.

'Always, sparrow. Trust me?'

'Don't push it.'

His smile made her laugh despite herself.

'I can't believe our date was here.'

'Oh, baby,' he laughed. 'You ain't seen nothing yet.' When he held his meaty hand out to her, she placed her hand, and her trust, firmly within it.

19

CALLUM

'Ugh! That smelled like paint stripper!' Her face was scrunched up tight, the lemon drop shooter they'd just necked still fizzing on his tongue as he watched her. 'Gah!'

He handed her one of the bottles of water he was holding. 'Here, wash it... down.'

She grabbed the bottle and drank half of it before he finished his sentence. 'Ahh... that's—' She smiled, half a second before letting out a very loud burp. 'Oops.'

'Better?' Callum's shoulders were shaking with laughter he was trying to hold in.

'Much.' The bartender was laughing too, and she shot him a 'sorry' look. 'So, what are we doing here exactly? Other than drinking flavoured poison?'

The place was filling up already; the Monday crowd were a bloodthirsty lot. A couple of women were busy murdering Gloria Gaynor on the large, raised stage that ran along the back wall. Around the outskirts of the room there were cosy booths on both sides, with the last wall containing the long, neon lit bar and front doors. It was a huge, high-ceilinged space, the acoustics making even the most off-key of singers sound half decent.

'Well.' He led her over to the end of the bar, where a woman was tapping on a touch screen in front of her. 'We came here when the place first opened. I worked on the whole project, got VIP tickets to the opening.'

The woman noticed him, throwing the pair of them a warm smile. 'Callum, good to see you! We have your booth all ready. Everything's set up for you.'

'Thanks,' Callum replied, handing over his credit card for her to swipe. 'Appreciate it. This is my Alice, by the way.'

'Hi.' Alice held out her hand. 'Nice to meet you.'

'Oh, honey, we already met.' She shook her hand. 'And we are very glad to have you back with us. I'm Heather, and all our staff are ready to make your night special. We got a booth away from the speakers, all ready for the two of you. VIP, from the boss.' She led them towards the booths at the right of the stage. Furthest from the DJ.

'You didn't have to do that,' Alice protested. 'Please tell your boss thank you.'

'Nonsense.' The server grinned back. 'I'm the boss. Callum here got this place looking good and came in under budget.' She stopped in front of a booth decorated with a flower centrepiece: peonies in a glass bowl. A bottle of champagne in ice and two flutes sat next to them. 'Besides, last time you were both in here, I made serious bank at the bar.' She turned to Callum. 'Just give me the nod when you're ready.'

'Ready for what?' Alice's eyes were bulging out of her head at this point, and for a second he wondered if this date would go off as planned. He felt sick to his stomach, and it wasn't from the lemon drop. 'Callum?'

They sat in the booth, the high walls like an insulation from the music. The singers on the stage finished, and then the audience broke out into applause when Heather took the stage.

'Hey guys, so – what do we think? Who sang it better?' The crowd started to clap for each of the singers, the place going wild with cheers and whistles.

'Oh my God.' Alice suddenly realised what was going on. He could see the dawning realisation and resulting horror playing out on her. 'Callum, what *exactly* did we do on our date, the first time here?'

'Thank you, Teri! Better luck next time, Henry. And now,' Heather said into the microphone. 'Here at Killing Me Softly, we have the honour of having one of our wildest,' she looked straight at Alice, who cringed and shrank further towards Callum in her seat, 'our wildest, funniest battlers, replaying an old classic. Alice is defending champion, and tonight,' Heather was working the crowd up to a frenzy, pointing her finger out into the crowd, 'the winner will be crowned, by you lot!' The spotlight fell on them, and Callum tucked his arm behind her, effectively pushing her out of the booth in front of him. 'Let's hear it for Alice and Callum!'

Callum went to move to the stage, and bounded right into Alice, who was rooted to the spot in front of him. 'Come on, sparrow, you have a title to defend.'

The opening bars of Elton John and Kiki Dee filled the speakers. Callum could see the moment the song sparked something in her. He saw it, the moment her brain offered her a crumb. He held his breath as the crowd chanted their names.

'I won,' she said, so quietly he barely heard it over the crowd. 'Opening night. I remember.' Her face was full of awe, and he watched her beautiful face take in the crowded venue again. 'We sat there, didn't we?' She pointed to a booth across the way, before turning and giving him such a dazzling, happy smile, he forgot how to breathe for a moment. 'I remember, Callum! It's working!'

'You remember?' He lifted her up into his arms, and the crowd erupted around them. Callum might as well have been standing on the precipice of nowhere; he didn't hear the crowd, or Heather's laugh down the microphone. *It was working. She was coming back to him, piece by piece.* 'Your brain works!'

'My brain works!' She laughed in his arms, looking down at him as he held her aloft.

'Come on, guys! Battle time!' Heather's voice boomed from the stage. 'Restart the song!' She nodded to the DJ in the booth, and the opening bars of the song rang out.

'You ready?' Callum asked, slowly lowering her to the ground in front of him. The second she was on her feet, she was off towards the stage steps. She took one of the microphones from Heather and threw the crowd a mischievous look.

'Callum Roberts,' she said into the mic as he reached her side. 'Are you ready?' She flexed her arm muscle man style. 'Because, baby, this sparrow is about to sing her heart out.'

Callum took the other microphone as the song started, leaning down to grab a quick kiss. He wouldn't have been able to sing without touching his lips to hers at least once. He took a pair of huge novelty glasses out of his pocket, putting them on with a straight face as the crowd laughed.

'Oh yeah?' He turned to the crowd face on, letting them all see his gaudy Elton John-style face furniture, complete with parrots hanging off the hinged corners. 'Bring it on, woman.' He made his glasses waggle on his face as he leaned in close to her microphone. 'Parrot trumps sparrow.'

The room erupted.

* * *

She won, of course. The woman had a set of pipes on her. He'd been lost early on. 'Don't Go Breaking My Heart' hit a bit different the second time around. When she'd sang the lyrics about not breaking his heart, she'd really looked at him. Sang it right to his face. It was all over once that happened; he was tongue tied. Alice was still on a triumphant high when Lew had dropped them off home.

'Well, Mr Roberts.' She took her heels off the second the front door locked behind them, dropping them to the floor and then going back to line them up neatly. The little ritual half emptied his lungs. The little bits of her were all coming back. He swallowed, resisting the urge to ruin the easy moment by telling her. Bringing up the memory loss when they'd had such a good night. 'That was a *lot* of fun.' She raised her trophy, a goofy look on her face. 'Now, where do we display this little beauty? With the other one, perhaps?'

'Oh, sorry,' he teased, heading to the kitchen for a bottle of water. 'I'm pretty sure we binned that. Want one?'

She followed him in, barefooted and beautiful. 'Yeah, please. Need to keep the old pipes lubricated.' He rolled her eyes. God, she was even cute when she was being smug. She narrowed her eyes right back.

'Where is it really?'

'In your office. On the far shelf.'

'I knew it,' she giggled. 'Well, if you'll excuse me, I have a couple of winners to introduce.' Taking the trophy and the water he offered, she padded up the stairs, pausing at the top. 'You coming?'

Callum's heart did a little stutter in his chest, but he nodded. 'Right behind you, sparrow.'

20

ALICE

'There you go: a little friend for you!' She put the trinket next to the other on the shelf in her office, taking in the sight of them together. Clinging to every little detail her mind was throwing out at her. She remembered getting both awards, so well, so vividly she would swear both wins could have taken place tonight. Seeing the inexpensive award trophy had fired something in her synapses, and she remembered the feeling of winning, the crowd cheering and whooping. None louder than the man with her now. He'd picked her up, twirling her around, high in his strong, sturdy grip.

She ran her finger over the placard at the front, the forgotten year etched on it reminding her that the memory was a win too. She had them both now, together. She heard Callum's footsteps come up the stairs. Closer.

'Thanks for tonight. I had a really good time. Again.' She turned to look at him, and what a sight he was.

Callum filled the doorway, his shirt open at the chest, bottle of water dangling loose from one hand.

'You're welcome. It was amazing. *You* were amazing.' He took a step closer with every word. 'Even though I'm pretty sure I let you win.'

'Let me win?' She sniggered, a little tipsy from the drinks. She'd had the lemon horror, and two glasses of champagne. Oops. Post-coma Alice was a lightweight. 'Dream on, Roberts. Read them and weep.' She finger-gunned her awards. 'Pew pew.' She pretended to holster them against the sides of her dress, making herself laugh all over again.

'You unarmed now?' He stopped a few inches from her. 'Permission to engage the enemy?' He leaned in close. She got the familiar hit of spice, of him. It made her light-headed.

'Permission granted, loser.'

'Really,' Callum rumbled, his voice low in his chest. It reverberated through her body, making her feel warm. 'Are you tipsy?' His brow furrowed. 'The champagne was a bad idea. Doctor B said—'

'I'm fine.'

'You sure?'

'Stop fussing,' she tutted. 'The doctor said I didn't have to live like a nun.'

'Oh. He did? I always did like Doctor Berkovich.' He dipped his head, taking her in a kiss so intense that she felt her feet lift up from the floor.

He moved down her neck, dropping lazy little touches of his lips, like stitches through fabric. 'You were great tonight. Migs said you'd go mad, but I knew you'd love it.' He traced his way back up to her lips, deepening his kisses as he pulled her closer in his arms.

'I did,' she hiccupped. 'Kicked your ass too, Roberts.'

His lips quirked. 'Again with the Roberts, eh? Now I know you're drunk. You only call me that when you are. Come on, bedtime.'

'Weeee!' She giggled when he lifted her into her arms. He carried her across the landing as if she were a pile of feathers. 'It's not bedtime yet. I'm not tired. Come on, tell me what the next date is!'

He put her down on the bed. 'Not a chance.' He nodded to the bottle of water. 'Drink it. I know you remember hangovers. I think your brain's been through enough drama lately.'

'Eugh,' she groaned. 'Yeah, I hate hangovers.' She swigged in big gulps, watching him take some clothes out of the closet. She felt a little wobbly, the fatigue from the day's adventures catching up with. He passed her one of his T-shirts. 'You okay to get changed?' He nibbled at his lip. 'I can stay, help if you like.'

I bet you could.

'I'm good.' She started to unzip her dress. 'I am an independent woman.' *A woman who is a bit squiffy and high from winning.*

Thankfully there was only one of Callum in her field of vision, and she used his forearm as a handrail while she whipped the dress down past her hips. Callum's eyes bulged out of his head, and he looked away.

'Okay.' He stood staring at the closet door as she took off her bra. She wanged it towards the laundry basket, but misaimed and practically threw it at his feet. He looked down at it, and she felt his forearm tense beneath her grasp. 'Puppies.' It was faint, but Alice's ears caught it.

'Did you say something?'

'Nope.' He mumbled something else when she turned around to bend over and retrieve the purple T-shirt he'd brought her to sleep in. Something she'd obviously misheard, because *she'd thought* he'd said 'Great-auntie Edna.'

Her arms half in the spicy-smelling cotton, she turned back in his direction, just as she was pulling his top over her naked bod. 'I know you said something then.' She fluffed her hair out from the neckline. He was standing there, dumbstruck.

'I did, but after that, I'd be hard-pressed to remember my own name.'

It was then she realised, albeit belatedly, that she'd just given him a free show of pretty much all her goods, without even batting an eyelid.

'Oh shit.' She smoothed down the T-shirt, aware that he hadn't taken his eyes off her. Tried to tug the hem a bit lower over her knickers. 'Would it be weird if I said I totally forgot about the not-getting-naked-in-front-of you thing?'

'Well,' he said after taking half a minute to swallow. 'I had noticed that, yeah.' He bit down on his bottom lip, and she felt something under the hem that wasn't embarrassment.

'I mean.' She was hot and bothered now in more ways than one. The fact that she'd felt so well, normal about it. It was a big thing for her. Even pre-coma her was a bit stiff that way; not a prude – but doing a striptease? Maybe not. Her ex, Ashley had pointed it out on more than one occasion. Which was presumably his reasoning for not being faithful. *Jerk*. It was a shame she couldn't pick which memories to lose during her coma. Ashley would have hit the cutting room floor faster than he dropped his pants for someone else. She focused back onto Callum. Here was a man who was still here, after the coma. Still looking at her like he wanted to lick her from head to foot. 'I mean...'

'You mean what, Ali?' he pressed her, his voice soft and sultry. 'Tell me.'

'I mean,' she continued. 'I know we've been naked before, together. In bed.'

He went still, he hadn't moved an inch since she'd managed to get the words out. A memory of them playing silly statues popped into her head. His big, brown eyes were just looking right back at her. That look on the photo flashed into her mind, back when they were kids. He looked... like he loved her. Like a penguin ready to go look for a perfect pebble. Pure and simple adoration. *How did I never see this before?* Probably because she was normally too busy ignoring him, or preoccupied with winding him up. 'I'm rambling. I meant, since I came home.' She noticed the bra on the floor. 'Tonight.' He nodded his head, just once. Barely there, and back to stone. 'Are you in there?'

He blinked three times, like rapid-fire rebooting was happening behind those long dark lashes. She'd always been a bit jealous of them. She used to threaten him with mascara all the time when he wound her up. Secretly, she'd kinda wanted to see how it would look. 'Yeah, I'm here. I'm just... letting you talk. Figure it out.'

She closed the space between them. 'I just meant things are coming back. I remembered the trophy tonight. Little bits are coming back to me. It's good, right? I mean, it's scary, but...' She felt his arms go around her, wrap around. It felt like they'd been made just right. This man, so burly and surly, once. Even as a kid, he'd always been there. 'You know, even with everything I've forgotten. All the dates, and the little things we did to torment each other. Even without all that, I still have a lifetime of memories of you. You were always there.' She pulled his gaze to hers. 'I get this, why this happened. Every memory I have is of you.'

She did get it. Right here, right now. The boy she'd lusted after and faux despised had melded into the man before her, and he was still him. He knew her, *really* knew her. When they were together, in their house bubble, it felt right. Like now. The other stuff just melted away, but it still lingered in the background. She wanted the bubble to last a bit longer. The Callum from her past was still there, but she didn't feel the flicker of irritation she used to. He was so loving, tender. Obviously into her. She felt... seen. More than she ever had before. Maybe it was the alcohol talking, but things were changing between them. She could feel it, almost touch it in the air around them. The doctors, everyone – they all said that she should try to embrace her new life. That included the man standing before her. Right now, she wanted that life. She wanted more of those memories to come back. Of him, her. Them. What was it her mother always said? The proof of the pudding? Well, looking at Callum now, his eyes fixed on hers, she decided to reach for a spoon.

'Callum?'

'Yeah,' he exhaled.

'Do you want to stay up here, tonight? With me?'

21

ALICE

'Migs, I'm telling you. He's avoiding me.' She buttered a slice of currant toast and shoved it straight into her mouth. 'And!' Both women watched as the bit of half-chewed currant that flew out her mouth hit the table between them. Alice leaned forward and flicked it off the table. 'And...' She swallowed, making her own eyes water and her words get louder. 'I feel like a... a... vixen!'

Migs rubbed her bump, leaning over to the rather shocked-looking gentleman on the next table, who was currently leaning over his laptop with a shocked expression.

'Sorry, she has a brain injury.'

'Migs!' Alice shouted.

Migs narrowed her eyes. 'For God's sake, lower your voice. You are not a,' she glared at laptop guy till he stopped staring, 'vixen,' she half whispered, 'but right now, you are acting crazy. Callum loves you. Lewis said you had a bit to drink, right?'

Alice frowned. 'Yeah, I suppose.'

'Sooooo?' Migs led her to a conclusion.

'So, he might have been being a gentleman.'

'Exactly.' She pointed at her. 'He probably feels awkward. Alice, the man loves the bones of you. He's always telling you, right? We told him not to, so much. We know it's been hard, but I think he's just trying to do the right thing here. You know him, right? You've just been telling me the dating's working.'

'It is,' Alice huffed. 'It was. Or I thought so. He was right there, in my – our bedroom. His shirt was open, I was standing there wearing his T-shirt for the love of God. He just stared at me. His jaw hit the floor, and then he shut me down. It was sooo bad. I didn't even mean sex, I...'

'You wanted him to sleep in your bed.' Migs took another sip of her green tea, sticking her tongue out when the taste hit her buds. 'God, I miss coffee.' She took another sip, this time pinching her nose between her fingers and swallowing audibly. 'Look, I get it. You felt a bit awkward, but I bet he felt bad too. He just wants it to be right, that's all.' She chuckled, waggling her eyebrows. 'Maybe your titty dance took him by surprise.'

'Not helping,' Alice scowled, before cackling right along with her when they locked eyes. 'God, I'm so glad you called me. I think Callum was too, to be honest. He had his keys in his hand before I had chance to hang up the phone.'

Migs shook her head, an apologetic look crossing her features.

'So it's really been three days, and nothing?'

'Nope. He's been attacking the rockery as if he's trying to dig his way to Middle Earth, though. Every time I enter a room, he either tries to feed me, tells me to rest or put my feet up like I'm infirm. Then he rips his shirt off and goes running off, all oiled up, tools in hand.' She bit at her lip, staring off through the coffee shop window. 'He swings that pickaxe like it's a lawn dart. All sweaty. Glistening. Moist.'

'Wow.' Migs broke her out of her rather pleasant daydream. 'You need to get laid.'

'Oh God.' Alice dropped her head. 'I'm fantasising about my

boyfriend. Help me. He's coming back in an hour. He's planned date five for today.'

She was all dressed up ready. Having no clue from the gruff exchange of words informing her of their date later that day, and given that it was now Thursday, she was winging it with a nice dress and pumps combo. She just hoped they weren't doing something outlandish. She didn't fancy some kind of mishap where she ended up flashing him again and scaring him off.

'I thought you weren't speaking?'

Alice jabbed her finger around like a conductor.

'Exactly! I said that. I said I didn't want to go.'

'You didn't!'

'I did.'

'What did he say?'

'He asked me why, and I bottled telling him I felt like a vix... you know. So I said I had to wash my hair.'

'Good one,' Migs chipped in. 'What did he say then?'

Alice huffed through her nostrils like a dragon.

'He told me to wear a hat.'

'Bastard!' Migs gasped sarcastically. 'Sorry.' She aimed that at Laptop Guy.

'Then he told me we had to go regardless because of the deal. The date was something we couldn't put off for another day.'

'Date five, I can't believe you're halfway there.'

'I still can't believe my parents are getting married again for this whole thing.'

Migs went white. 'Oh God, I knew I shouldn't have told you!' She slapped herself on the forehead. 'Stupid baby brain! I've done it twice this month. I asked Fiona at work the other day when she was due.'

When Alice didn't say anything, Migs looked at her pointedly. 'You know, pregnant Fiona? You met her last year at the work thing.'

'Nope,' Alice said gently, humouring her friend. 'Can't recall a Fiona. What were you saying? About the baby brain?'

Migs finished off her croissant, her face falling when she internally replied to the conversation. 'Oh yeah! Right, so I said to Fiona, when are you due? I was thinking we might be due the same time. You know.'

'Okay.'

'Well.' Migs looked scandalised. 'She'd only already had it, hadn't she?'

Alice gawped at her, then burst into laughter. Migs huffed. 'It's not funny. She'd only come in to get some paperwork filed, she's on ruddy maternity leave! I've even held the baby; she'd brought her to work!'

Alice was crying with laughter now, which made Migs crumple like a paper fan. Soon the pair of them were laughing so hard, Laptop Guy moved his mini office to a table further away.

'And you say *I* have a brain injury!' Alice dissolved again.

Migs pulled it together first. 'It's not funny. I'm glad I'm on maternity leave soon. HR sent an email around the next day about combatting fat-shaming in the workplace. I ate in the toilets at lunch.'

The pair of them were still laughing their heads off when a shadow appeared over their table.

'Hi.' Callum was smiling, but his face still looked pinched. Moody man. 'Sorry I'm a bit early, but there's a bit of traffic reported. We need to get on the road if we're going to be on time.'

Alice waved Migs off; she was on her way back to work anyway. Probably to hide in fear of bumping into HR. They didn't get chance to finish their chat, and Alice felt cheated. She needed her friend to tell her what to do. Give her some clue how to not let the day suck.

'You had a good time?' It was the first time either of them had spoken, all the way to his car. He clicked the sat nav on the dashboard, then typed in a postcode and pulled away from the car park.

'Yeah, I did.' Alice was feeling decidedly spiky. 'Speaking to me now, are you?'

He looked away from the road. His scowl softened. 'I always speak to you. I've been busy, working, you know.'

'Yeah, anything to avoid me.' Talking it over with Migs had stoked the fire. 'Are we going to talk about the other night?'

He raised a brow, his eyes firmly on the road. 'What about the other night?'

She waited for him to cave, but when she saw his fist clench on the gear stick, she knew he wasn't going to. 'Fine. Where are we going?'

'You know I won't tell you.'

She folded her arms with a huff, turning away from him to look out of the window. 'Fine.'

He sighed. 'Lot of fines going around.'

'Yeah,' she fired back. 'Lots of games being played, too.' She looked at the time on the sat nav. Wherever they were going, it wasn't a quick journey. They had just under two hours to be stuck in this car together. Each way. She turned away from the screen with a pout. 'Can we at least have the radio on?'

His eyes were on hers now, the traffic lights on red. 'What games?' He frowned, but this time he looked genuinely puzzled. 'You think I'm playing a game?'

He focused back on the road when the traffic started moving, but his jaw was tight. 'This isn't a game, Ali. It's my life, our life. I want this. No games.'

'So...' She tried to piece it together. Migs had told her the same, but his actions were confusing. 'So why didn't you stay with me?'

His eyes bugged out. 'That's why you're mad? Because I went and slept on the couch?'

'Well, yeah. And since then you've been avoiding me like the plague. I know I shocked you, but—'

'You didn't shock me,' he said, his voice low.

'Oh really?' she scoffed. 'You said goodnight and was out of there before I could blink.'

'I wasn't shocked, Alice. I wanted to stay with you.'

'So why didn't you?!' She watched his hands flex on the wheel, him squirm in his seat. 'I didn't mean to rip my clothes off, but we had a good night, and...'

'You'd been drinking, we both had. I just... thought it would be better not to, that's all. We made a deal, to do the ten dates, like before.'

He focused back on her before flicking his gaze back to the road. 'If you want me to stay with you, I will. I just don't want it to be like that, okay? When I get back into our bed, I want you to remember it. To know exactly why you're there, and why you want to be.'

The flames fuelling Alice's emotions sparked into flickers of something far warmer...

He reached for her hand, pulling it back with his to the gear stick.

'I don't want to fight, okay? Ever. It's not us, not like this. We don't ever fight about being together.' He swallowed, bringing her hand up to his mouth to kiss. 'We fought too damn hard to get there in the first place. We were solid, and I want you to feel that. Even if it's before me feeling you in bed again. You didn't shock me, sparrow. You fucking turned me on.'

'I... did?' She thought back to how weird he was, muttering to himself. 'Great-auntie Edna?'

He blushed, and the pink hue met his hairline. 'I say things, to distract me. You know, usual stuff. Dead puppies. My Great-auntie Edna, God rest her soul. Devout Christian. Works every time.'

'Been saying it a lot, have you?'

He threw her a quick glance, before concentrating on the motorway coming up ahead. She didn't miss the fact his eyes dropped to her lips. 'You have no idea. I want this to be right, that's all. It's working, the memories are coming back.' He looked happier now. She felt relieved too. *You fucking turned me on.* More than relieved. *Excited.* 'I just think if we rush things, if things go too fast, we'll regret it. I know I will.'

She digested what he was telling her. He was trying to win her, the right way. His surety was sometimes what scared her the most, she realised. He could remember everything, though. He had a lot more to go on. She was still half in, half out. Still thinking for the most part that she was stalwartly single. A workaholic. Not someone who wrote little notes for the man she lived with. She'd seen them, all over. In drawers, on the fridge. Some simple.

Buy milk, babes, see you later

Some not.

Can't wait to grow old with you! Will be counting the minutes till you get home.
    Love sparrow

He was trying to recreate all these dates, be patient, and she'd got a little tipsy and thrown caution to the wind. She had to let him take the lead, because she didn't know how.

'So, no sleepovers.' She kept her tone light, her face neutral but instead she was a maelstrom of emotions. Some of which she couldn't even name right now. So she squashed them down. 'Noted.'

'Just for now, yeah.'

'Cool!' she shrilled, slapping him on the arm a little harder than she meant to. 'Cool, cool. Breezy.' Breezy? 'Well, not breezy.'

'So just cool.' He arched a brow, and she could see his lips trying their best not to pull into an amused smirk. 'Okay.' He poked her in the side.

'More than okay.'

'Good. Besides, the new couch is pretty nice to sleep on. I might just wait till you carry me to the bedroom.'

The rest of the journey was a lot smoother. They sang along to the radio, Callum laughing as she heard a song that she didn't remember hearing before. Callum ended up hooking his phone up to the truck, and he clicked play on the dashboard. 'Sparrow', the playlist was titled. It was all her favourite bands and artists, everything from her blip. Pushing the anxiety of the secret she kept firmly to the side, she focused on the present. The date. He'd made her a frickin' playlist.

'When did you make this?' she asked, blown away.

'I had to plan for the trip, and channel my sexual frustration.' He shrugged, making her laugh. The bubble sagged a little. That's what he'd been doing in his office. It made her think of her office, and back to the plans hidden in her desk. Trying to avoid it had lasted all of twenty seconds.

'Sorry.' She shot him a rueful smile. 'I forget most of the time how difficult this is for you, too.'

He was already shaking his head, turning off the motorway under the sat nav's instruction. 'You don't have anything to be sorry for. I'm in this, Ali, for better or worse. Sickness and health.'

Alice frowned. 'That's marriage.'

He shot her a look she couldn't decipher. 'Yeah, well, er... we're a couple. It still stands. You didn't cause this any more than I did. We do this together, like always.'

He flicked his intense eyes back on the road, and she just about remembered to breathe again. Right now, it was pretty easy to see why she'd wanted a baby with this man. A whole big life. When he said things like that, was so sure and committed, every sensible notion and flicker of panic were doused. Not to mention the fact that she was now squirming in her seat and flushed from the power of his rather sultry gaze. She pulled herself together and dug a little further.

'Now the air is clear, I wondered.' She put her hands loose on her lap, tried to relax her shoulders to avoid detection. 'Is there anything else we need to talk about?'

She kept her eyes forward. If he so much as glanced across the car in her direction, she'd get too tongue-tied to focus. God, he was still so infuriating! He was the only man who had ever got under her skin so deeply she couldn't tell the difference between them any more. She went from wanting to punch him in the face, shake him till his bones rattled to making him pull his car over and jumping on him like a starved hyena.

'Like what?'

'Oh, I dunno. Stuff, you know? Plans, maybe?' She cast her eyes around, trying to be all nonchalant. Thinking about the baby thing was stressing her out too. Pre-coma her, the one she remembered, didn't dream about big white weddings, cute little babies. She dreamed of travelling around, seeing clients, building her dilapidated shack into the dream house she'd dreamed of since she was a girl. 'We had plans, right? I just want to know what's going on with the...' She gave up when she saw he wasn't buying it. Whenever she felt herself flapping about the dates ending, he was there. Just... calm.

'If you're fishing about the date, we'll be there in ten minutes. I promise you'll like this one.'

'No, not the date! Just...'

'Spit it out, sparrow. Nine minutes now.'

'I don't think... maybe we should talk later. At home.'

'Not a chance. It's obviously bothering you, and I want to have a good day today.'

She bit at her lip. She'd been doing that so much lately, the inside of her lip was all swollen.

'I really think...'

'Eight minutes, sparrow. Cough it up.'

'The new plans for the house, the ones I found in my office.'

The car jumped, as if his feet had tightened on the brake. He dropped down a gear and when the navigation barked out another command, he followed it, but his speed decreased. A driver honked from behind, but Callum ignored him.

'I knew seeing Migs might trigger this.' He sighed, beeping back at the driver and cursing when the old dude driving flipped him off.

'Migs didn't trigger it. I mean, it was a shock. Finding out I was going to be an auntie was weird, and Lewis as a dad is something I just have to see, given that he forgot to feed his pet hamster Woody and it died.'

'I mean about the baby plans. I didn't know. If that's any comfort, it was a bit of a shock to me too, but it wasn't like we didn't talk about it. Don't freak out, Ali, it's not like we have to do it right now. I think your body's been through enough for one year, don't you?'

Her hand reached up to touch the scar on her face. The one her eyes were always drawn to when she looked in the mirror. When she glanced across at Callum, she could tell from his clenched jaw that he'd clocked the action too.

'You're beautiful.' He reached across, pulling her hand away from her face to hold in his. Their hands changed the gear together.

'I just... worry. We can't even talk about sex properly, or even read each other right. I really thought you ran away the other night. I felt like some kind of failed seductress. I was mad.'

'I could tell. I will never run from you Ali. Never. No matter what.'

There he goes again. Being all... dreamy. It was getting harder and harder to lean into her inner cynic. 'You were mad too.'

He frowned. 'No, I was horny, and missing my f... girlfriend. My very hot girlfriend, who is not only a two-time champion at Death Match Karaoke, but an absolute knockout.' He squeezed her hand. 'Battle scars and all. We don't have to go buy a stroller. I didn't know about the plans, but I love that you did that for me. For us. I know you're freaked out, but things change. People crash cars, go into comas. Fate doesn't give a shit about people's five-year plans.'

'Yeah, but I do. What if I'd been pregnant when the crash happened?'

The way his face blanched told her he'd thought about that too.

'But you weren't.'

'Yeah, but I could have been.'

'No, you couldn't, and you wouldn't have been out drinking that night if you had been. You'd have been at home, waiting for me to finish work.' Another jaw flex. 'I don't like thinking about the crash, Ali, but you weren't pregnant, and I am not pressuring you to do anything you don't want to do. The ten dates are not about trying to fast-track things. It's about showing you what your life was like. What *our* life was like.'

He took another right, and Alice realised where they were. She'd seen signs for it on the way, but not connected the two. Every year, Manchester held a huge exhibition. All of the interior designers went there, where companies and property firms show-cased the latest innovations in home design and decoration. Smart homes, climate change friendly set-ups, and the latest trends and must haves. Basically, it was like porn for her. A huge exhibition centre full of dopamine-inducing marvels.

'The expo?' she checked. 'That's where our date was? Really!?'

He grinned, but it didn't quite reach his eyes. She hated herself for putting that troubled look there. He drove through the car park, pulling into a space and killing the engine. He didn't let go of her hand.

'Yep. We came here for our fifth date, and we've been every year since.'

'Thank you.' She beamed. 'Really, Callum. Thank you. For the dating, the effort you're going to. I'm sorry I'm such a mess all the time.'

He huffed. 'Alice, you have never been a mess. Your whole life, you knew what you wanted. I was in awe of you when we were kids. Lewis and I, Migs even, we just seemed to wing it most of the time. I knew I wanted to be a builder; it was hardly a surprise, given the family business. I grew up around construction sites; hell, the only quality time I ever spent with my dad was when I went to work with him when school was off. I could build a brick wall by the time I was a teenager, but you...' He brought her hand up to his lips, brushing his hot lips against her knuckles. 'You were always so driven. Stubborn as a mule, too.'

She tried to pull her hands away as a joke but his grip was tight and she couldn't budge.

'Hey, it's a good thing.' He waggled his eyebrows, making her laugh out loud. 'Most of the time anyway. My point is, you have always known what you want in life, and when you want it. I don't want that to change, but what you've been through, what you're going through, it would kill most people off. Most people I know would have just given up, wailed at the world. I read about one woman who upped and left her life, moved to another country.'

'You read about other coma victims? I did the same. There are some scary stories out there. I read about one woman who woke up and her partner had ghosted her, moved on with someone else while she was still in the hospital. Just moved out of their place and left her to wake up alone.'

Callum didn't say anything at first. He got out of the car and was at her door before she could blink.

'Well, that's awful, and it's not us.' He took her hand and they headed out of the car park to the main doors of the exhibition. It was pretty busy already, and Callum took her into his side, his arm protecting her. 'That guy was a dick who didn't deserve to be with her anyway.'

'At least she remembered him,' Alice countered. She felt his voice whisper against her neck.

'We're soulmates, sparrow. Your mind might have lost me, but your heart didn't. Give it time.'

She shuddered at the touch of his lips against the shell of her ear, heard his low laugh.

'Your body is not quite as forgetful as your mind, I see.'

'Tease,' she whispered back as they walked through the main doors.

'Always.' He smirked. 'Come on, baby, let's have some fun, eh?'

* * *

'Wow.' Alice sighed contentedly from her chair. They'd been walking around the different stands for hours, and they had collected bags of brochures, samples and freebies. Callum passed her the sushi they'd bought from one of the bespoke companies catering the event. 'Thanks. This looks delish.'

He raised his triple burger in her direction. 'I can't believe you passed up the burger.'

'It's sushi though, you love sushi! You did nothing but rave about it last time. You even made us buy extra to take back home.' She tucked in heartily to a salmon skin roll, ravenous.

Callum's head snapped back. 'You remember that?'

'Remember what?' she said between chews. She replayed it in her head. 'Oh wow, yeah! Callum, I remember!'

His eyes were shining, the burger forgotten. 'What else?' The busy food court disappeared from around them as they sat there, across the table from each other. She could see it, them before. They were sitting smushed up to each other, on the same side of the table. Him feeding her bits of wasabi, laughing when she tried to pretend her mouth wasn't on fire.

She thought for a moment. 'I remember coming here. Wasabi. You were talking about expanding the business, your building business.' She kept focused, allowing the memory to take her over. She willed it back into her brain. 'We took more sushi home. Ate it with wine on the back doorstep of the house.'

Callum's smile was radiant. 'Yeah. It was one of the best days of my life. We talked about your house plans, what you wanted to do. You were so excited. The whole day you were like...'

'A kid in a candy store,' she finished for him. 'You said that to me, didn't you? That day.'

He nodded. 'Good date, eh? You always did love being here. In your world.'

Callum opened his mouth to say something else but a man dressed in a very expensive designer suit came up behind him. Patted him on the shoulder.

'Callum Roberts! I'd been hoping I'd bump into you today.'

Alice smiled reflexively at the stranger, but the look on Callum's face told her something was amiss. His relaxed gait and sexy, easy smile disappeared, and she suddenly both hated and feared the man.

'Oh hi, Mr Abbott.'

'Oh Roger, please!' The man, who was definitely going for the silver fox look turned to Alice, hand outstretched. 'Roger Abbott.

Sorry to interrupt your lunch, but I wondered if I could borrow Callum for a moment? I have some clients with me that I would love to introduce him to.'

Alice shook his hand. 'Of course,' she started to say, just as Callum stood from his seat.

'Er, sorry, Roger. I can't. We have plans, and I'm not working the centre today.'

Roger ignored him, shaking Alice's hand far beyond what was comfortable.

'You look well; we were sorry to hear about your accident. Coma, eh? Must have been rough.'

Alice slowly but firmly pulled her hand from his grasp. 'Er no, not exactly a barrel of laughs. Sorry, have we met before, or...'

'Oh no! No, Callum and I were due to do some business together but...' For the first time, he looked a little uncomfortable. 'Well, things were put on hold, so to speak.' He eyed her up and down. 'You look well though, eh, Callum? Doesn't she look well? You must be thrilled. Wedding back on and everything?'

Callum had come around the table to stand at her side.

'I don't know what you're talking about,' Alice cut in. 'Sorry, Roger, but what wedding?'

Callum cut in front of her, ushering Roger away from the table.

'I won't be a minute.' He threw over his shoulder at her as Roger headed straight to a small group of suits. Alice sat for a moment, picking at her sushi, watching him talk to the men, shake hands. He looked over at her now and then, and she could see the tension in his face. Pulling out her phone, she dialled Migs.

'Hey, girl! How's the expo going? Killed each other yet?'

'Not yet. I do have questions though. Who is Roger Abbott, and why was he just talking to me about a wedding being back on?'

The voice at the other end of the line went silent. She could hear frantic tapping.

'Migs! Don't you dare be texting Lewis!'

'I wasn't!'

'Or Callum! I'm not an idiot, I still have a brain, it's just not completely back. Tell me!'

Migs sighed. 'You have a better brain than I have; this baby is leaching the intelligence out of me a bit more every day.' More tapping.

'Migs, if you tell Callum I'm asking questions, I will tell my new niece or nephew lots of very embarrassing things about her or his mother that I do remember. Things *so* embarrassing that they are etched onto my grey matter *forever.*' She checked to see where Callum was; he was being corralled by the group of businessmen over to a housing development company with a big gaudy banner, depicting a row of bright homes all with differently coloured roofs. 'Come on, Migs! You used to tell me everything, and this stuff I already knew anyway, right?' More tapping. 'Migs, I swear, if you text Callum I will buy your kid the noisiest, loudest toy for every Christmas and birthday!' She checked, but Callum wasn't reaching for his phone. 'I already knew, so just tell me!'

Migs sighed. It was so deep that Alice could have sworn she felt the wind off it through the phone.

'Fine. Roger Abbott is a huge deal, Ali. He's running a whole bunch of projects, one of which is a small eco housing estate. A pilot that will soon become his new standard. Before... everything happened, Callum had been courted by him. He has a whole heap of investors, and he wanted Callum to head the crew running it. Oversee the whole thing. When you were in the hospital, he pulled the job. Told Roger he had to focus on you.'

Alice sat back in her chair, taking in the group of men again. They were all hanging off Callum's every word, and she was hit once again by everything that this man had done. Was doing for her.

'You there? Alice?'

'I'm here. Sounds like a big deal. Callum loves all the sustainable living stuff.'

'Yeah, it was, but don't be blaming yourself for that. Callum is a big boy, and it was his decision.'

'Hmm.' Alice's mind was whirring now. The memory she had of them eating, he'd been talking about it then. His plans for expanding the business, taking on less of the smaller jobs. He wanted to step back, take more of a manager role. Running a large crew instead of being knee deep in dirt and plaster dust on the sites. He'd pulled it off. His career was where he wanted it. Only to walk away from it for a woman who didn't remember him or his dream. He was still building hers. He was still finishing the house, and that was *her* dream. She hated herself for it. In that moment, she wanted to go over and tell Roger that he was still in. He was the man for the job. 'Still here. Is that all of it? What about the wedding stuff?'

Migs emitted a little squeak. 'Ali, you really should talk to Callum about all this.'

'I will, but we've already had baby talk and a memory today, I'd rather not give the guy a stroke.' Callum was now looking her way, his brows furrowed. 'Tell me, Migs, please. I have no clue what I'm doing from one day to the next.' She took a deep breath. 'I don't want to hurt him, Migs. I care.'

I care a lot more than I thought I would. Every memory, every day she spent with him, seemed to pull them closer together. They were halfway through this, but would it be enough?

'I know you do, but don't freak out, okay?'

Callum was saying his goodbyes, his eyes firmly on hers as he shook hands and patted backs. He'd be back any minute.

'I wish people would stop saying that to me. I'm not that bad.'

'I know, but this is...'

'Migs, I have about thirty seconds before Callum gets back here.'

'Fine,' she huffed. 'Just so you know, I'm telling this kid how much of a pain in the arse their auntie is.'

'I'll take it. Teeeeelll meeee!'

'When you were on your way home that night, the night of the accident. Do you remember anything yet?'

Alice wracked her brain but all she could think of was Callum's clumsy pass. 'No, it's still jumbled from two years ago. Why?'

'You were talking to Callum on the phone. We think that's *why* it was so jumbled in your head. Callum had asked you to marry him, Alice. The housing project, he wasn't just going to do it because he loves it. He was doing it for the money too, to start off your married life.'

'What? He did it for me? What am I supposed to do with that, Migs? He's throwing away jobs, his life goals. He proposed! He wants the whole thing, marriage – forever! I never even thought about being with someone like that. The last memory I have is of being a singleton. I was browsing rescue websites for a damn cat! Now I'm a bride, making nursery plans? What if I can't do this? I'll destroy him! What if this all goes wrong? I woke up thinking I was alone. I was okay with that, but now?'

'Not just for you, Al. He was doing it for both of you. That was still you, making those plans. Wanting those things *with* him. You love each other so much; it's meant to be, Alice! God, you don't get it yet, do you? You're going to talk yourself out of something you've wanted since you were a kid, Alice McClaren! That stubborn teen you were still wanted him, even when you wanted to throttle him. Do you really not see that?'

Callum was still having his ear chewed off by Roger, but he was still looking over at her. An unreadable look across his face.

'I think I'm starting to.' She waggled her fingers at him, and his face relaxed into a smile. 'I said yes, in the cab, didn't I?'

'You remember it?'

'No,' she muttered. 'I don't need to remember to know. I... I feel it. Thanks, Migs.'

'Call me later, okay? It's Callum, remember. He's loved you since he was in short pants. Trust that. Trust him. He doesn't do a thing he doesn't believe in. That includes you.'

'Love you, Migs.'

'Love you back. Bye.'

The line clicked off and Alice turned back towards the table. The burger was cold now, abandoned on the plate.

'I said yes,' she repeated.

'Said yes to what?' Callum said from behind her.

* * *

The rest of the day was quiet. Too quiet. Alice went to buy sushi to take home with them while Callum was distracted by Roger coming back over with yet another enthusiastic suit. She could see his irritation, his fists clenching by his sides. She knew just by looking at him what he was thinking, feeling even. She wondered how long she'd been able to do that. Did her body still recognise him, even though her mind held things back from her?

She'd been saved from answering his questions, escaping to get more food. It was sitting on the back seat now as they pulled into the drive. He killed the engine but made no move to get out.

'You haven't asked about Roger. Who snitched?'

'I called Migs. Why didn't you tell me about the job?' *About me saying yes to marrying you seconds before the damn taxi was totalled?*

'When she has that little rugrat, we'll be having words.'

'Oh, I know,' she agreed. 'I was mad too, believe me.' She reached for his hand. 'Callum, we're halfway through this. Aren't you scared?'

He started to shake his head, as he always did, but she reached for his jaw. Turned his face to hers. 'I care about you, I know that. More than I did. More than I ever thought I would when I woke up in that hospital.'

That got a laugh. 'You were a bit prickly.'

'I didn't recognise you, with the beard and everything. I remembered the wrong night. I woke up mad at you.'

He leaned in, and she pulled on his jaw to close the distance. Kissing him hard, and with meaning. 'I said I would marry you that night, didn't I?' He'd only just pulled back, and she saw the shock horror on his face. 'Migs told me. I made her. Threatened to tell her baby all her embarrassing secrets. I did, didn't I? And then I forgot everything, forgot you.' She kissed him again to stop the damn broken-hearted expression on his features. He pulled her to him, till the gear stick stuck into her leg.

'Let's go inside,' he said, opening the door. 'We can eat and talk there.'

A little while later, they were both showered. Alice was in her pyjamas, him in a T-shirt and grey joggers. The bags of goodies from the exhibition left in the hallway, the remnants of the sushi containers out on the coffee table.

'It was nice that you got that.' He pointed to it.

'Well, it's what we did the first time.' She smiled, taking a deep pull on the beer he'd gotten out of the fridge to go with it. 'I figured I could do my bit. I'm sorry about the baby stuff, the freaking out.'

'It's fine.' He moved a little closer on their couch, wrapping his arm around her. She relaxed into him, tucking her legs up underneath her. 'It freaked me out too, just for a second. I was worried you were going to run for the hills. I'm glad you told me.'

'That why no one told me about the proposal?'

'Yeah. I asked them not to the second I realised you didn't remember it.'

'I wish I could remember. Why did I have to lose the whole of us? It's not fair. It's like some sick joke, like a movie or something. It could have been six months, a year.'

'Or nothing. Life's not fair, sparrow. We just have to work with what we've got.'

'Yeah well. It sucks. You didn't take the job with Roger cos of this.'

Their faces were just millimetres apart now, and she tried to concentrate on his words rather than falling into those mesmerising brown eyes.

'Roger's a big boy. He was a little butt hurt, sure. He was trying to change my mind today, but in all honesty, I don't think my heart was in it. You'd already told me not to do it.'

'I did?'

'Yep. You said it wasn't my dream, and you were right. The money was so good though, and I wanted to shore us up. Your business was doing great, but you were focused on the house. We both were, really, and I wanted to give you the best. Lew's wedding was so fancy.'

'I don't care about any of that. Lewis is a solicitor; he earns more money, but he doesn't have the spare time either. I know that neither of us ever wanted to be chained to a desk, or a job. Why do you keep compromising your dream for me? Callum, we're halfway through this. My memory isn't back.'

'It's coming though, right? Today you remembered something. I see more than you think. You made me a drink the other day. Remembered my favourite mug, how I take it.'

'You've had three sugars in your tea since you were a kid. I used to change them for salt, remember? It's hardly ground-breaking news.'

'No, true. But you remember my goals, the sushi. Things are coming back.' He was rubbing her shoulder now with his hand, and she shivered a little. 'Your body remembers me. When you were in the coma, I'd just sit there. Day after day. Night after night. They kept trying to kick me out, but I refused and they gave in in the end. Dr B told me that you could probably hear me. I held your hand as often as I could. Watched while they changed your casts. Your face was so cut up, I couldn't stand not being able to touch it. I hated it but I knew you were in there.'

She sank down further into the couch, resting her head on his shoulder. Felt him kiss her hair. 'When I told you I loved you, you'd squeeze my hand sometimes. Not every time, but those words seemed to get through to you. Even when you were so far away from me, you still reacted to those words. That's why we can't just give up on this. I know we said ten dates, but I'm not expecting you to snap back to the old you at the end of this. To lov... to be who we were like some kind of spell's been broken.'

'Spell?'

He chuckled, and she felt his whole chest move with it. Heard his heartbeat. Strong, steady against her ear. Just like him wrapped around her.

'I watched a lot of TV in the hospital. Some witchy show with three sisters in it. It was quite good.'

They laughed together then, wrapped around each other tight on their couch.

'I'm sorry I forgot you, Callum.'

'We're together now, back home. That's all I ever wanted, sparrow. My little hot birdie back in the nest.'

'Hot, eh?' She smirked up at him. He kissed her forehead, chuckling.

'Out of all that, hot is what you heard?'

'Hey, scar face here will take what she can get.' She laughed but his brows knitted together. 'I was kidding.'

'I still don't like it. You don't realise just how gorgeous you are.'

He leaned down further, kissing every little scar in turn. 'A sparrow with a broken wing.'

She turned her head up till their lips met. She could taste the lager they'd been drinking, and him. His spice was ever present, and she wondered whether it was even the aftershave that made him smell like that, or if it was him that changed the scent. It was unique, and every time she got a taste, she just seemed to want more.

'I'm pretty tired,' she said when they'd finally stopped making out on the couch. 'I think I'm going to get some sleep.'

'Oh... okay. Night, Ali.' He kissed her again.

She got to the doorway and turned back. 'Come with me. No more nights on the couch. I'm not suggesting anything else, but I... want you with me. Deal?'

He stared at her for a long moment, finally standing and coming to take her hand. 'Deal.'

She led him up to their room. When they got under the covers, he turned to his side, wrapping his strong arms around her. The warmth of him instantly relaxed her little spoon body.

'I missed this,' he said simply.

'I think I did too,' she replied honestly. 'Goodnight, Callum.'

'Goodnight, sparrow.'

22

ALICE

The next week passed by in a blur. Callum finished removing the rockery, levelling the ground ready for it to be transformed into her vision. Alice watched him from the back windows as she worked in her office. Her clients were thrilled to hear from her, and she'd even planned a few projects. Nothing too bulky, a few home offices needing an expensive-looking update for the workers who now called their home their office. It was interesting, draining, but the painters and decorators, furniture dealers and movers handled most of the strain. She got to sit in her office for the most part, discussing colour swatches on Zoom. She soon got to love her lunchtimes with Callum too. If he was working on a job, he was only taking on small projects too. No large eco-housing estates, for a start. Roger was still courting him; she saw his name pop up sometimes when Callum got a phone call. He was always polite, but firm. Whenever he said he was focusing on his girlfriend's recovery, it made her heart skip a beat. For good reasons and bad. Pre-coma Alice had told him that she didn't think it was his dream, and she had to agree with herself. Those estate buildings could be pretty soulless, and her cynical business head knew that this was about getting the tax breaks and ecology grants for Roger and his business cronies, not true sustainability and leaving the planet in a better place.

The easy rhythm between them continued. Lewis and Migs had come round for a pizza one of the nights, and they'd all reverted pretty much back to their teenage selves, larking about, talking about old times.

Callum hadn't slept on the couch since the night of the expo, and neither of them mentioned it. The spare blankets and pillows were firmly back in the closet. Their midnight kisses growing into more too. Caresses, lips on her neck. They were playing a game of sorts. One little move lower each night, but she was still feeling frustrated. Not as frustrated as she feared what moving too fast would do though, so make-out sessions and heavy petting was as far as anything went. She'd made him laugh when she'd told him that. That her awkward teenage self would have been thrilled to get this far back then. As usual, he was in awe that she'd hidden it so well behind the put-downs and the glares. How blind they'd both been. His sullen, moody, near-silent nature a cover for his frustration just like her barbed, spiky one-liner self.

'See, sparrow,' he whispered to her one night as they fell asleep together. 'It was always there. That kind of love doesn't disappear.' She didn't answer him, but she knew exactly what he meant. Ever since he had come back into their bed, she'd never slept better. Waking up in his arms, she felt so safe, so happy. The panic and worry kept at bay. He soothed her overthinking brain with a touch of his body, and she was like a little junkie, craving her nightly fix. Then the next date rolled around, and she was reminded of the self-imposed clock on their future. Date six was here, and she could feel the ticking of time once more.

* * *

'You ready for this?' She said to him as they stood on her parents' doorstep two weeks after their last date. 'We could have literally done anything else.'

'Nope, this was our date. We stick to the plan.'

He was grinning from ear to ear, and she could see the cellophane on the bunch of flowers he carried jiggling in his arms.

'You're loving this, aren't you? Who takes a date to her own parents' house? I am amazed we ever got to date seven.' She was seething, and not looking forward to this at all. Her parents had kept their distance since she'd gone home, so she knew that they would be eager to see her. *More pressure.* She was just starting to enjoy the calm of her and Callum at home, and now she was right back in the land of overthinking and uncertainty.

'Let's make a run for it. We could go for a pub lunch. My treat?'

Callum's arched brow told her he wasn't biting.

'Please! You know what my parents are like, come on! I'll even go see yours.'

Callum chuckled. 'My parents are still on a cruise, and you know it. Besides, you chose this date.'

'I did not!' The horror. This was self-inflicted? 'God, I hate pre-coma me sometimes! Why on earth would I pick this for a date?'

Callum shrugged. 'To put me off, I think. You have some twisted ideas, McClaren.'

'Fuck,' she said under her breath. 'You know, sometimes you really get on my tits, Roberts.'

She could see movement behind the frosted glass of the doorway and waited for the door to open and her nightmare to begin. Callum was still laughing when the door handle finally moved down, and she just managed to get an elbow into his ribs in the nick of time.

'Alice!' Her mother practically jumped on her the second she saw her. 'Ohmydarlingyoulooksowell!' Her words came out in a torrent, and Alice was hugged so tight she thought her head might pop off. When she finally let her go, Alice reached for Callum's free hand instinctively. He rubbed his thumb along her palm. 'Callum!' Her mum continued to gush. She went to hug him, but he lifted the flowers, gripping Alice's hand tighter. Louisa tittered loudly. 'Oh sorry! Where are my manners!' She turned and bellowed, 'Gerry!' just as Alice's father appeared in the doorway behind her. Gerry winced, waggling one finger in his ear.

'I heard you, Lou. Half the street did.' He turned his attention to the pair on the doorstep. 'Hello, love, you look well. Come on in.'

He patted Callum on the shoulder as they walked over the threshold. 'Hello, lad.' Alice saw his face crinkle with affection, and her heart leaped. He'd always had a soft spot for Callum. It seemed that had deepened over the years. 'How about that score last night?' The two of them started to talk sport, and her mother took the flowers from Callum and headed off to the kitchen to put them in some water. The second she was out of earshot, her father led them into the lounge.

'Sorry, she's been cooking all morning. Cleaned everything to within an inch of its life. I fell asleep watching the snooker and woke up to her hoovering the biscuit crumbs off my cardigan. I thought my time was up.'

Callum laughed easily, his thumb keeping up its soothing movements. Alice tried to focus on that, and not her mother's slightly deranged humming from the kitchen. He ushered her with him over to the floral-covered sofa, and tucked her into his side as they sat down.

'Thanks,' she whispered to him, and he squeezed her hand, bringing it to his lap.

'Any time, sparrow,' he whispered back from the corner of his mouth. 'Alice was asking me on the way over why we would have come here for a date.'

Her dad pulled his glasses down his nose. 'That's my Alice. As inquisitive as she is stubborn.' He grinned, dipping his head to Callum. 'Shaking this one off, of course. Not that it worked. He was already part of the family.' He leaned forward in his armchair, steepling his fingers. 'Bear with your mother, eh? She's been chomping at the bit to come round and see you. She's baked enough muffins to feed the whole village. I ended up taking some of them up to the church. When Callum called to say you were ready for the next date the other day, it was the first time I've not seen her without a mixing bowl in her hand.'

Alice nodded, taking everything in. Not just her mother, and the fact that she'd been baking her worry away, but the surroundings of her childhood home.

'You've decorated. It looks... different.' She'd been numb before, not even registered the changes. Perhaps her newly revived self had protected her from the visual assault she was currently experiencing.

It looked like her mother had looked at a floral swatch catalogue and decided to go for every single one. In the same room. It was dazzling. She felt a bit sick.

'Oh.' Her dad looked around. 'Yeah, last year.' He turned his attention back to her, chuckling as her mother was clanging things about in the other room. 'You hated it then too. Didn't she, Cal?'

Callum was saved from answering when her mother walked back in. 'Dinner's ready! Come through.' She was rubbing her hands together. A sure sign she was anxious; she'd done it since Alice was a kid.

'Living room looks nice, Mum,' she tried, hoping to break the tension. Her mother dropped her hands.

'Thanks, darling,' her eyes filled up, but she blinked them away. 'Come through, eh?' She glared at her husband. 'Gerry! Have you not even offered them a drink?'

Her dad shot them a wink. 'Was just going to, dear, no need to get the Dyson out.'

* * *

Dinner had been nicer than Alice had expected. Probably helped by the fact that her dad had poured her mother a glass of brandy somewhere in between the prawn cocktail starter and the roast beef main course. And had kept topping it up whenever she wasn't looking. By the time the sherry trifle was out, her mother's perfect hairstyle was looking a little tousled, but she'd stopped looking at Alice like she was a china doll hanging off the end of a shelf. The talk had been extensive, and Alice had soaked it all up. What her parents had been up to, anecdotes from the church and her mother's craft and chat group, which was always a hotbed of gossip and intrigue. For a benign group of women, they sure got up to some antics. They'd talked about the house, and Callum had come to life, telling them how the place was shaping up. How the garden was almost done, how much Alice had put into the details of each room. He looked so proud of her, his eyes constantly finding hers. Sitting on the same side of the table from each other, her mum and dad at the other side, it felt normal. Intimate. She wondered just how many nights they'd spent like this.

Once dinner was finished, and they were back in the sitting room, she'd almost forgotten that they were even on a date. Her dad had refilled their glasses and had unbuttoned his trousers before settling down in his armchair.

'Jesus, Mother! Do you have to?'

Louisa had walked in clutching a stack of photo albums.

Gerry puffed out a strained breath, rubbing his belly. 'I think that trifle finished me off, Lou. Give the poor lass a break, eh?'

Her mother silenced him with a tut and a swift tap to the shin as she breezed past. She stood expectantly before Callum and Alice, who were back on the sofa. 'Scooch over, you two!'

Alice tried to convey to Callum her panic, but he gave her a wink and moved aside. Louisa parked herself between them, moving various trinkets aside on the coffee table to make room for the volumes of photos. Her dad turned the TV on, muting it, and a recording of snooker filled the screen.

Alice tried to mouth 'help' at him, but he just shrugged his shoulders with a rueful look. He reached into his side table, pulling out a bottle of cognac.

'One for the road?'

Callum shook his head. 'Not for me, thanks.'

'Oh, go on.' Louisa nudged his arm. 'There's no rush to get home, is there? Lewis said you were both off tomorrow. It is Sunday.' She bit at her lip. 'You'd better not, Gerry. Early service tomorrow.'

Gerry looked crestfallen but put the bottle back in the drawer. Alice was pretty sure she heard him mutter something about Jesus liking a tipple himself, water into wine, but he soon returned his gaze to the snooker. By the time they were halfway through the first album, he was snoring softly.

'Oh look, this is the one!' Her mother slapped the cover of one album near the bottom of the pile. It had a couple of cats photographed sitting in a basket on the front. The words 'Puuuur-fect' printed across it in swirly pink lettering. 'Look, Alice, I think this might help.'

Alice cringed but tried to keep it off her face. Her mother was sitting tight against her, and she could smell her Rose Garden perfume, the one she asked for on every special occasion. It was mixed with the sharp whiff of brandy, and something sugary. Probably all the baking – it had seeped into her pores and been pickled with the booze. She looked across at Callum, and he was watching her. He mouthed, 'Are you okay?' and she smiled before looking at the first page.

It was her and Callum, sitting on her mother's old couch. They were snuggled up against each other, his arm around her. Just in the same way he did these days. She looked... different. Sure, she was scar free, but that wasn't it. She looked... happy. Her mother was grinning at her like a lunatic.

'See, that was the date you had here. We were so surprised when you rang, asked if you could bring Callum to dinner. We thought you were going to terrorise him, but it wasn't like that. Not really.'

'It was really my idea?' she checked.

Her mother nodded, pointing out the Twister mat in the corner.

'It was strange at first, you insisted on playing the games you did when you were kids. We all played Twister till dinner was ready. It was like you were challenging him, but soon you were laughing together, mucking about. Teasing each other.' Her mother went a bit misty-eyed. 'I saw it, you know. Well,' she looked across at her husband, who gave a little snort and smacked his lips together, 'your dad did, actually. I think he saw it before anyone.'

'Saw what?' Callum asked softly. When Alice looked across at him, his eyes were roving over the photos of them. Laughing as they were contorted over the Twister mat. Callum's hands were caught in action, reaching for Alice as she fell from her stance.

She looked across at him, covering his hand with hers.

'That the pair of you were meant for each other. I'm so glad you came home, Alice in Wonderland.' Her nickname for her only daughter.

Alice said nothing for a second, and then reached for her mother. This time it was Louisa that was squeezed half to death.

'Me too, Mum. I love you. Always have.'

'I love you more, baby girl.' She booped her on the nose. 'And don't you ever forget it.'

23

CALLUM

'Roger, I already gave you my decision. It's not the right time. Alice still needs time, I've been polite, but—'

He banged the printer, hoping it would decide to stop being a dick and spit out the documents he needed. Why was it the bloody things never worked when you wanted them to? He checked the lights on the Wi-Fi router, but it was all working. He banged the printer again, and it whirred.

'Ha ha! I win, you little bastard!' He forked the machine with two fingers in a reverse V as it printed out the tickets he needed. Alice had gone out to see a local boutique about a redesign, and he'd been working on the last bits of the hallway. The house had been a real labour of love, but with the pressure of their seventh date that evening, he was starting to feel more than a little under the cosh. Since the dinner with her parents, they'd become even closer. Waking up every morning with her in his arms felt like a dream, one he'd sometimes doubted would happen again all those days by her bedside. She wore his sweatpants around the house, slept in his T-shirts every night. Kissed him to distraction in the dark every night. They didn't speak about the long term, and while he loved their bubble, he still felt the fear.

'What? Callum?' Roger's voice brought him back to the present.

'Sorry, I wasn't talking to you.' He heard Alice's car pull up, the front door open a few minutes later.

'Callum?' she called.

'Just a minute,' he called back. 'Roger, I have to go. We have plans tonight.' Roger carried on, oblivious. 'What? How much more?'

Roger gave him a figure, and he felt his hand close around the corner of his desk. 'Well, Roger, that's very generous, but as I said—'

Alice appeared in the doorway to his office, looking as gorgeous as ever. He felt his whole face break out into a grin, and suddenly he didn't hear Roger's voice any more.

'Roger, I have to go. Something's come up.' *Yeah, in my pants.* He clicked off the call, and strode over to her.

'Hey, don't crush my dress!' she chided as he lifted her into the air, not even seeing the garment bag she had hanging over her shoulder. He took it from her, hooking it onto the door frame and lifting her onto his desk.

'Hmm, you bought a dress, eh? For tonight?'

He pulled her to him, kissing a line down from her lips to the collarbone of her purple Bardot top. 'Job went well then?'

'Yep.' She giggled, then moaned when he sucked at a sensitive part of her neck that he knew she loved. 'I got the job, I start in a couple of months. Mmmm,' she breathed, reaching for him to pull him in. 'How do you know...' He licked at her collarbone, making her shudder. 'Oh, right.' She giggled again. 'We've done this before.'

He waggled his eyebrows at her. 'Oh yeah, baby. All this...' He nuzzled at her neck once more, eliciting a delicious little moan from her that he didn't realise he'd craved till now. 'And much,' *kiss,* 'much,' *lick,* 'more.'

'Tease,' she murmured.

'Always,' he retorted, reluctantly putting her down before he lost all control. 'So, are you going to show me the dress?'

'Nope.' She laughed, swatting at his backside as he shoved the tickets from the printer under some papers. 'Unless you want to tell me where we're going tonight.'

He threw her a dirty look. 'Nice try, sparrow. Just be ready for six. It's a bit of drive, but you'll love it.'

'Okay, Mr Secretive. Well, let me just get a shower, then. You eaten? I called at the sandwich place you love. Got you a sub, it's on the counter.' She picked her dress hanger up off the wood. 'Looking forward to it, Cal.' She blew him a kiss and he reached up to catch it. The minute she was gone, he scrambled on the desk, triple-checking that the tickets were all correct. He couldn't risk getting there and having something wrong.

He was lucky that he'd managed to pull it off. He had worried that this date would be a non-starter, but fate had intervened and the band they'd been to see were touring again, only a couple of hours' drive away. He'd already planned the eighth date for the following weekend, and from the amount of emails her mother had been sending him, Migs and Lew, the thrown-together vow renewal to replace Lew's wedding was being organised faster and more efficiently than a military operation overseas. It was all coming together, but that was the problem. When he'd proposed the deal, he'd been grasping at straws. He knew Alice, and how proud and independent she was. How much waking up like that, to all that trauma, would make her retreat back to her default self. The protective, I-don't-need-anyone stance she'd held around her like armour since she was old enough to know her own mind. Now, she was a strong adult who literally *didn't know her own mind*. He just didn't plan on this. She was getting closer to him every day, but with the baby plans and the proposal bombshell, he knew she was as gun-shy as a mare right now. Roger was offering him more money, and it was so tempting. More than ever now he'd barely worked for the last few months. The funds were dwindling. He'd not used any of Alice's money, something about that didn't feel right, so aside from checking her bills were paid, and a loan from his ever-absent parents, he could really do with the money. If she ever did decide to marry him, he wouldn't be able to give her the best. That tore him up, even though he knew she wasn't one for a big affair anyway. That wasn't the point. Alice was his everything, and he wanted to hand her the moon on a damn stick.

It wasn't till he was out of the shower later that he realised the sub on the counter wasn't a new thing. He hadn't eaten there since before the accident. Alice had remembered his favourite sandwich, had gone out of her way to get it for him.

'It's going to work,' he said to himself, reaching for the after-shave she loved. 'It has to.'

24

CALLUM

'Lincoln Sparks!' As soon as they left the motorway, the jig was up. The banners were huge, her favourite all time band from her teenage years and beyond smiling out from the billboards around the exhibition centre. They were sitting in the best seats, right near the front. 'I still can't believe it!' She grabbed his face and planted a huge smacker on his lips. 'I swear, I could spit from here and hit them in the eye!' She was bouncing up and down in her seat.

'Please don't,' he laughed. 'I had to pull some strings to get these seats at short notice. You want another drink?' She'd almost drained her bottle of water and the band weren't even on the stage yet. The support act had been an up-and-coming US band, and they'd whipped the already ebullient crowd up to a near frenzy. They were both wearing merchandise T-shirts to match, and he'd snapped a few photos of them laughing and smiling into the camera. He'd filled his phone over the last few weeks, part of his promise to himself, and her by her bedside. That when she was awake, and back with him, he'd record the moments. Not get bogged down by the day-to-day grind. Looking at her now, he knew that he would lift the earth up onto his shoulders if he needed to.

Would carry it till it broke him, just to see that smile on her face every day for the rest of his life.

'Best date ever,' she laughed, just as the lights went down and the first bars of the song started.

They danced and bopped their way through the songs, oblivious to the audience. Everyone was standing up around them, and she came to stand in front of him, wrapping his strong arms around her and nuzzling into his front. This was her favourite place, she realised with a jolt. Not the concert hall or being back out in the big wide world. Surrounded by people, when she had spent weeks being alone, trapped in her own body. Barry had taken a lot, but he'd given her a gift too, in a way. In a stupid selfish act, he'd opened her up. Reminded her of just what she'd lost. Reminded her never to take that for granted ever again. The song ended, and the lead singer wiped his brow and spoke to the crowd.

'We have a special request tonight, for you all. From a very determined man who blew up our PR people. We sing about pain, but we write about love too, and this couple have had more than their fair share of both lately.' He clicked his fingers and the spotlight came up, lighting him against the dark and the mobile phones, all showing their torches in the expanse of the crowd. 'So this is for a very big fan, and the man she loves. They are here tonight, on a very special date.' The opening bars of their best song, her favourite song, 'Always', begin to play. 'Alice McClaren, this one is for you.' For a second, Alice panicked. Was she still in the damn coma? Was she going to wake up, single? From a very weird, prolonged dream? The next words had her reaching for her arm, giving herself a sharp pinch. Just to be sure.

'This is from a man who has his own little songbird, sparrow.' The crowd erupted and just before the opening line was sang, Hammer, the lead singer and songwriter of the band, leaned in close to the microphone. 'Glad you woke up, Alice. Welcome back to wonderland.'

She turned to Callum as the song played, his arms never losing their grip on her body. She gazed up into his eyes, blinking and failing to stop the joyous tears from escaping.

'You did this?'

He dipped his head and kissed her like his life depended on it. Maybe he thought it did. *This man*, she thought to herself. *You've been tormented by him for more than half your life. Maybe fate was trying to tell you that our story wasn't done yet.*

'I basically made a nuisance of myself,' he laughed, and she felt the rumble of it even over the crowd, the music. 'It was worth it too, to see that smile. I love you so much, Ali.'

He pulled her back into his arms as she turned back to the stage.

'I think I'm falling for you too,' she said, but the crowd drowned out her hopefully cautious words.

25

ALICE

'Can we at least stop for coffee?' she asked grumpily. After the concert, the whole week had been a thrill. They were like teenagers, canoodling whenever they were alone, which was a lot since they were content to hang at the house together so much. The hallway flooring was looking amazing, and Alice had to admit that seeing the house nearly finished was both making her happy and sad. After today, they only had two dates left. She still didn't remember her old life, just memories here and there. She was starting to fear that it would never come back, and what impact that would have on her life. On their life. Her life wasn't that of a single woman any more, but how could she put that on Callum forever? Was it fair to ask? She kept trying to think what would happen if he'd been in the crash. Would she have done all of this? She wouldn't even have thought of the ten dates in the first place. She was too stubborn back then, far too focused on the plans and not the moments that came in-between. Callum lived in the now; he didn't waste his time overthinking. Even now, when he'd dragged them both out of their warm, cosy bed at the crack of dawn for their next secret adventure, she had been nothing but grumpy.

'Sorry,' she said as he pulled off the motorway, following the signs for the coffee shop drive-thru. 'I didn't mean to be morning-y.'

He raised their linked hands to his mouth, dropping a kiss on the skin he found there.

'I've been around you enough mornings not to be offended,' he laughed easily. 'I added time for coffee, so it's all good, baby.'

A couple of hours later, and they were pulling right up to the beach front at Filey.

'A date at the beach, eh? Wonder whose idea that was.'

'Well, it was mine, but given that you should have been born with fins and a tail, I figured it out pretty quickly the first time. I even brought your cossie.'

She pulled a face. 'Oh God, what about my—'

'You look perfect. If anyone even looks at you funny, I'll be there. Ready?'

She reached for him, cradling his jaw in her hands. 'I don't deserve all this, Cal. I know I've not made this easy.'

He kissed her in the car till she forgot her own name, never mind worrying about showing off her battle-scarred body. He always made her feel beautiful.

'Nothing easy was ever worth having, baby. Come on, let's go have our perfect eighth date all over again. We ate fish and chips on the seafront, fed each other ice cream. Made sandcastles till the sun faded. Then we drove home and spent the night on the couch watching trashy TV and eating junk.' He brushed his thumb against her cheek. 'We went to bed still smelling of the sea. Curled up together.'

She drew him closer, laughing. 'God, whoever taught you to speak like that deserves a medal.' He belly-laughed at that. 'I mean it; how do you know just what to say to calm me down, every time?'

He touched his forehead to hers. 'I paid attention, sparrow. When you want something bad enough, you can't stop looking at it.

I will never stop looking, baby. Now come on, get your sexy arse out of the car before I give the seagulls something to really watch.'

* * *

The sun was warm; it felt good on her bare skin. Callum had nipped to the stand nearby to get them some drinks, and she'd been woken from a dozing, sexy dream involving Callum, ice cream and sand in places it didn't normally go on an average beach day by her phone ringing.

'Oh come on, it's beach day,' she moaned, expecting it to be her mother with some little detail about the wedding. Or her father, calling from the shed at the bottom of the garden to moan about the fact his wife had seemingly turned into Bridezilla. The hospital number came up, and she answered it with trepidation. She'd been seeing Doctor Berkovich every few weeks, and had just had a repeat scan to check on how she was healing.

'Hello?'

'Good afternoon, Miss McClaren. Do you have time to go over your results?' A seagull made a loud laughing sound overhead, and she heard the doctor pause. 'Er? I can call back?'

'Oh, it's fine. I'm just at the beach with Callum, actually.'

'Oh!' Dr B sounded quite happy to hear that. 'Well, a good time to tell you that your scans are normal. Everything came back fine. I will write to you in more detail, of course, but I must say, I am more than pleased with the progress you're making. Have you had any more memories come back?'

'Not really, no.' She had cause to pause herself then. 'Do you think they ever will?'

She heard him sigh before he answered, a sure sign she'd come to learn from talking with him that there wasn't an easy answer.

'The brain is complex, Alice. We have no absolutes, unfortunately, but getting to this point is a very good sign. It's important to remember that you are still healing and will be for a long time. When the brain's normal functions are disrupted from trauma, things can take time. Some things are never gained back, but it's important to stay positive. Be aware of making decisions; life upheavals like this can often result in confusion. New ways of the brain coping. Impulsive behaviours can occur, and great swings of mood, as we discussed.'

Impulsive behaviours. She looked across at Cal, who was on his way back to her. Looking gorgeous and sun soaked in a pair of swim shorts, his bare chest glistening from the oil. Something in her mind started to kick the cogs into turning.

'By impulsive behaviours, do you mean emotions?'

'Yes, of course. Emotions are a big part of the mind, and recovery from a trauma like yours has been known to disrupt these thought patterns, interrupt our usual ways of reasoning. Are you experiencing anything like this? As I said before, I do recommend therapy. I know you're not keen, but...'

'So you're saying my brain still might not be processing properly.'

Another tell-tale pause, a sigh. 'Not necessarily. Things are going well, Alice. Everything else will simply be down to time.'

Time was the one thing she didn't have, and now she didn't even know if what she was feeling for Callum was real. What if it was just a trick of her mind? She could fall in love with him; God knows she was falling already. What if she went all in and then woke up one morning to find it was gone? What if she was married to him by then, or they had kids? There was no timeline to her brain, but there was a timeline to his heart. He was barely working, and although he'd been offered a fantastic job with Roger, he'd hidden it from her. At the rate he was abandoning his own life to focus on her, he would be bankrupt in months. He had built his business up from nothing, just like her. Even when he was her counterpart in being annoying, before all this, she'd admired his drive, the passion and hard work he put into everything she did. She saw it every day, walking around their beautiful home. She went into this swearing that she wouldn't break his heart, and her brain was something she didn't trust any more. What she did trust in was him, and she knew he would never leave her. She would have to be the one to do it.

'Alice, are you still there? I can arrange an appointment to discuss this in more detail; perhaps Callum would like to come along?'

'No!' She swallowed, taking a deep breath. Cal would be in earshot any minute. 'No, I understand. Thank you.' She cut the call off, and tried to calm down her rapidly beating heart.

'Everything okay?' he asked, kissing her before dropping down on his towel.

'Yes, yeah,' she replied, putting on her sunglasses to hide her eyes from him. If he looked into them, he would suss her out in a second. 'Just Mum, wedding stuff. You know what she's like.'

He leaned on one elbow, running his soft lips over the tip of her shoulder. 'Your dad has called me from the shed a few times. I think they might end up having to host the wedding there. He says if she doesn't stop talking to him about centrepieces, he's going to move into the shed.'

She laughed, lying back down and running her hands through the sand. Inside, her guts were churning. They had two dates left. If she was going to walk away from Callum, let him live his life without her, she was going to have to enjoy every moment.

Getting up on her feet, she reached for his hand. 'Come on, let's go swim in the sea. I kinda like the idea of you smelling like the ocean.' He grinned, and lifting her into his arms, he carried her to the water. She let him, while she still could. *He told me he would carry the world for me. I love him too much already to make him try and be broken under the weight of it all.*

26

ALICE

The expectation had already been bearing down on Alice before they entered the hotel suite. It had ever since Dr B had called her on the beach. Before she saw their cases sitting side by side. The large king-size bed, covered with rose petals and a couple of towels shaped into kissing swans screamed romance, and she didn't know where to put herself.

The wedding had been amazing. More than amazing. But now they were alone, she couldn't stop dwelling on the reactions of the guests, the fact that it was all ending.

The people at the wedding had been so full of joy. For her parents, for Lewis and Migs and their impending family. For her and Callum, and the love story they all thought so beautiful. It made her want to scream. To thrash and rage and wrench everything out of her head. But she didn't. She lived in the moment, went along with their joy while her own was slipping through her fingers. Just like the sand on the beach.

They pretty much all knew the couple version of Callum and Alice, the pre-coma version. Exclaimed how well she looked, how delighted they were that the two of them were back together, happy.

As soon as they'd said goodbye to the people left behind and headed to the lift, she'd not been able to think about anything else. They had one date left. One. After that, what then? They called it quits? End of the line? She didn't have her memory back. Callum would be crushed. However she ended it. It was almost better when they played at hating each other. Easier. He wouldn't try if he hated her. Maybe she had to make him. Perhaps even that would be kinder.

All this effort, all of the conversations, the tiptoeing around each other. Living together and chasing the ghosts of their past around every room. She felt wretched. Broken. She thought waking up from the coma had been bad. This felt worse. At least then she had hope alongside the fear. She might never get every piece of those two years back. She would always be one step behind everyone else. Missing the in-jokes, the anecdotes of the memories she couldn't laugh at. Didn't get. Like being on the outside, never quite fitting back into her own existence. Looking at Callum now, as he stood beside her, pulling off his fancy tie, she wondered whether he would feel that too. Like he never quite got all of her. She cared too bloody much to put him through any more pain.

She'd read about people in comas. She'd done nothing but Google the best- and worst-case scenarios. Most people didn't snap back to their old selves. They changed their lives. Marriages broke down. Parental relationships stretched so taut they weakened; some snapped altogether. The people moved on, made their lives bearable. New partners. Ones who didn't even know them in their lost years. Easier, she'd thought, reading them. That seemed easier. Callum was entwined in her life, and those around her. The people in her life all loved him. As the months and years went on, would he resent her for not remembering? Deem it too hard? What then? What would all this be for?

One more date. It would have to be a hell of an event if she was going to pull this off. If she was going to keep Callum. Keep him forever. Marry him, have babies together. Live in their dream house and grow old together. If they could get to that, get to sit in their rockers and tell *this story* as an anecdote, it would be more than she could ever wish for. She needed her brain to remember him. Properly. All of them, then she didn't have to live in fear. If she got it all back, it would just be a funny story, right? Like leaving the stove on and burning the kitchen curtains. Or putting diesel in the petrol tank.

Remember that time you forgot me, sparrow?

Yes, love, I do. Ha ha ha. What a lark, eh? What do you want for dinner?

Maybe not.

'Ali?' He was standing in front of her now, his tie discarded on the bed. His open shirt releasing the spicy scent that was now her favourite aroma. She wanted to bottle it, so she could keep it forever. She wanted to keep him forever. She pushed the thought aside.

'You okay? You didn't say a word the whole way up here.'

'I'm good.' She smiled, but he wasn't buying it.

'Ali,' he pressed.

'I was just thinking about stuff, that's all.' She motioned to the petal-strewn bed. 'I see my mother's insistence about booking the rooms had an ulterior motive.'

He reddened, lifting his hand to trail his fingers slowly up the skin of her bare arm.

'I didn't have a clue till Lew spilled the beans earlier.' His full, sexy lips twitched. 'I get why she practically threw the bell hop at us the second we arrived. She obviously didn't want us up here till after.'

That made her laugh, and his fingers on her arm were thawing out the ice running up the length of her spine from overthinking.

Oh the irony. A brain injury, and the damn thing still ran like a motor. Overran. *One. Last. Date. One.* Uno. *Single.* No plurals to cushion the fear that bubbled within her.

'She's one of a kind, I'll give her that. It's not many parents who throw themselves a wedding to help their daughter.' She said it to lighten the mood, but hearing the words were like a knife to the heart. She could feel it there, every shaky breath she took pushing the tip closer to her organ. The one she feared breaking in the man in the room. Her face gave her away, as it always did to Callum.

'Ali, they wanted to do this. They'd been talking about it, before.'

'When I didn't remember,' she finished for him. He pressed his lips together, a slow nod of his head. 'I get why. The ten dates were important. I just wish everyone hadn't spent so much time and effort on it all.'

'Yeah. About that...' Oh God, this was it. The big talk. She couldn't do it yet. She just couldn't. She needed every second she could get till the dates were over.

'Do we have to talk about it tonight?' She pulled away, kicking her heels off and putting them under the vanity unit. 'It's been great tonight, but it was a lot, you know?'

That look again. She couldn't bear that disappointed look on his features. The one he always tried to hide from her. She constantly put it there, without even trying to half the time. Just the fact she was who she was now caused him daily pain. His own butcher knife jabbing his aorta, but this time she held the handle. Pushed it further, just a little more each time. She couldn't bear it. He deserved so much more. From the minute she'd woken up, she'd given him shit. Yelled at him, snarky comments fired like cannon shots into the bow of their relationship. Sure, she'd been happy and excited most of the time, but she couldn't trust it. Couldn't risk trusting it.

She couldn't do it any more. She couldn't ruin his life like this. Because she didn't want to lose him. She was madly in love with Callum Roberts. Not because she used to love him or remembered exactly how that felt. Nine dates were all it took this time. Nine dates. They'd broken their own personal best, and she couldn't even tell him. She couldn't bring herself to claim him. She had to wrap her fingers around that handle and cut his heart in half. Sever it forever. From her, from them. Even if one day, he would heal. Give it to someone else. She would watch him from afar, keep him close. In the family, as he was. She would fade herself into the background. Her parents, Migs, her brother – she would make sure that they looked after him this time. She would go back to her old life. Back to work.

She'd always thought the old saying was a crock of shit. A lie people said to each other to make the hard times more bearable. An empty platitude. She replayed it over and over in her head, and she knew what to do. She'd figured it out. *If you love something, set it free.* Till then, she had tonight. Tonight and one more beautiful date. She would fall apart after.

'Tell me about the wedding night, before. Lew's wedding. What happened when we left?'

Callum's brows shot up to his hairline, and she resisted the urge to smooth them out. Kiss them better with her lips by stepping backwards. She took a seat on the bed, pushing the swans off the side, and patted the sheets. 'Come sit with me and tell me about the ninth date.'

27

CALLUM

Something was wrong. Callum knew the woman sitting on the bed better than he knew anyone. Himself, even. Pre-coma her, and now – he knew her every movement, every thought. He could see the storm brewing within her. This was it.

He felt... broken. Just like the night that before all this, when Barry the sodding drunk had smashed everything apart.

Tonight should have been a good night. This night, the first ninth date, at Lew's wedding, was the night they'd finally slept together. Declared their love for each other. It was the night she became his, in every sense of the word.

Looking at her now, he felt like he'd climbed the summit of a mountain for the second time, only to find the view bleak. A muted version of the original. Because there hadn't been a tenth date. Last time, they'd never needed it. After that night, she'd come to his apartment. Given him a key to her house. Told him that she loved him, wanted a future with him. Every day after that was the tenth date. It was perfect. He'd hidden it all this time, wanting it to be just like before. Not wanting to pressure her or shorten their time together.

He couldn't lie, couldn't fabricate a last date out of thin air. All through their time together, he'd never lied. He'd hidden some of the truths that might have shocked her, sure. The little ones mostly, the big ones. The proposal. The pieces of their entwined past that would have sent her scuttling back into the safety of a shell. Like a tortoise when it sensed a dark shadow overhead. He wasn't about to start now. He took a seat beside her, feeling the mattress dip beneath him. Kicked off his dress shoes and left them where they landed. One half on its side, the other half under the bed.

'You really want to know? Do you want to tell me what's bothering you first?'

She nodded her head. 'Tell me about the night.' A half-answer, but he took it anyway. He breathed deep, feeling his chest crack open with the power of his feelings.

'Well, we came back to our hotel room.' He ran one hand over the cover, picking up a petal and putting it into her hands. 'We had a twin room, and we'd had a bit to drink. More than tonight, but we weren't smashed.'

'Okay.' Alice nodded, pushing her feet out in front and lying back on the bed. He matched her, and felt her fingers slip into his. Interlock together. It warmed him from the inside. 'What else?'

He chuckled, a low rumble emanating from him. 'Well, we were pretty happy. We goofed around a fair bit, dancing to music. You were hungry, so we ordered burger and fries from room service. Champagne.' He had asked the hotel manager to put a bottle in the fridge tonight, but he didn't mention it. He was too busy reliving the night himself. How easy it had been, how sexy it had become.

'Champagne, eh? Romantic.' She squeezed his fingers. 'Go on.'

'We pushed the beds together, sat cross-legged and ate the food.' Another chuckle erupted from him. 'You ripped into yours like a hungry bear as always.'

'Cheeky.' She turned to her side, resting her head on her elbow and focusing on his eyes. He forgot what he was saying, just for a moment. She always had that effect on him. Made him feel like a lusty schoolboy all over again. Feeling moody and irritated, frustrated for the confusing feelings he had around his best friend's little sister. Teenage angst amplified whenever he was around Alice. He'd loved her for most of his life, and now he felt like this was the last night. He couldn't bear it.

How the fuck am I going to tell her this is it? There is no date ten. End of the line. I can't lose her now. I need her to love me. I'll die without it.

'Cal?' she asked, leaning closer. 'Are you okay?'

His throat felt like it had closed up, his vocal cords disobeying him as he tried to form words to explain how lost he felt. He recognised the feeling. It had been his silent companion for weeks. Those long months when she was in that hospital bed had been the darkest time. Until now. He realised what it was. It was fear.

'I'm terrified of losing you, sparrow. I went through it once. I won't survive that again.' He felt a tear run down the side of his face, drip down near his ear as he gazed across at the woman he adored more than anything. 'I don't want to survive that again. I love you sparrow. That night, Lew's wedding?' It was tumbling out of him now, his emotions spilling out. 'You asked what we did, after the wedding, and the dancing. We came up to the room. We ate burgers, and fries. We drank, and then we were together.' He brushed another tear away before it could escape. 'Really together.'

He waited for her to stiffen up; his shoulder was flush against hers and he waited to feel her muscles tense. Like they often did when he got into the deep stuff. Aside from the night after the karaoke, when she'd wanted to go further and he'd practically run out of the door to stop himself from taking her there and then. Even all the nights they'd slept together, limbs entwined, they'd never discussed going further. This time, it didn't happen. She didn't flinch. This time, he felt her soft lips against his. Their joined hands rested on his chest as she half leaned over him, her side jammed against his as she kissed him softly, tenderly.

'We're here,' she said when they finally came up for air. 'We're together now, right?'

He wanted to say no, it wasn't the same. One night of kissing her in this bed would never be enough for a start. He'd planned to spend the rest of his lifetime with her, not say goodbye come the morning. She didn't love him. She hadn't said it, and he didn't want to ask the question. Put pressure on her. Hear what he already felt in his gut. She didn't love him, didn't feel as she did. He felt wretched but if tonight was all they had before the sun rose and reality set in, he would take it.

'Right,' he muttered. 'We're together now.'

Her smile at his words was bright, radiant. It lit up her whole face.

'Good,' she breathed, rolling over till she was lying on top of him. 'Then I think we should stick to the plan.'

'What?' He tried to get up. 'No, Ali. That's not what I meant.'

'I know it wasn't.' She clenched her jaw. 'I'm sick of making plans in my life. What's the point? You plan your life; you follow a path. Then you get hit by a car and it all turns to shit.'

He held his breath. Waited for her to tell him just how she felt.

28

ALICE

She locked eyes with him. 'I want to be here, Callum. I wouldn't be here if I didn't. I chose this.' She kissed him with everything she had. Holding the tears back. She would cry a river when she was back in her house, alone. When all of this fairy tale was over. When she'd walked away from the Prince Charming she never knew she wanted. Then she would let herself feel the pain. Now, she wanted to drain every second of joy and love from him that she could. 'I choose you, Callum.'

He reached for her then. 'Are you really sure?'

She wanted to say she had never been surer of her decisions, but she didn't want that replaying in her head when this was over.

'Yes,' she breathed instead.

'Good.' He smiled. 'Because we never got to ten dates, sparrow. Nine was all we needed the last time.' His smile was so peaceful, so happy it made her want to cling to him forever. Take a photo to remember how he looked. She'd never see him look this way at her again.

Tonight is all we have.

She didn't trust herself to answer. Everything she said would be a lie. So she kissed him instead, and then there were no more words to speak.

They undressed each other in the lamplight, Callum kissing every scar, every inch of her as they lay together. She tried to memorise every inch of him, her fingers running over his skin. Reading every part of him like Braille on a page beneath her fingertips.

Callum was strong, but so tender and gentle. He caressed every inch of her, touched her till she hummed and begged for more. When he finally slid into her, they moved together in sync. Each bringing each other to the brink over and over, moving and touching, licking and tasting each other till they both found their release. Callum telling her over and over how beautiful she was, how much he'd missed her. How it would never be enough, even if they stayed in this bed forever. He surpassed every daydream she'd ever had. *He was right. It would never be enough.*

Hours later, sated and utterly wrapped in each other, she lay with his head on her chest. Watched the shadows from the morning light gradually creep across the stark, white ceiling. It had been perfect, and she'd been there. Fully there, in the moment. She'd heard his breathing slow, felt his limbs relax as he fell asleep. Thought over and over about what she'd been through. All the moments she'd missed, and the ones she hadn't. All precious memories that meant so much, even to a cynical stubborn woman like her. She breathed in his scent, ran her fingers through his thick brown hair. Watched his eyelids flutter as he slept.

Finally, when the dawn broke, she snuck out from beneath him, gathered her things, and left. The door barely clicked behind her, and then she was running to her car.

29

ALICE & CALLUM?

'Stupid, stupid woman!' She banged her hand on the steering wheel, trying to wipe the torrent of tears away from her eyes as she drove away from the hotel. Her stuff was slung all over the back seat; she hadn't even packed her case up properly in her panic. She was wearing one of Callum's T-shirts, the one he'd packed for her to sleep in, and his soft grey joggers. Her hair was still tousled from his hands, her lips still swollen from his kisses. All she could smell was him, the spicy scent she wanted to bathe in for the rest of her life. 'Stupid, fucking, woman!'

She squealed out of the hotel car park, heading for home. He'd come after her, she knew that. He'd wake up, find her gone and come looking for her. She couldn't go to Migs and Lew; they were still sleeping in the hotel like the rest of the guests. Where could she go? A coma might have been convenient right about now. Her unreliable brain couldn't even do that for her. Couldn't even throw out a helpful clot, or another death nap to shield her from the pain in her chest, and the horror she'd left behind. So she drove, and drove. Away from the hotel, taking the corners a little too fast. Clipping a kerb here and there. All the while crying hysterically. Maybe she could drive herself to the hospital. Plead with Dr B to stick her in the arm and knock her the fuck out. Stop her from feeling... anything. Maybe he could go to the hotel, stick a needle in Callum too. Before he woke up to find her gone. He'd hate her, probably. She'd hate him if she'd had the best night of her life and woken up alone, the scent of him still all over her. Every time she took in a shuddering breath, she just inhaled him. Her whole body was shaking, and so she headed for the country lanes. Pushed her foot down on the pedals, harder and harder. More and more. The roar of the engine not enough to block out the thoughts spinning around in her head. Callum calling her 'sparrow', the groans and growls he'd made the night before when she'd touched him, when he'd pushed into her and made her feel complete. Finally complete. She cried harder and stabbed at the radio button to block out the sound of him. Her own thoughts.

'Always' started playing. She tried to turn it off when her phone started ringing. She'd shoved it into the cup holder when she'd jumped in the car. Callum's face popped up on the screen, a picture of the two of them from the concert taunting her as the phone rang and rang. His name flashing up on the screen over and over.

Callum. Callum. Callum. She grabbed for the phone through watery, blurred vision, to hit the red button but knocked it instead, right under her legs. She reached down to grab it, not even seeing the oncoming car coming from the other direction till she heard the honk of the horn.

She looked up just as the car loomed into view.

'Shit!' she screamed, slamming hard on the brakes and turning the wheel. She slammed to a stop, the two cars screeching as their tyres grasped for purchase on the road. She shut her eyes, tight.

I'm so sorry, Callum. I love you was her final thought as she waited for the impact. The smash of the glass. The second her eyes closed; she was out of the car. In her head, she was in the back of that taxi. Barry barrelling towards the cab, an unseen destructive force.

* * *

'What did you just say?' She was tipsy in the back of the cab, eager to get back home after a fun night. She was ready for her bed.

'Marry me,' Callum repeated. 'I'm sorry, I couldn't wait till you got home. I want to marry you, sparrow. I want you to be Mrs Roberts, I want to love you till we're both old and wrinkly and need to wipe each other's arses. Remind each other where our keys are. I want to make beautiful babies with you, that have your stubborn streak. Marry me, Ali. I will love you...'

'Always,' she finished for him, tears in her eyes. 'Of course I'll marry you, Callum, I lov—' There was a screech of tyres, she heard herself scream, and then the glass. The awful sound of twisting metal and shattering glass. Callum's voice, shouting her name. 'Alice! Alice!'

* * *

'Arsehole!' the driver screamed at her. 'You could have killed us, you stupid feckin' arsehole!'

The woman driver spat the words at her before driving off. Alice was in her car. Alive. She'd missed the other car and the wall at the side of the road by inches. She pulled the car out of gear and turned the engine off until her hands stopped shaking. Her phone, somewhere in the car, kept ringing. Ringing off, and then ringing again. She took deep shuddery breaths, willing herself to breathe normally. When she could turn the wheel without shaking herself off the road, she turned the car around, and drove.

She pulled into the car park just as Callum was storming out of the front doors. Lewis was following behind, yelling at him not to drive. To wait till he got his keys. Callum was wearing his suit trousers, the jacket open showing a bare chest. A concerned-looking hotel porter was standing in the doorway. All three men stopped when she pulled up, and she got out of the car slowly. Her legs were still like jelly.

Lewis spoke first.

'Where the hell did you go? Did you drive like that? What the hell is wrong with you?' He went to step forward, but Callum stopped him with a meaty hand against his chest.

'Don't speak to her like that,' he growled, and Lewis stepped back. The porter shrank back behind the doorway. Callum rounded on her. 'Where the hell did you go? Did you just drive away?'

'I'm sorry,' she started, but he took a step back.

'No, Ali. Leaving me without a word is one thing, but driving away in a state? What the hell were you thinking?'

Lewis piped up behind him, 'Kinda what I said, mate.'

'Lew,' he spat back. 'Piss off a minute, will ya?'

Lewis raised his brows but started to walk backwards. 'Fine. I'll go tell Migs you're back.'

He left them alone, standing on the gravel path. Callum looked angry, so angry, but when she started to cry, he sagged. A deep ragged sigh left him, the fight draining out of him.

'Don't ever drive off like that again. Leave me? Fine. But I don't ever want to pull you out of a wreck again.'

'I love you,' she rushed out, taking small steps towards him now. Getting bolder with each step. 'I panicked. Dr B said something about my brain never being right, things being jumbled. I thought we had another date. I was going to see it through, but then last night happened and... I left. I drove too fast, I almost crashed.'

Callum's hands were over his face now, his body bent low. 'Jesus! Alice!'

'I know, I'm sorry. I was upset, you rang my phone. I didn't see the car, but then I stopped, just in time. But I remembered. That night, us. I remember the night in the cab, and I couldn't let you go.' She kept taking small steps, till she was a metre away. 'I didn't want to leave you, really I didn't, but I don't want you to ruin your life over me. I didn't want you to live some half-life, when I might go nuts and leave you, or move to Peru or something on a whim, but I remembered. I remember how I felt in that taxi, Callum. I felt it.'

She took another step, wiping at the tears rolling down her face. 'I don't want our story to end like that.'

She bent a knee, right there on the gravel. Right in front of the man she'd been obsessed with one way or another for most of her life.

'I love you, Callum. I loved you then, and I love you now. More, if that's even possible. Marry me, please? I promise I will never run again. From anything. I want to get old with you. I will happily wipe your saggy, wrinkly arse. I want to give you beautiful babies, ones that are as stubborn as me and love as hard as you do. I want it all, Callum. Forgive me?'

She looked up at him, imploring him with every part of her soul. His brown eyes just stared at her for a long moment. He closed the gap between them, his face unreadable. *It's too late*, she thought as she felt her heart start to splinter in her chest. *You've broken him.*

'Get up,' he said after what felt like forever. She stood up, holding her breath. He studied her face, and broke into a broad grin.

'You remembered the proposal,' he said. 'Those were my words.'

She nodded, a hopeful smile competing with her wobbly bottom lip.

His brows furrowed. 'You love me?'

She sighed. 'I've loved you in every version of me. I will love you forever, if you'll let me.'

He stepped closer. 'Well, it's about damn time, sparrow.'

He lifted her into his arms, and she threw her arms around his neck as he dipped his head and kissed her like he never wanted to stop. She was okay with that.

They heard applause behind them, whoops and cheers that grew louder. He pulled away reluctantly, turning them around to the hotel main doors. Her parents, Lew and Migs, and half the hotel guests were all standing there in their pyjamas, cheering them on.

Callum groaned, and Alice laughed through her tears. He nuzzled into her neck, and she pulled him close. She was never going to let go again.

'What do we do now?' she whispered to him.

He kissed her scar, his face the picture of serenity. He raised a dark brow.

'I vote for going back to bed, sparrow. We have some making up to do.'

She kissed his soft lips, inhaling the spice in the air.

'Lead the way, Roberts. That sounds like a perfect plan.'

ACKNOWLEDGEMENTS

Well, 2022 has been quite a ride! One that makes you throw up and never want to go on again, but books have been a bright spot thankfully. I am thrilled to have *Ten Dates* published with Boldwood Books, and I loved telling Alice and Callum's story. I wish I could keep Callum forever, but I know you all love him now too.

Big thanks to my amazing editor Emily, Nia and Amanda, and the rest of the fantastic team of people who all helped to bring this story into your hands. Huge thanks to Rachel Gilbert and the fab bloggers on the tour; keep sharing that book love and sharing the joy!

Gratitude to my friends and family for putting up with me talking about this book for weeks on end, and finally a huge smacker goes to my boys, who are both so amazing, and my husband Peter. He is the muse for all my heroes, and I get to keep him all to myself forever. Love you, baby.

Also, to my readers, who have stuck with me book after book. I thank and love you all so much. Till the next book, my friends, see you soon.

And to Georgina Barker-Mander, my lovely friend and very knowledgeable nurse, who helped me with the technical and random questions I sent her at all hours. Stay weird G; it's the best way to be xx

Rachel Dove

ABOUT THE AUTHOR

Rachel Dove lives in leafy West Yorkshire with her family, and rescue animals Tilly the cat and Darcy the dog (named after Mr Darcy, of course!). A former teacher specialising in Autism, ADHD and SpLDs, she is passionate about changing the system and raising awareness/acceptance. She loves a good rom-com, and the beach!

Sign up to Rachel Dove's mailing list here for news, competitions and updates on future books.

Visit Rachel's website: racheldovebooks.co.uk

Follow Rachel on social media:

 x.com/writerdove
 instagram.com/writerdove
 facebook.com/racheldoveauthor
 tiktok.com/@writerdove

ALSO BY RACHEL DOVE

Ten Dates

Summer Hates Christmas

Mr Right Next Door

LOVE NOTES

LOVE IN EVERY CHAPTER

WHERE ALL YOUR ROMANCE
DREAMS COME TRUE!

THE HOME OF BESTSELLING
ROMANCE AND WOMEN'S
FICTION

 WARNING:
MAY CONTAIN SPICE

Boldwood

Boldwood Books is an award-winning fiction publishing company seeking out the best stories from around the world.

Find out more at www.boldwoodbooks.com

Join our reader community for brilliant books, competitions and offers!

Follow us
@BoldwoodBooks
@TheBoldBookClub

Sign up to our weekly deals newsletter

https://bit.ly/BoldwoodBNewsletter